Praise for *Confessions of a Bronx Bookie:*

"I laughed, spit my beer across the table and then laughed some more."
— Ray Krzyzek, CEO of Proteggo

"Finally someone who really gets that it's never too late. Everything we ever wanted is on the other side of fear."
— Laura Beth Walker, author

"Anyone who has ever raised a glass, bent a knee, or just plain lost their way should read this book."
— Trillium writer's guild

Confessions of a Bronx Bookie

Billy O'Connor

Copyright 2014 by William P O'Connor. All rights reserved.
No portions of this book, except for brief reviews, may be reproduced, stored in a retrieval system, or transmitted in any form or by any means—electronic, mechanical, photocopying, recording or otherwise—without the written permission of the publisher.

For information, contact oconnor.williamp@gmail.com

Published by POETS Press
20050 N. Cave Creek Rd, Suite 310
Phoenix AZ 85024

Cover design by Kastle Olson kastleo@gmail.com
Back cover photo by Steve Johnson Productions at University of Florida
Edited by Erica Litz ericamlitz@gmail.com
Interior layout by www.go-word.com
Bronxbilly.com website by Jessie Kilker jessica@brightsidecs.com
Media consultant: Adam Scott Waddle awaddle05@msn.com

Printed in the USA

Issued in print and electronic forms
ISBN 978-0-9908480-0-4 pdf
ISBN 978-0-9908480-1-1 pbk

At 66, I'd like to dedicate this, my first book, to the 343 of my brother firefighters who died on 9/11, to A.A. and all recovery programs, and last but not least to the unsung heroes on the front lines of education, especially Mike Foley and the professors who taught me at the University of Florida.

I'll never forget.

CHAPTER ONE

Lost causes are the ones we pray for the hardest.
Throughout Mom's Alzheimer's, I prayed every day.
A year after her death, I was done praying.
I didn't need God. I needed a drink.
When I left a Westchester bar stewed, it was 2 a.m. and pouring rain.
Despite the nasty weather, I lowered my passenger window and hoped the howling night air would keep me alert. Through my Buick's slapping windshield wipers, I squinted at the flatbed truck paused ahead of me at the stop sign.
Not completely plastered, I slowed up and pulled behind it. I didn't spot the red flag attached to the 12-foot pipes that extended past the end of the truck's bed.
The steel exploded through my windshield, rocketed an inch from both my ears and blew out the rear window. I sat frozen. The silence became palpable and merciless in its depths. The only sound came from my car's radio. The Temptations towed me to tears.
"People get ready, there's a train a coming. You don't need no ticket. You just get on board."
With decapitation two inches from both ears, covered in broken glass and as frightened as a lost child, my sodden fingers formed the sign of the cross, but I refused to bless myself. Instead, I sat alone in this windowless wreck with nowhere to turn, nowhere to go and watched a drunken gamblers' life flick before me like a deck of cards.

* * *

"Wait, Hank. Don't hang up. Wait for your repeat. You got Pittsburgh minus four, 400 times. That's $2,000 on Pittsburgh minus 4."

To take illegal action, the three of us needed aliases. Steve's was Red. Carmine's was Gobbo, and mine was Mars. As soon as I cradled the phone, it rang again. All four phones were singing. Before I grabbed one, I barked frantically,

"Red, that makes over $18,000 on the Steelers. We better bump that price to four and a half."

"It's only five minutes before kick off. Calm the fuck down. What difference does it make now?" Red said.

Annoyed, I shook my head. Ever since my other partner Carmine left, Steve had been off the chain. To Red, the business wasn't as important as getting his action in. This thick, Polish prick was only worried about his own bets.

In truth, I was almost as bad. Because we both gambled heavy, our bookmaking business suffered.

I shrugged and lifted the nearest phone. A sharp, calm voice said,

"This is Brian for Mars."

My heart fluttered.

I focused.

"Yeah, Brian."

"What are you using on the Steelers – Raiders?" he asked.

Even though I needed Raider action for $18,000, I couldn't give Brian a four and a half. He was a bookmaker and a big one. Although all he'd get from me was $2,000, his games were smoking hot. This guy hit at an 80 percent rate. The only reason our office gave him a price on a game at all was so we could get down on that game ourselves. I couldn't let him rob me.

"Four," I said.

"Let me have the Raiders plus the four for two dimes," he said.

"Brian, you've got Oakland plus the four 400 times, $2,000. Is that it?"

"Yeah," he said. The phone died.

Elated, I yelled,

"Red, Brian just bet $2,000 on the Raiders."

My partner leapt to his feet.

"I gotta get me some of that," he said.

Red's shoulders were as broad as ax handles and attached to a short-neck that struggled to support his keg-sized head. He wore his cropped-blonde hair close, like a drill instructor.

Red screamed, "I can't get out."

Every time Red picked up a phone to place his bet, a customer was already on it.

"These fucken customers are screwing up our business," he said.

I laughed at the irony of that sentence, but I knew where he was coming from. I had the same problem. I wanted to bet $20,000 on Brian's hot side too. Even though our office already needed the Raiders for $18,000, I couldn't get enough of a sure thing.

With only four minutes left til kickoff, I was afraid I'd get shut out. I answered one of our four phones and tried to write the ticket quickly, but my mind was on two things. Get this mook off the phone and get $20,000 down on the Raiders.

Frantic, I said,

"Yeah, Artie for Red, you got it. Dallas minus the 11 for a nickel."

My index finger pressed the cradle button, and I heard a dial tone. The other phones hummed, but I didn't answer them. With a free phone at last, I scrambled to dial out. I was stuck $18,800 for the week. If Oakland won, I could bail out. I dialed one of my outlets.

Busy.

I redialed.

Busy.

I checked the big clock above our long metal desk. Two minutes till kick off.

Panicked, I redialed . . .

Busy.

I had a twisted feeling high up in my chest, as if something heavy was pushing against my lungs.

Our phones rang off the hook. No one answered.

Red already had 20 dimes on the Raiders but wanted more. He wasn't answering any phones.

Neither was I.

I dialed again . . . at last,

"Hello this is Mars for the Pimp. Whatta ya got on the Pittsburgh game?" I said.

"Four? Great. Let me have the Raiders plus four for 20 dimes."

I listened to slight murmurs of protest.

"He'll only take 10 dimes?"

Too late to call another bookie and I needed more.

"Listen, tell the Pimp to do me a favor," I said. "We're loaded up on the Raiders. We need to layoff some of this." I lied. "Tell him if he takes this that in future we'll use him exclusively to lay off all our excess."

Seconds seemed like hours.

"OK, man. Tell him thanks. Yeah, tell him, no problem. We'll settle up Tuesday. See ya," I said.

I pointed my index finger and extended thumb at Red and slowly squeezed my forefinger in the gangster's salute.

"I got 20 dimes. How about you?"

"I've got 40 dimes so far, but I'm looking for more than just $40,000."

The hard part done, the butterflies fled. Now I could relax, write the last few tickets, watch the game and collect my winnings.

* * *

"Red, I can't believe it. Why the fuck didn't they run the ball into the end zone instead of throwing two passes on the two-yard line?"

Oakland lost by six. I was fucked.

Besides the office taking a beating, I was down over $40,000 for the week. I didn't have dollar one. Making it worse, Tuesday was only two days away. I had to come up with the bread.

These guys were "serious" people.

If we had a chance in hell of digging out, Red and I had to

pay the customers first. We had to stay in action. To leash the both of us that night, I posted a sign above the phones.

Suckers bet. Winners write.

"I don't give a fuck if the game was played already, and I know the score," I told Red. "No way I'm making another bet."

He agreed, but his eyes hedged.

I knew this hump. No way he'd just shut it down. I wasn't honestly sure I could either. Fuck it. I needed to call a hooker.

* * *

I was so busy trying to raise cash that I barely had time to ignore my creditors. I had to make something work and fast. If not drunk, which wasn't often, I was at the gym. Anything to get rid of stress.

While pushing weights one morning, I spotted my 17-year-old niece punishing a Stairmaster by the gym's plate-glass window. I strolled over, and we swapped hellos.

I resumed my zombie-like workout. My cheeks dented and puffed during sets.

After 12 repetitions, I dropped the barbell onto the bench-rack and sat up.

I noticed a middle-aged, 300-pound black man talking to my niece.

Neither racist nor paranoid, I knew that watching her wouldn't help me get in shape. I methodically added ten-pound plates to both sides of the bar and decreased the number of repetitions. On my fourth set, I noticed the black giant and my niece were still at it.

Finishing my bench presses, I headed to the floor-mats to do some stomach work. After three sets, their conversation hadn't faded.

What's this guy all about?

I'll just slide over. Make him aware he hasn't gone unnoticed.

I closed in.

"Hey Jill, how's your Mom doing?"

Both turned.

Jill said fine and smiled. The giant black man stared soundless with a stoic expression. He was barrel-chested with large eyes and carelessly shaved dark jowls. His baleful look helped deliver a monotone warning that slapped me senseless,

"Brother, the Holy Spirit needs to reach you. Someone is praying for you very, very hard."

This wasn't the first time I had heard that alarming sentence. It shocked and segued me to another prophet who had told me the same thing years earlier in a Bronx Protestant Church.

The black giant, Elijah, continued,

"The Holy Spirit compels me to talk to you."

My eyes fell to my shoes. I thought,

Holy shit. Not again.

The black prophet's next line cut to the chase.

"You're a dissolute gambler, womanizer and alcoholic."

What the fuck did he just say? Again with this crap? I thought.

The steep, rounded slope of his massive shoulders made his body seem conical. Elijah caught his breath and stared at me calmly,

"For a deep tragedy in your life, you blamed God. You disavowed your Creator and disregarded the sanctity of your immortal soul."

Not again, no, no, no—just like that first warning by that other seer, Trudy. I thought this shit was behind me. A half a decade without warnings. I don't need this shit now, I thought.

I stared at the black rubber floor-mat and mumbled,

"Yeah, something like that."

Elijah couldn't know these things about me. My niece couldn't have told him. She didn't know anything about my personal life. These aren't things I discussed with Jill. Our conversations were banal. We talked about her Mom and Dad's health or the weather.

Besides, I saw it in Elijah's face.

This guy was on a mission.

* * *

The seven-footer spilled his story.

A football player at Grambling University, the black giant dreamed of turning pro. Sports were all he thought about.

Elijah's fiancé told him to spend more time on his knees and less time in a three-point stance—to be thankful for God's gifts and not ask for more.

Then the enormous prophet told me his kicker.

During senior year, doctors found bone cancer in one of his huge legs. To save his life, he'd have to lose the limb.

Weeks before the operation, like Christ in Gethsemane, he sweated blood. He promised that if God saved his leg, he would devote his life to the Lord. Mystifying the doctors, the day before the operation all signs of cancer miraculously disappeared.

Making good on his vow, Elijah preached. At the moment, I was sitting in his pew.

He gave me a blow-by-blow account of things he had no business knowing, along with things that I had barely remembered. As he continued, I got more and more uncomfortable. When silent, Elijah searched skyward for divine intervention, or revelation, or maybe his next startling sentence. Throughout my ordeal, he praised God, thanked God and meditated.

Then his praying stopped.

In a hushed, calm tone he said,

"God gave you a gift, the ability to connect with other people, and you used it immorally. Your creator's disappointed.

"I am a warning."

"And I may be your last warning."

"The Lord saved your life in Asia, plucked you from disaster in Florida, and again in New York. Why do you ignore your Savior?"

This got my attention and how. Once more, he praised Jesus skyward.

"Yes Jesus. Thank you Jesus. I'll tell him, Jesus—The Holy Spirit wants you to read the Bible, Jeremiah, Chapter 1.5."

"The Bible?"

"Jeremiah Chapter 1.5," he continued, "God wants you to stop the drugs, the drinking and the gambling. Fulfill what He planned for you before your birth. Thank you Jesus. Praise Jesus."

I got the message, thanked Elijah for his time, and motored

my legs toward the lockers as fast as they would carry me.

In the shower, I reflected on this earth-shattering revelation.

God gave me a gift.

God is pissed off.

This guy's my last chance.

Holy shit.

The shower's hot water calmed me. My mind meandered to the many times that guys came up to me and reminded me of advice that I had given them years before, advice that I had long forgotten.

God gave me a gift?

Elijah's warning got my attention, shook me up. This was twice now, no accident and no coincidence.

Wait until I tell my girlfriend, Colleen, about this. This is "my last warning." That doesn't sound good.

I went from the gym to a bar and had a few pops. When I saw Colleen, I told her the whole story.

Colleen reacted unexpectedly.

"You can't ignore this warning. You know how strong your mother's prayers are. You've got to get to the bottom of this. God wants to reach you."

Colleen's an academic, a lifelong student, and a brilliant girl who when focused could memorize a book during a nuclear attack. Nothing normally shook her.

I told her to calm down. I'd check it out when I got around to it.

This happened Monday.

I had to see a knee doctor in Manhattan Wednesday. I called Colleen,

"I have a 2 p.m. appointment in the city. How about dinner after?"

* * *

We met in an Indian restaurant. All went well. Now it was late afternoon and rush hour had started. I dreaded the trip upstate so I suggested a movie.

Wednesday was a slow night at the office. Red could handle the action.

At the curb, I spied a newsstand. Colleen jumped out to buy a paper and check the movie listings.

Back immediately, "No more papers," she said.

This guy ran out of papers in Manhattan? I spotted a candy store, shot through the green light, and pulled over to the curb.

Two minutes later, she said,

"No papers. He's all out."

"Are you fucken kidding me? Forget it. Let's get the hell out of Manhattan before it's bumper to bumper. We'll just catch a movie in Yonkers."

Driving up the FDR Drive was predictable, two hours to go 10 or 20 miles. In Yonkers, I saw a multiplex and pulled over. I bought two tickets for *Good Will Hunting* with an 8 p.m. start.

"Baby I'm not drinking. How you want to kill time until the movie begins?"

"Look, a Barnes and Noble," she said. "Let's browse the books."

Walking through the parking lot, an afterthought,

"We should look up that Bible reference the black preacher told you about," Colleen said.

"Yeah, why the hell not. What was it again, Jeremiah Chapter 1.5?"

Inside the bookstore, I said,

"Find the section marked Religion."

I strolled through. I was shocked.

Not one Bible.

From the other aisle, Colleen shouted,

"Here's a whole section with nothing but Bibles. Over here."

I joined her among rows and rows of Bibles: King James, Webster, Young, Darby, Living, Good News and Hebrew. Bibles in German, French, Dutch, every language imaginable, hundreds overwhelmed me.

She said, "Grab any one."

I reached randomly for a Bible at eye level and paused.

Looking down at the book's roughly 3000 pages, I noticed one dog-eared page.

I got a cold chill.

My knees weakened.

I hesitated to open the book.

I said, "Impossible, it can't be. If this dog-ear is Jeremiah Chapter 1.5, I swear to God I'll drop dead."

Colleen's emerald eyes turned eggshell-white.

I turned to the marked page.

Before me like a neon warning sign, Jeremiah Chapter 1.5. The print screamed the prophet's words.

My head pivoted in denial.

"What the hell is going on? I can't fucken take this."

My terrified girlfriend chanted,

"Oh my God. Oh my God. You can't ignore this. You can't. You can't. You've got to do something. Do something."

I did . . .

I listened to my skin crawl.

God's first words to Jeremiah read,

"I knew you, before you were born."

God commanded Jeremiah to preach his message.

The prophet would be the most unlikely of messengers. As a temporal profligate, Jeremiah pleaded mistaken identity. He claimed he was the wrong man for the job. But the Lord used divine insistence, and Jeremiah finally relented.

"Before I formed thee in the belly, I knew thee, and before thou camest forth out of the womb . . . I ordained thee a prophet. Do not fear them. I will put the words in your mouth."

* * *

The following week, I spotted Elijah at the gym and rushed up.

"Hey man, wait until you hear this. You won't believe it."

I told him the whole tale.

His visage made my anxiety worse.

"Why are you surprised that the Holy Spirit contacted you?" He said smugly. "You think the Lord can't show you signs?"

"Yeah, I know," I said. "But you've got to admit what happened was pretty weird."

He pointed his enormous finger into my skeptical face.

"Don't you dare let the Lord down."

For emphasis, he moved inches from my face and tightened his cheek, exposing the teeth on the right side of his lip.

"Not again. Don't you dare let the Lord down, again," he repeated.

* * *

I couldn't believe it. This incident really shook me up.

Don't you dare let the Lord down, again? How did he know about my past warning?

Then he had stuck a finger as big as a cucumber in my face.

What was that a curse or something? Sonofabitch might just as well have said,

"Let it be on your head."

Jeremiah's passage had gone on to read that God sometimes chose unlikely orators to deliver his message. God warned Jeremiah that he had no choice. If the chosen prophet ignored God's command, he and his descendents would be severely punished.

I didn't need God's punishment and neither did my son. So, if the Lord demanded an unlikely orator, maybe I could be his boy. No one had ever accused me of sainthood, but I couldn't see this marriage of God and man working. Not with Connor Kelly as the groom anyway.

Another hedonistic Irishman, Oscar Wilde, once famously said,

"Nothing succeeds like excess."

I had spent the better part of my life trying to prove him right.

So let me start my story on more empirical ground . . .

The day I called that hooker in Myrtle Beach.

CHAPTER TWO

My divorce lawyer had appealed by phone,
"It's last minute, but someone dropped out. I remembered that you're a golfer. I thought you might be interested."
I had almost agreed, just a few more questions.
"Anyone else I know besides you?"
"No, the 15 guys are doctors, lawyers and psychiatrists. They look forward to this trip every year. Some of them get pretty wild."
"How many days?"
"Just four days, a long weekend. Come on. We need a guy for that fourth foursome," he said.
A year divorced, I had rented an apartment in the same Bronx building my family moved to when we came from Ireland nearly four decades ago. I was literally back to square one.
My lawyer had done me a few favors, and I might need a few more.
"Yeah, what the hell."
He warned me,
"Don't be prudish. On vacation, these guys blow off a lot of steam."

* * *

We arrived in Myrtle Beach about 9 a.m. and teed off at noon. Golf went well. The three guys I had played with seemed a bit stiff yet amiable enough. At the hotel, I roomed with a cardiologist.
Eugene was one of those polysyllabic prigs, the type of phony

who said sibling instead of brother or sister.

Between screwdrivers on the plane, six beers on the golf course, and three shots of sambuca in the clubhouse, I had a pretty good buzz on. Naturally, for this trip, I had brought a full cache' of contraband.

Bookmaking now, I earned great money, but my expenses kept rising with my income. Considering my mania and addiction to excess of any form, my "expenses" were predictable.

As the good doctor neatly unpacked his clothes, I broke out my stash and rolled a joint. I lit up and began to flip through the phone book.

Since Vietnam, I had no qualms about using escort services. During the war, prostitutes were $4 apiece. At 19, I had gotten all I could while I could.

Blatant and unimaginative ads devoted to working girls plastered page after page of the phone book. *Holy shit, was this the Bible belt or Bangkok?*

Astounded, I erupted,

"Eugene can you believe this? Look at all these prostitutes."

Doctor Eugene adopted a "who farted" expression, and said, "You don't use those services do you?"

Making a minuscule attempt at reconciliation, I lied.

"Rarely."

I rang-up the least offensive ad.

"Hello Temptation, what are your hourly rates?"

I covered the phone and asked the cardiologist if he wanted to spring for a $100.

"I don't pay for sex. I'm going to dinner. Do what you like."

Ignoring his contempt, I continued negotiations.

"How long will it take her to get here? My name's Fred, room 202. That's right, Holiday Inn."

* * *

The knock signaled the doctor's exit. Despite his apparent disgust, I suspected curiosity about the hooker's looks caused him to stall. When Eugene opened the door, I was on the bed in boxers.

A syrupy voice from the hallway said, "You Fred?"

"No," he said condescendingly, letting her enter. "Fred's over there on the bed."

She entered the room, stopped and screamed, "Connor Kelly, I can't believe it."

I yelled out,

"Shane. What the hell are you doing here?"

She laughed and said,

"Selling my ass, what are you doing here?"

"I guess I'm buying it. How long has it been?"

"Almost 10 years, you got any drugs?" she said.

"Yeah, Quaaludes, grass, a little coke, and I got beer and vodka on ice."

"Cool. I'll call my boss, tell him I couldn't find the John, and take the rest of the night off," she said.

Eugene sprinted to the dresser. He shuffled clothes into his suitcase and stammered,

"I'm going downstairs to get another room. I've had enough of this."

Good. The guy was a stiff anyway.

Shane was a real sport. She would never make the cover of Vogue, but she had a fine body and a face that wouldn't frighten children.

She ate a down, rolled a joint, and made a drink. We reminisced about old times in New Orleans. We caught up throughout the night and interrupted our chat only to exchange currency and commerce.

Shane asked me if I'd do her a favor. She had already done me two, so I said,

"Sure."

But because she was "Shane the Insane," I was a bit apprehensive.

"Would you put on my underwear and nylons? It turns me on."

Reluctant but whacked, I figured who was going to know? The downs had kicked in. I was as drunk as a bridegroom, and I knew this chick 15 years.

Besides, she was a pro. I didn't want her to think I was a

Puritan or couldn't keep pace.

Minutes later, I was lying on the bed dressed like a Victoria's Secret model.

Garnished in panties, garter belt, nylons and a black bra, I reached for my vodka: a dead soldier, empty.

I said, "I need another drink."

I staggered to an ice bucket as empty as my glass.

It was past midnight, and the ice machine was only two doors down. Shouldn't take more than a minute, so I decided to take a shot and sprint. I hit the hallway like an Olympic gold medal winner.

The door across from mine opened. I stared dumbfounded at Eugene the cardiologist. His stunned face looked like a cobra had just crawled up his black-silk pajama bottoms and bit him on the prick. Despite the lingerie, it was obvious by my hairy chest and spindly legs that I wasn't Angelina Jolie.

Besides the thin veneer of Shane's unmentionables, I wore nothing but an effulgent smile. I cradled the ice bucket like an infant. I shrugged and said indifferently,

"Just say oops, and close the fucking door."

"Oops?"

"That's right, oops. Now close the fucking door."

* * *

Next morning my head was as big as a school bus. I showered, did a short line of coke and headed for breakfast.

On the way, I started piecing together last night's events.

I dreaded the "wild professionals" reactions but decided to brazen it out. I barely remembered Eugene spotting me in the hallway, but I was sure my name was mentioned over coffee.

A gaggle of golfers traded small talk at the table. When I entered, all voices ceased. All eyes fastened on me.

I parried their garrulous silence.

"Nice day for golf gentlemen. Shall we drink the coffee or just snort the beans?"

* * *

Golf mercifully over, I couldn't wait to hit the sack. I didn't bounce back like I used to. I was in bed by 3 p.m.

About 10 p.m., I awoke from a miserable, restless sleep.

Clutching my throat with my fingers, I gasped for water. My mouth felt like I had gargled with sand. I vaulted for the cooler, grasped a beer, popped the top and drained it. The foam had barely settled when I heard a commotion outside in the hallway. I threw on shorts and opened my hotel room door.

Three of the "professionals" from our golf trip were inspecting five hookers like they were bruised fruit. All three men were drunk, and the heretofore-contemptuous cardiologist, Eugene, had turned abusive. He inspected each girl with dull dead eyes. With a wicked and sullen mouth, he spat meanness.

"You—too short. You—no tits. You—take a civil service test."

I stopped him cold.

"Hey Doc. You might know about heart surgery, but you're clueless about how to treat a working girl. What's the matter with you? Take a tip from Beau Brummel. 'Treat a queen like a tramp and a tramp like a queen.' You'd be better off."

As I stepped into the hallway to rescue one charming, wide-eyed girl, Eugene's face held a peculiar emptiness. I gripped her tender little hand and led her to my room.

As I ushered her through my doorway I said,

"Never mind that asshole, honey. Come in here. You're safe with me."

Eugene protested, "Hey, I called these girls. You can't do that."

"The problem with you guys who shower before work and not after is that you treat everybody that you deem 'beneath you' like shit." I told the other girls. "Gals, you don't have to put up with this abuse. After you finish your labors, knock on my door. See how a blue-collar guy treats a lady. You gals need to organize. We'll have a few drinks and hold a union meeting," I laughed.

Eugene screamed, "Mind your own business you socialist bastard."

I shrugged, turned, and this time it was me that said "Oops." I shut my door.

* * *

Weeks later, retelling the story to the few people I could. I turned to my best friend and bookmaking partner, Gobbo, and said,

"Can you imagine the coincidence? I've never even been to Myrtle Beach. What are the odds of running into a hooker I know?"

Gobbo didn't hesitate. "With you? I make it even money."

I laughed like a 10-year-old for a while, but when I stopped, I thought,

Maybe what that shrink told me was right?

CHAPTER THREE

The joint smelled of old beer, stale cigarettes, and freshly mopped ammonia floors. The only dim light bled from the bar's propped-open front door, and I stared into the gray Bronx Street. I turned my attention from the door to the front page of the Daily News. The headline read,
"Iran to Release Captive American Hostages."
An unfamiliar voice caught my ear.
"Connor Kelly. I can't believe it."
Happy for a bit of company, I parked my freshly poured Bloody Mary on a bar napkin and turned to see who else needed a drink at 10 a.m.
"I can't believe it's you." The stranger exulted, "Shit. How long has it been, three years?"
Who the fuck is this guy? Three years? He acts like I just rose from the dead.
"Yeah, at least three years," I bluffed. "Sit down man. I'll buy you a squirt."
I have to play along here.
"So, what the hell you doing in the Bronx?" I said.
He was a big-boned, full-faced man with messy blond hair, maybe 35, handsome in a brutal, sloppy way.
"My brother lives about a mile from here. He has a dentist appointment around the corner. I came into French Charlie's to kill some time. I can't fucken believe it. One guy at the bar, and it's Connor fucken Kelly."

* * *

Over two more Bloody Marys and an hour of gratuitous

chatter, the thick-minded stranger finally copped on.

"Wait a second, you don't know who I am. Do you?"

Busted.

"No man. I really don't. I'm sorry."

I pandered,

"Look man, it's no reflection on you. I have a bad memory. I drink a lot, and I do a lot of drugs. So it's nothing personal. I just don't remember you."

"Are you fucking kidding me?"

"No. Look man, I'm sorry. Don't take it personal," I said.

"But I tell everybody you're the craziest fucker I ever met."

"That might be. I've been told that before, but I swear to God, until this moment, I've never seen you before. Where do you know me from?" I asked.

"We spent four days together in the Hamptons," he said.

The sentence smacks me like a locomotive.

"Four days? I spent four days with you?"

"Yeah. I can't believe you don't remember me."

"How fucked up was I?"

"You were really fucked up. You were drinking Beefeater Martini's out of a plastic thermos, and you had a baggie full of cocaine."

"I never liked cocaine, just the smell of it," I quipped.

But I covered my unfinished drink with a coaster to indicate to the bartender that I had had enough. I made my apologies and fled. Introspective, I thought,

Four days? And I didn't even know him? If I'm not careful, this alcohol shit could start to become a problem.

I was beginning to think that this might be a long day. I was right. How long a day I'd find out in two hours. Good thing that mook came in. I'd need a clear head for what my ex-wife was about to hit me with.

* * *

My neck veins bulged. I screamed into the phone,

"What do you mean Liam's suicidal? Who the fuck told you that shit?"

I didn't shoot messengers . . .

I hacked them to pieces.

My ex-wife, Lorraine, stuttered to explain, "Llliamm's ffffriend at sschool tttold a teacher that he was talking about suicide."

Frantic, "What can I do? Who can I see?"

"His school counselor, Mrs. Patrick, wants to meet with the three of us, you, me and Liam."

I continued my tirade. Lorraine uttered a sound that wasn't quite a word and hung up.

* * *

We met Friday at the counselor's office. Mrs. Patrick, my ex-wife and I did all the talking. The turmoil's source, my son, said nothing. After meeting us collectively, the counselor insisted on seeing us individually. My son went first. After a short time, Liam exited and Lorraine entered. Same result, my ex-wife came out within 10 minutes, my turn next.

I rushed in and got in Patrick's face,

"What did Liam have to say?"

She wore a gray suit and a white silk blouse with a star shaped Brighton-Silver pendant around her neck. Her hair, streaked blonde, was cropped as if cut with sheers. Her eyes were hazel and charged with energy.

The counselor said, "He wouldn't talk." Patrick's expression was sincere as if all she was concerned about was my welfare.

"I'll break his ass. He'll talk."

My response gave Patrick a clue about the real problem.

Patrick said, "Tell me a little about yourself, Mr. Kelly."

Determined to help my son, I opted for complete candor. I launched a 20-minute soliloquy. I held nothing back: women, booze, drugs, gambling an avalanche of vice. During my rant, Patrick's face contorted. Her eyes became baleful. Her jaw dropped.

The counselor scribbled fitfully. She flipped the pages of her yellow legal pad so fast she almost tore them. Finally, Patrick looked up. She knew she had hit the mother lode.

I paused to catch my breath and saw the disbelief chiseled on the counselor's face.

Perhaps I've overplayed my hand?

Patrick suggested more therapy. She recommended an analyst in Ardsley.

I grimaced, "That's going to be tough on the kid. No one wants to be told they need a shrink."

"Mr. Kelly, I'm afraid you misunderstood. The psychiatrist is for you."

* * *

I was thrilled to see a shrink. For my son's welfare, of course, but also because for years I'd suspected that I wasn't completely on the level. I was skeptical yet, as always, optimistic. I wanted to meet these demons that drove me.

These same devils had driven my mom, Nora, to her knees every day. She had prayed in vain that her two sons would change their ways and win their war with whiskey.

* * *

In the shrink's outer office, I sat and scanned the Wall Street Journal. The headline read, "Iran Hostages Freed."

I turned to the inside story and read the first sentence,

"After two long years . . ."

But the receptionist interrupted, "Dr. Welsh will see you now."

The psychiatrist's inner office was predictable. Wearying the walls were four or five degrees from various universities. I scanned a few to ensure the shrink wasn't all- Caribbean educated. Two deep, leather chairs sat to his left. To his right sat the stereotypical matching leather couch.

The small, unimposing, owlish doctor perched behind a huge oak desk where a framed 8 x 10 photograph of a woman and two children screamed for attention. The unfortunate woman had a manatee's body and a face that resembled Andre the Giant's.

The doctor must have pissed off the Almighty because the two children in his photo shared the woman's features. I knew my views were insular, superficial and shallow, but I couldn't help it. I couldn't get past this image.

I was here for my son, not because society thought I was

crazy. I wasn't particularly concerned about what the "Fred's" think. To me, the back-of-the-liners' opinions meant less than nothing. I'd be below the ground a lot longer than above it, and so would they. In the meantime, I was having as much fun as the law allowed, most times more.

While the psychiatrist prattled, I sneaked peaks at the 8 X 10 photo. It fixated me so entirely; I couldn't hear a word he said. When the doctor's lips stopped moving, I asked the inevitable.

The psychiatrist proudly bellowed, "Yes, my wife and kids."

* * *

Dr. Welsh said,

"Tell me something about yourself, Mr. Kelly."

"Well Doc," I began, "I'm 33, no wait I'm 34, or is it 34 last year and 35 this year?"

The psychiatrist interrupted, "You don't know how old you are?"

I reached for a lifeline.

"Well my birthday was yesterday and with all this going on, I haven't had time to think about it."

After this inauspicious beginning, I launched into a brief summary of my life so far—no pulled punches and no embellishment.

The doctor listened attentively to the sordid tale and produced, like a rabbit out of a hat, an instant diagnosis.

"You sound manic depressive."

I protested, "No, Doc, I don't think so. I never get depressed."

"Well then," Welsh continued, "You're not bipolar manic depressive. You sound unipolar. From what you've told me, you experience delusions of grandeur, a propensity for risk, and a tendency to see everything through rose-colored glasses."

"Well," I muttered, "I don't know about that."

From a collection of books on a shelf to the left of his desk, the doctor stood and snatched a volume.

"Let's take a look."

He paged to unipolar manic depression and read,

"Hyperthymic Temperament is the personality associated

with this disorder. It consists of the following attributes: cheerful, exuberant, overoptimistic, carefree, extroverted, people seeking, overconfident, grandiose, high energy level, uninhibited and stimulus seeking."

I perked up, "Yeah that sounds like me. What's the problem with that? It sounds like a disease people would send away for in the mail."

Dr. Welsh said, "It's fine for you, but it's very tough on the people around you."

We alcoholics are selfishness. If you're doing it right, the disease demands total attention. It's a hard lesson I learned as a child dealing with my old man.

Grasping at a final sanctuary, I defensively crossed my arms, "Look Doc, if people don't want to be around me, fuck 'em."

He ignored my remark and continued,

"The big problem resides in the stimulus seeking. Your disease feeds on excitement and therefore treads on dangerous ground. A patient with this disease would likely seek drugs, gambling and alcohol as stimulants."

I said nothing but thought,

I've been doing this all my life. Taught by experience, I've got these things under control.

Welsh interrupted my thoughts.

"Fortunately, science has a cure. Because your brain lacks salt, the medication lithium gradually increased over time, will correct your chemical imbalance."

Salt? Is he kidding? Salt? What am I fucking popcorn?

According to this guy's diagnosis, delusions of grandeur crippled my consciousness, yet all that I needed was salt?

I vehemently disagreed with his bullshit.

"Well . . . do you gamble?" he asked.

I nodded.

"Do you drink?"

My head bobbled again.

"Do you take drugs?"

Same response.

"Do you have problems remembering dates?"

I reminded him of what happened when I entered the office. This time he nodded.

Welsh said, "The only thing you haven't mentioned is infidelity. It goes on to read here that you should have a heightened libido and a tendency toward infidelity."

"Doc, give me the Goddamn pills."

* * *

The first week on the lithium I told my girlfriend, Paula,

"This is the drug I've been searching for all my life. I feel great."

Then I left the house.

Introverted, quiet, not myself, I blamed sobriety.

The second week of the treatment, to eliminate the uncharacteristic ennui I experienced in bars, I snorted a few lines of cocaine. I was still on the wagon, but to my mind, self-medication wasn't cheating. A cocaine and lithium cocktail wasn't the concoction Welsh would have recommended, but because I couldn't drink—I wrote my own prescription.

The effect was dramatic. I walked into my bar feeling like a mental patient in a stadium full of butterfly nets. Everyone was a potential enemy. My eyes darted from corner to corner, face to face.

Worse, even if I could've overcome my anxiety and had a conversation with a woman, I couldn't have closed the deal. I found that out earlier with Paula. The drug had a side effect that the good doctor didn't tell me about. Lithium was salt, and a large dose of it acted exactly like saltpeter. Screwing was as tricky as trying to thread a needle with dry thread—not impossible but difficult.

In my mind, chastity and lunacy were synonymous, and because one of the symptoms of Hyperthymic Temperament was a strong libido, celibacy wasn't an option. Screw those pills. If I were already crazy, not enjoying a woman's company would only make my madness worse.

* * *

When I returned to the shrink's office,

"Hey Doc, you didn't tell me about the sexual side effects."

"They shouldn't be a problem, Mr. Kelly. You won't traffic in those circles anymore."

Shouldn't be a problem?

At the moment, I'm pushing $10 or $15 thousand a game on sports. Even though I'm recently divorced, I have a 23-year-old girlfriend, and I'm cheating on her with two other broads. I'm a bookie, and 90 percent of my business consists of dropping off and picking up money in bars. Yet because this guy has a college degree, he thinks paranoia and celibacy aren't problems?

Thanks to this asshole's pills, I'm so paranoid that when I'm driving I don't think I'm being followed, I wonder if the guy driving in front of me thinks that I'm following him.

"Does normal mean I get to be more like you, Doc? Are you normal?"

The doctor looked up, removed his glasses, blew his nose and said, "Exactly."

For the last time, I glanced at the photo on the desk. The faces unchanged, I said,

"Thanks for all your help."

This Welsh guy might have been a great shrink, but he wasn't my kind of man. An overactive libido and constant optimism were gifts from God, not problems. I'd get to the bottom of what makes me tick, and I wouldn't use salt.

I decided to start in the old neighborhood. That was where it all began.

CHAPTER FOUR

My childhood drowned in whiskey.

Sometimes my old man came home violent. Other times, the unpredictable giant would stumble home with comic books or pizza. When dad's key tumbled the lock, I didn't know whether to grin or grimace.

Whatever mood he was in, Big Tom reminded my brother, Timmy, and me that,

"Small boys are seen and not heard."

When I saw him start to mouth it, I'd shudder.

I'd rather he just smacked me.

The old man said it first in English and then for emphasis, he'd repeat it in Gaelic. To make matters worse, like many alcoholics, he'd forget he said it and repeat himself in both languages.

At home, a small boy I'd always be—but not out in the streets.

Free from rules and restrictions on that Bronx asphalt, heaven became reality. The price of my paradise was 25 cents, the cost of a rubber ball. We kids played ball all day, every day.

Street games developed camaraderie, loyalty and most importantly, love.

Within those four blocks, if a guy was Irish, Italian, German, Jewish, Hispanic, or "funny" (Homosexuals weren't gay yet), whatever, no matter.

Only three things counted—was he one of us, was he a stand-up guy, and how many sewers could he hit a Spaldeen?

Those early years were magical. Only someone who came

from those streets could ever hope to understand that common bond. If you grew up as Gobbo, then whether you were unemployed, a Sergeant on the NYPD, or a Fortune 500 CEO, you'd always be Gobbo.

Future glamour couldn't outshine the beauty of our past.
And how did we express our love?
We broke each other's balls.
It was beautiful.

To survive, we developed sharp wits, thick skin or both. You either broke balls or learned to take it because the only way to stop a ball-breaker was to break his balls worse.

No matter how far you went in life, your old buddies would always remember you for who you were, not who you had become.

And they'd still break your balls.
I tell you it was glorious.

* * *

My old man left Ireland's stone, green fields to migrate to the glass, concrete canyons of New York in 1950. Ten months later, Big Tom sent for his two little blond blaggards, Timmy and me, and my mother, an uncanonized saint.

Our family moved into a three-bedroom fifth-floor walk-up. Timmy and I each had our own bedroom. My two windows overlooked the street. One window had a fire escape, the other a whiskey bottle hiding on a string hanging from a nail.

To prevent my mom from watering down his whiskey, Big Tom would scratch a mark at the liquid level on the amber bottle and hang it out my window. He swore me to secrecy, and as a reward for my silence, he'd let me finish his beer.

I was four.

One morning I awoke to yells. I rubbed my eyes and staggered down the long hallway that led to the kitchen. In that hallway, my brother held his index finger to his lips and stopped me cold. The old man said to my mom,

"I need money for work."

"Money for work?" Mom said. "You need money for drink. Get out of my sight. I have no money for stool-fools. I need money to raise my children."

"Your children? They're my children too," Big Tom said. "If it were up to you, you'd only have one child. Sure, you never wanted Connor."

"Why would I want another child after the way you acted when Timmy was born? Not one dime, now get out of my bloody sight."

I remember sniffling at that, but Timmy put his arm around my small shoulders.

"Pay no attention, Connor. Mom was just mad, and the old man's a drunk."

Timmy was always right, so I put it out of my head. But what happened next never left me.

"Give me lunch money, or I won't go. I just won't go," Dad screamed.

"I don't care if you go or not," Nora said.

We started for the back bedroom and heard a scream. The front door slammed. Timmy and I charged for the kitchen. Our mother knelt. Her hands covered her face. Deep purple wads of blood seeped through her spread fingers and stained the checkered linoleum.

* * *

The following morning, a stranger's voice crept from the kitchen.

"I'll have a chat with Tom, but you must stick it out for the sake of your children, Nora."

"I have to leave him, Father. No woman can put up with this," Mom said adamantly.

In pajamas, puzzled, I rubbed my eyes and wobbled to the kitchen.

"Go back to bed, Connor. It's too early for you to be up," Mom said.

"Why's the priest here, Mommy?"

"I asked him to come. He's leaving now. Back to bed and I'll read you a story."

I turned and pretended to leave but instead eavesdropped. From the hallway, I heard Father Moriarity say,

"Mother Church doesn't recognize divorce, Nora. Your soul is at stake here."

Divorce? Are my parents getting divorced?

I didn't know much about souls or divorce. I just wanted my mother's black eyes to heal and Mother Church to leave us the hell alone.

After the priest left, Mom took me to bed, tucked me in and turned the pages of "Peter Pan."

"Read every day, Connor. That's how you learn."

I reached up and caressed her broken nose.

"Why did he hit you, Mommy?"

"Your father's a good man, but the drink makes him crazy. We must drop to our knees and pray he gets smart to himself and gives it up."

"Don't call him my father. I hate him." I said.

"Shush, you don't know your father the way I do. He works hard and loves us very much. Shuh, in Ireland if he had one pint of Guinness a week, it was a lot. This is between your father and me."

"I hate priests too," I whispered meekly.

"Connor, don't you ever say that. That's an awful thing to say. Priests save your almighty soul."

Maybe so, but my little mind wrapped around one thought. I'd avoid my father and the priests and stick closer to my brother. Timmy would be my North Star.

Mom tried to read aloud but started crying.

Before I knew it, I was crying too.

* * *

Despite the turmoil at home, I felt blessed to grow up in the Bronx.

The Irish Immigrant's ballad proved true. The streets of N.Y. were paved with gold. Not success or money though ...

To this day, I pity people so poor that all they have is money.

No, the teeming Bronx tenements spawned lifelong friends, true treasure.

With 20 to 30 kids surrounding me daily, boredom was inconceivable.

"What you want to do, Gobbo?"

"Let's play stickball till dark, then round up a game of ring-a-levio, or manhunt."

"Screw that. Let's play off-the-wall, or king-queen, then kick-the-can or maybe Johnny-on-the-pony. And after dark tonight, we can play manhunt."

I'd point disgustedly at my fifth-floor window.

"What time does it get dark? I've got to be up by 10 p.m."

In the tenements we went up and down, never in and out.

None of us ever wanted to go up. Up meant supervision and restraint.

"Why's your shirt outside your pants?" Big Tom would badger. "What a stupid thing to ask," he'd say. And when he gave me a clout, "Don't start that crying crap. If you want to cry, I'll give you something to cry about."

* * *

Down meant freedom.

Once I fled those five flights of interior stairs and dashed into the streets, my world changed. Playing with kids from every imaginable ethnic group seeded social skills that would sprout and serve me later.

First we'd choose sides.

If picked first, a kid had street cred, clout.

If picked last, he sucked. If he wanted to play, he had to practice and get better. No one cared about self-esteem. Criticism was harsh, unrestricted and merciless.

Often, money set the tone.

I can't remember a time that I didn't gamble.

Cutthroat competition and betting led to fierce fights.

Sometimes we'd wager a soda or 50 cents a man, a fortune to a child of the '50s, so we treated each bet like life or death. If we had no money, we'd gamble on "shots."

We called it "moons up." The loser had to face a wall and put his ass up while the winner fired a ball at his keister. Even when we had no money, we still gambled.

Gambling just made victory sweeter.

When we played nickel poker or blackjack, we'd even

compete for the best seats. The two seats where players could lean their backs against tenement walls were premium. The other players just filled out the circle.

We'd gamble baseball cards too. We'd both flip them and toss them. We gambled on every fucken thing, and to me it came naturally. I honed my gambling chops on those city blocks.

I had shoeboxes full of Mickey Mantles, Hank Aaron's and other '50s baseball stars, hard currency for a seven-year-old kid.

Degrees impressed our parents, but we kids respected street smarts more. Our classrooms were the stoops and storefronts, not nearby Fordham University.

Besides the college, our backyard had Yankee Stadium, the Zoo and the Botanical Gardens. Our Bronx neighborhood screamed working poor, but with landmarks like that within walking distance, our estates rivaled any tycoons.

We were always broke, but we found ways to get by.

For us kids, Halloween was the ultimate legal shake down. Timmy and I never bought Halloween costumes. We burned wine corks and covered our faces with charcoal, then grabbed two of the old man's hats and trick or treated as hoboes.

Candy was currency too.

When neighbors ran out of candy, they tossed pennies in our paper sacks. Like everything else we did, Halloween was competitive. Bragging about how much shit we garnered became as important as the loot itself.

One Halloween, after two hours of "begging," my bag was stuffed, but I tried one last apartment.

My tiny hand rang the bell.

"Trick or treat."

From a bowl by her door, a generous woman shoveled candy and shouted,

"Mark, come see this little boy's costume. The homemade ones are the best."

I thought,

A burnt cork and an old hat?

"Clever," she said. "See the patches ironed to his worn out jeans and the black electrical tape wrapped around his sneakers?"

Happy enough with my haul, I fled from the woman's door but felt a bit odd.

The patched dungarees and taped sneakers were my everyday clothes.

* * *

The Bronx streets also had rich, wonderful smells and delicious delicacies nonexistent anyplace else—egg creams, pizza by the slice, Italian Bread, great Jewish Rye and rugala from the German Bakery.

But the neighborhood had drawbacks too.

My father and his buddies had access to dozens of "gin mills," such as The Jolly Tinker, The Bedford Chophouse, Darby O Gills, Louie's, O'Brien's. And none of them ever wanted for customers.

Although despised by our mothers, the saloons were irreplaceable sanctuaries for blue-collar workers. In the days before ATMs and cell-phones, saloons were way stations used to receive messages, drop off keys or packages, and serve as a place where a man could cash his check or get spotted $20 until payday.

Connections made over a few beers could also insure that a laborer had a job on Monday. A man's union leader or shop steward was just as likely to be sipping suds in the local oasis as he was.

When dinner was ready at home, the phone would ring, and the bartender would give a patented response,

"Big Tom? He just left."

Three terse words let the caller's husband know that recess was over.

These men took the sting out of a hard day's work with boilermakers.

This concoction consisted of an ounce of whiskey, preferably Fleischmann's, followed by a beer chaser. Boilermakers worked quick and cheap.

My old man saw open whiskey bottles as mistakes and did his best to erase them.

Big Tom came from nothing, barely knew his mother, was proud of his heritage, and wore the title "hard man" like a badge of honor.

His peers could bestow no greater compliment.

We knew at home just how hard he really was, but his friends didn't.

Big Tom was tough, most times too tough.

At times Dad had a callous instead of a heart, but then Big Tom would cry when other men wouldn't.

He bawled openly at my Communion.

* * *

To our parents, we had no real identities. Children were merely reflections of an immigrant's ambitions.

Big Tom and Nora took pride that their kids were well-behaved, schooled and groomed for new-world success, yet Timmy and I felt stunted, restricted and most times intimidated.

We loved baseball, books and TV. We were "Yanks," not "Micks," and saw ourselves as New Yorker's, not kids.

But kids we were.

To a child's wide eyes, Big Tom was a titan. He'd bellow, roar and scare me shitless.

Though drunk often, Big Tom never missed work, which would have been a sign that he couldn't handle his drink.

Calling an Irishman a drunk is like calling another man a junkie. The tag "alcoholic" carried awful connotations.

All our dads drank heavily, but none of my pals, not even when alone, would dare mention the forbidden word alcoholic. Yet the more my old man drank, the harder it was to keep it out of my vocabulary.

* * *

The animated little girl ran toward us.

"There's a drunk in the hall."

My buddies and I laughed. Our ballgame could wait. We sprinted after her. This was unusual, a bit of excitement.

The four of us leapt the stoop's steps and ran into the foyer. Jimmy and Bobby spied the drunk first.

"Look, the bum can't even stand up," said Bobby.

My buddies howled. When my best friend, Gobbo, and I caught up,

Gobbo said, "Holy shit, Connor. It's your dad."

The smile dripped from my lips.

I looked at my friends' faces, and for that rare, singular moment, I hated every one of them.

"Alright you guys. Back outside," I said.

Gobbo helped me lift my dad's dead weight.

* * *

Despite these painful memories, when I came of age, I cheerfully followed the same soggy course. Whether my genes, my spirit, or my demons drove me to alcohol, who knows? Alcohol and my friends molded me more than my education or my parents. Always anonymous at home, the streets furnished me with a distinctive voice.

* * *

We can't apply for passports to the past.

Too bad, in the '50s, the Bronx streets were heaven.

Eisenhower was our avuncular and apolitical President.

He governed in innocent times when even teenagers singing harmless doo-wop in storefronts were considered juvenile delinquents. New York to California took 12-hours by plane, 30-cents bought a movie ticket, newspapers cost a nickel, and even the rich paid taxes.

Although most Bronx neighborhoods were similar, ours was tighter than most. It consisted of a four-block imaginary boundary created by our neighborhood's Catholic School parameters.

We didn't grow up in New York. We grew up within those treasured four blocks.

But if a kid could play ball, like political gerrymandering, we'd reassess our borders.

The neighborhood guys knew your roots, knew about those cold winters when you banged on the pipes for a bit of heat, knew if your old man was a drunk, knew if Charlie's dad beat his wife.

Our friends knew, and we didn't care. We were too close for secrets, part of something special, part of those four blocks.

And those blocks were part of us.

* * *

We fought like hell but no matter what, we always stuck

together against outsiders, always that common bond, always a glorious unity. Neither time, nor distance could ever separate us. I talked my way out of most scuffles, but no one ever called me a punk either.

In the Bronx, that word had consequences. When someone called you a punk, it was as bad as saying something about your mother.

A kid had to fight.

In a few years, some of my childhood friends would be given a crash course in what a real fight looked like. The professors wouldn't wear corduroy jackets or bow ties. Their teachers would be Vietnamese and wear black-pajamas and sandals. Those lucky enough to graduate would remember their curriculum forever, but there'd be no make-up tests for those left behind.

My Italian pal, Vinny, had a big mouth. Sometimes, he'd start a bar-brawl and bail out. Vincent didn't start the fight at Khe Sanh, but he didn't run from it either.

He should have.

He was 18.

Charlie was another one who never came back. When Charlie strolled into a bar, heads turned. He had a tall strapping figure, a movie star's looks, and a voice bold enough to quell a riot.

After the Tet Offensive, an army private washed away what was left of his faceless remains with a garden hose.

Kennedy warned us that freedom had a price.

* * *

Soon, I'd be in Asia to fight my own enemy.

I'd declare war on boredom.

Although not near as high a price as Vinny or Charlie paid, the cost would be dear enough.

CHAPTER FIVE

Decades after I left Vietnam, I darted down a Dublin hospital corridor and spotted three Irish nurses sharing a smoke. I glanced again at the paper with my cousin's room number and asked for directions.

One green-eyed colleen exhaled smoke from her fag and pointed a slender finger toward a long hallway. The trio stood under a no-smoking sign, I laughed and said,

"Wow, no smoking in hospitals any more, huh?"

Bridget took another drag and said,

"Yeah, it's awful really, a real nuisance. Next, they'll be forbidding it in pubs."

The curly blonde nurse smoking next to her laughed and said, "Talk sense, Bridget. Talk sense."

* * *

Back then most Irish shared her sentiments. Irish police flouted and rarely enforced the smoking ban. Because the Brits made many of our laws, we Irish historically have disdain for authority. It's almost a patriotic responsibility to disobey the law.

In the United States, gambling laws garner the same reaction.

We must seem schizophrenic to foreigners.

Lotto thrives in every state. In Las Vegas, Reno and Atlantic City, gambling drives the local economies yet betting is illegal.

Most good-sized towns have off-track betting.

The clergy condemn a gambler's character, yet sponsor and depend on raffles and weekly bingo.

Bureaucrats condemn gambling, then buy boxes in Super

Bowl pools. Office workers, policemen, stockbrokers, doctors, teachers, even priests—everyone wants a box.

Americans follow Super Bowl lines closer than presidential elections. Super Sunday creates a commercial payday for bars, beer distributors, and supermarkets, but bookmakers fear that miserable day because all the action rests on one game. Massive volume on one game can't compensate for the edge bookmakers have with a full schedule.

So, on Super Bowl Sunday old-school bookies juggle their lines to balance money, but our office's biggest fear was getting busted.

On Super Sunday, we write four times our usual slips. One regular customer might call in bets for 12 friends. No other day generates more action.

* * *

Cops hunger for big busts and the big headlines that accompany them. Law enforcers crave publicity. District attorneys, police captains and others, want the public to know the lengths they go to in order to protect their citizens. Big busts look great on promotion and re-election resumes.

So on Super Sundays cops love to break down doors and haul off the ticket-writers who only give the public the action they crave.

Cops seize the betting slips, add up the amount of action, multiply the total by 365, and release statements such as the following:

"The District Attorney's office has just shut down an illegal $12 million gambling operation."

Everybody takes a bow. Great story for the local paper, job well-done by the D.A., and citizens feel relief.

Meanwhile, the bookie's shell-shocked. He couldn't write $12 million worth of action if he had 40 clerks, a printing press and operated out of a warehouse.

* * *

Before we set up shop, Gobbo, Red and I needed some advice.

I called "Julius," also known as Jimmy Simpson. He was

the most degenerate gambler I knew. A former successful big time bookmaker on Staten Island, he swapped conveyer belts of cash for the economic treadmill that he plodded on now. His ardor for action was on par with a politician's for power. Julius earned dumpsters full of dollars but then shuffled the cash to other bookies. His weight was a testament to his compulsive behavior, but I needed Julius's hard earned expertise from his gambling compulsion.

* * *

Julius suggested that the three of us rent an apartment in the most drug-ridden, crime-infested section of the Bronx, which was only four blocks from where I lived. To expedite the process and ensure that no names were exchanged, we threw the superintendent $500. The apartment's rent was cheap, and the precinct cops were so busy with stabbings, shootings, and drugs that they wouldn't be bothered with us.

* * *

The apartment was a five-floor walk-up in a dingy tenement. We "decorated" accordingly. The living room had two old couches and a cheap television. In the other room, opposite the bed, sat two folding tables. Above those tables hung a wall-sized white-board and a large digital clock. Sitting on the tables were four rollover phones and a tape recorder.

Rollover phones were necessary. We supplied our customers with an 800 number, Gobbo's idea. A free number made access easier. If one phone was busy, the call rolled over to the next. On Sundays, all four phones rang off the hook.

Each call was written on a different betting slip. Our paper slips were 4 X 4 carbon triplicate forms. After we took the action, my partners and I each took a copy home to calculate. Separate locations insured "the work" was accurate. If mistakes were made in the player's favor, the bettor wouldn't say shit.

Any discrepancies my partner and I had were rechecked before Monday night's action. Monday night we'd tell the caller his weekly figure.

Any problems, we'd say,

"Call back after the game starts, and we'll go over the

work." Nine times out of ten, the players were wrong. If a bettor insisted he didn't make the bet, we played him his tape. Once the "figures" were correct, the hard part came—collecting.

That part of the operation would eventually prove our undoing.

CHAPTER SIX

"My name's Jack. I'm an alcoholic, six-years since my last drink."

"Hi Jack. Hi Jack," the chorus resonated from the folding chairs of the donated Presbyterian Church hall.

For the last two tedious months, I had wasted my time at the "Plug in the Jug."

Subjected to Jack's story, I took a long drag of my Marlboro Light and clutched the Styrofoam cup that held my fourth coffee in 30 minutes.

Jack said, "If anyone thinks that I don't belong here, let me tell you about my arrest. One night, I got drunk and robbed an appliance warehouse."

Jack would have been a good-looking guy, except his teeth were far too big for his mouth. He stuffed a cookie between his oversized uppers and lowers, chewed and paused for dramatic effect.

"I had three TVs stacked in the alley outside the warehouse. But by then, I sobered up a bit, and realized I hadn't thought this through. I had planned my getaway on a bicycle."

I turn to the weathered face next to me,

"That's it. I'm outta here. I can't be this screwed up. I don't belong here."

He said, "You don't belong here?"

"No way, I'm as pathetic as these guys."

"Your dad a drunk?"

"Yeah."

"His dad a drunk?"

"Yeah."

"But you don't belong here?"

"No."

Stone faced, he said, "I'll save you a seat. You'll be back."

In the packed parking lot, I spotted my car, slid behind the steering wheel, and thought,

Fuck him, "You'll be back."

I can beat this without A.A. I've been going it alone since I was a kid. I remember drinking in bars when I was a teenager.

* * *

The bartender pushed the pitcher of beer at Patsy. The sagging jowls, stained white shirt, and the careless cigarette hanging from Cliff's lips attested to his apathy. Cliff snatched my friend's fiver and asked,

"What's that funny smell?"

Less than 20-feet away at a small-round cocktail table, I sat with my other friend Bob and yelled,

"Turkish cigarettes, I roll them myself."

"They smell like prison laundry," the barman said.

"Yeah, but they're cheap."

Patsy grinned, winked at me, and placed the freshly poured pitcher of beer on the table across from us. He couldn't put the beer on our table. We couldn't take the chance it might spill because the table's left hand corner held the sheet of wax paper that I had piled high with a Jell-O and mescaline mixture.

It was my brilliant idea to mix the two. When we wanted to get higher, we simply touched our index fingers to our tongues and dipped them into the pile of strawberry concentrate and back to our tongue . . . perfect.

Bob passed me the joint.

I was 16-years-old in a Bronx bar, and the bartender was clueless about pot. He wasn't alone. In 1964, only Jazz musicians and hipsters smoked weed.

The legal drinking age was 18, yet only the ex-marine, Bob, was of age. Without us, this dump would have been empty. For proof, Cliff even accepted library cards.

I dated the ex-marine's daughter. After Korea, Bob did five

years in Dannemora for armed robbery. Released last month, Bob turned me on to pot.

I passed him the joint.

"No fucking way, Bob. Not after you've been drinking, no way. I don't care how old you are. Can't be done, impossible."

Bob said, "We'll bet $5 and do it right now."

As he made his case, his eyes brightened,

"I have a sophisticated palate."

"So you're saying that after getting loaded all night on mescaline, you can sip three glasses of draught beer and tell the difference between Rheingold, Schaeffer, or Budweiser? You've got a bet," I said.

We blindfolded Bob and lined up three 7-ounce glasses. He sipped,

"This one's Schaeffer."

I was impressed.

"This one's Budweiser."

I was astonished.

"Of course, the last one's Rheingold."

Remarkable. I handed him his pound and applauded.

Hours after Bob left, the flutters from the hallucinogen had fled, but I was still a little whacked. Cliff called me to the bar.

"I didn't want to start any problems before, but all these taps plug into Schaeffer. It was on sale this month, so that's all we got."

* * *

My old man was the real deal.

From my bed, I watched Big Tom reach out my window and pull in the fishing line. On the other end of the line, five-floors above the courtyard, hung his Fleischman's bottle.

Like Fagin from Oliver Twist, he fretted about his treasure.

His fears were well-founded. Knowing Big Tom was powerless against his addiction, the ever-vigilant Nora watered down her husband's whiskey.

* * *

"Hey mom, you know who died?"

"No, who?"

"Mike Fitzmaurice."

Her thick brogue sounded confused,

"Mike Fitzmaurice? Dead? Is he? But shuh, he didn't drink at all?"

"Mom, people die other ways besides drink."

* * *

I rode the packed city bus that took me to the Catholic Prep School where I was a senior, and amidst the confusion, the clamor and the cigarette smoke, I was squinting for the third time at the letter Timmy had sent me from France.

"Paris is getting a bit boring. I think I'll jump up to Belgium in August, maybe cross the English Channel, and have a few laughs in London."

I refolded the letter and replaced it back inside my blazer pocket. The gray, littered sun-bleached streets rushed past the bus.

My eyes waded through the sea of white shirts and ties. Weaned on movies about exotic locales, such as "Macao" and "Casablanca," I was green with envy.

I'm stuck in a five-flight walk-up with a lunatic for an old man, yet Timmy finds the Air Force and Paris a little boring. I gotta get me some of that boredom.

I loosened my tie. The Bronx in June. I should've sat by a window.

* * *

My old man's disease progressed along with my buddies' drug habits. My former sanctuary, the street, had changed dramatically. Drugs had poured in. No one played stickball anymore. Everything placed a distant second to getting high.

As I walked past the pizza shop, Kenny stopped me.

"Hey Connor, man, you gotta cigarette?"

I reached into my shirt pocket, and for the first time, studied the deteriorating mess who only a year before had been the neighborhood quarterback. Kenny's nose ran. His eyes nodded. His dirty fingernails scratched the undernourished arm that sprouted from a filthy T-shirt.

Kenny wasn't alone.

My friend Paul sat on the stoop with his face buried in a number-two-brown-paper bag containing plastic cement. I thought,

This guy's going nowhere fast.

I was wrong. Two years later, Paul, the glue-freak, became Ace Frehley, lead guitarist of the rock band KISS.

Other friends weren't as fortunate.

Vince and Charley had already "bought the farm" in Vietnam.

Shit, the war was real. Guys were dying. If I joined the service, maybe . . .

Nonsense. I was too "street-smart" to die.

* * *

When heroin began rotting the neighborhood, it was time to ship out. If I left the Bronx, I'd stay straight. Besides, as an immigrant, I owed my country. I decided to join the Air Force and help defend the Vietnamese from themselves.

After all, who was more qualified than a blue-eyed, blond-haired 19-year-old Irishman with a drinking problem to decide Southeast Asia's fate?

I'd defend my country, see the world, and get clean and sober. What were the chances Southeast Asia had drugs?

CHAPTER SEVEN

"What time ya got Deacon?"

A decade older and a more accomplished drunk than me, the Deacon's younger brother was Timmy's best friend. At 18, that made me feel like a big shot.

I had to shove off soon.

I was well past whacked, and the field we had been drinking on since noon was as black as a crow's wing. The Deacon normally had an alcoholic shine in his eyes and a rosy bloom to his cheeks, but even from five feet away I could barely make out the portly, amorphous frame that answered.

It was late. What time ya got, Deac?

"About 2 a.m., why, you worried LBJ will end the war before you become a hero?" he asked.

Jesus, I had to be at Whitehall Street in five hours. Manhattan seemed a long way from this open Bronx field.

I had never traveled on a plane before. Once aboard, I had hoped sleep would come easy. I'd need it.

When Deacon talked about the war, he might as well have been talking about another galaxy. Vietnam seemed fictional.

I hoisted the Jameson bottle to my lips. It brought tears to my eyes. I quickly wrenched the quart bottle of Schaeffer Beer from Deacon's hands to chase the Irish whiskey's harshness.

As the bottle emptied and the hour drew near, I started talking serious.

"You were in the Navy. The first day has to be a cakewalk, just orientation and shit like that, right?"

"Yeah, don't worry about nothing. Once they swear you in,

you're Government Issue, just another GI who belongs to Uncle Sam. He takes care of everything. For the next four years, you'll have nothing to say about how the government uses you. You belong to them now," he said.

I thought,

Bullshit to that. I'll have something to say about it. I'll figure out an angle. I always do.

* * *

Three hours later, I broke my mother's heart.

"Come here ma. Let me hold you one last time."

Her head rested on my shoulder, and her tears told me what her tongue couldn't.

"Don't Mom. I'll be alright."

Nora knew my enlistment was my ticket out of that fifth-floor walk-up. Mom also knew that the ticket was one way. Even if I came home limbless, I would never come back here.

My head was stuffed with bats, but when I felt my mother's vise-like grip, I knew it was her last unspoken plea. The pain in her eyes fed my nausea and chased me to the stairwell.

Whenever I thought of home over the next four years, it was with guilt. But I had to leave. The idea of open skies and water tormented me.

Because of novels and movies, my heart had desired distant shores and the beat of rough blue waves on long golden sands. My eyes had yearned for the distant views of mountains almost as much as my ears had longed for whispers of women and romance.

I knew it was all out there somewhere, and I wanted it . . . all of it.

Apart from my mother, I would miss the streets and my friends, but to paraphrase Thomas Wolfe, I should have known that the streets I would dream about were long gone, as dead as my childhood, and any memories of them only ashes.

The Air Force promised a chance to see the world, an escape from drugs, alcohol and my old man. But I'd learn a hard lesson ahead. No one runs from himself. No matter where we go, we bring us with us.

* * *

A sleepless flight landed me in formation at San Antonio's Lackland Air Force Base. The dark Texas night framed the barracks that I'd call home for the next three months.

A seven-foot, lanky sergeant barked incomprehensible commands. His Texas drawl, demeanor and the speed of his sentences confused my sleep-deprived brain.

The beanpole screamed,

"From now on you have no name. You are Airman Basic—11819876. You understand?" His mouth was inches from my ear. "Repeat it. Who are you?"

I managed to stutter,

"I'm Armen Basie, 118198?? I'm sorry, sir. I forget the numbers."

"Sir? I ain't no fucken sir, stupid. You call me Sergeant."

He moved on to the next GI in line . . . Then a thought struck him, and he was back in my face. His breath smelled like someone had set fire to a pet shop.

"Armen Basie? What the fuck kind of name is that?"

I thought,

Jesus, help me. I escaped my old man for this lunatic?

* * *

Finally inside the austere barracks at 3 a.m., two-rows of bunk beds stretched half the length of a football field. I wanted to collapse on one and bury myself beneath the covers to make this nightmare disappear.

I had just drifted into a deep sleep, when my ears awoke ahead of my eyes. A thunderous voice swallowed the barracks.

"Get up. Get up. Get up."

Each refrain louder than the one before,

"Get up. Get up. Get up."

Good God, someone's gone insane.

A fresh screaming face circled the barracks.

"You've got 10 minutes, scumbags. Shit, shower, shave and be in formation for chow—outside in 10 minutes."

This drill sergeant was shorter and louder than his counterpart. He wore a tan shirt with three stripes down and two up attached to both sleeves and a Smokey the Bear hat. The creases in his matching pants could've cut cheese.

I didn't need to be on the wrong side of this maniac, and he said 10 minutes. I sleepwalked to the latrine to secure a commode. The toilet bowls had no partitions, so I heard the guy with a Southern drawl who sat to my left.

"Man y'all stink. This is worse than the outhouse back home. At least there ya only got to smell your own shit."

Rubbing the sleep from my eyes, I turned and looked into the eyes of a country boy as big as any outhouse.

A voice from my right seemed more familiar. A mouth full of gold teeth from Philly spurted,

"Ain't this some bullshit, some fucken country turkey rapping about outhouses."

This is a bad dream, I thought.

Wait, I'm not here for a sociological study. These boys are ripe. I'd better concentrate on the business at hand.

My shower finished two parts of the morning trilogy, and in what turned out to be a big mistake, and because my face was bowling ball smooth, I skipped the shave.

I couldn't be late. I had to hustle-up and fall out. It wasn't smart to begin boot camp by drawing attention to myself. I wanted to remain anonymous, which for me was a formidable task.

Before we marched to chow, the Drill Instructor inspected our formation as closely as he would a jewelry piece. He stopped at me.

"You shave this morning boy?"

I had never shaved before in my life.

"Yes sir."

"I ain't no fucking sir, stupid."

"Yes, Sergeant."

"You're a liar, boy. Your face has more peach fuzz than your N.Y. ass. From now on, before the sun comes up every morning, you fall out and dry shave."

By the end of the week, my face was pulped—a baked, blood-raw disaster exacerbated by the white-hot Texas sun.

For the next three months, all I thought about was sticking a knife in this prick's throat. If that was the point of 12-weeks of basic training, the Air Force succeeded. For the first time in my young life, I wanted to kill somebody.

* * *

At last, after five weeks of boot camp, they allowed us a beer. At the Post Exchange, I was gulping a pitcher when the Tennessean who shared my table asked,

"They got drive-in movies in New York?"

He wore a button-down, blue dress shirt with an alligator logo embroidered over the pocket and a pair of tapered-black chinos. He was coarse and boring, but I would have drunk with the devil himself.

"Only one. In the Throggs Neck section of the Bronx, but I don't have a car."

"You don't have a car? What are you a virgin?"

"What does driving have to do with sex?" I asked.

The mountain boy looked smug and lifted his pitcher. He poured beer into his plastic cup until foam ran over its lip.

"Well if you don't drive, where do you get a little poontang?"

"We go up to our friends' apartments. I've been with lots of girls," I lied.

He leaned close and hesitated. I saw a bit of devilment in his eyes.

He broke into a jack-o'-lantern's grin and spit out the source of his glee,

"You got oysters in N.Y.?"

The phrase seemed so benign. I was surprised. From my experience on the streets, I expected a monumental put-down or set-up.

"Sure we got oysters in N.Y. I love oysters."

Relieved that I didn't have to lie to defend my nonexistent sexual prowess, I relaxed. Oysters were subjects I could talk about with some authority. I gobbled oysters like M&M's.

Unbeknownst to me, we were talking about two different subjects. Ottawa, Tennessee was a long way from any ocean. In the mountains of the South, eating oysters constituted a rite of passage. In Tennessee, oysters were a euphemism for hog's testicles. They'd fry them up and dare outsiders to eat them.

The mountain man's eyebrow rose with what seemed newfound respect,

"You like oysters? Really? How many can you eat?"

"I don't know. It depends. Usually two or three dozen."

His skeptical voice raised four octaves in disbelief. Words sputtered from his mouth,

"Two or three dozen?"

"Yeah, usually two sometimes three," I said.

"Wow. I never met anybody who can eat that many," he sang. "How do you like them cooked—fried, roasted, broiled?"

"No, I eat 'em raw."

"Raw?" He almost fell out of his seat and screeched, "Raw?"

"Yeah raw, just a little ketchup, squeeze a little lemon on 'em. I like 'em raw."

I left the table and headed for the bathroom.

I took advantage of the exchange's enclosed toilet to alleviate the constipation that had built up because of my shyness of shitting while staring at the other GI's.

My deed done, I washed my hands and headed back to my beer. The Tennessean had disappeared. We talked little the remaining months.

Weeks later when I had figured out what had happened, I cracked up. This guy must have thought that anyone who had eaten three-dozen raw hog's balls just might take a chunk out of his country ass.

CHAPTER EIGHT

A few years ago, the NBA busted one of their referees, Tim Donaghy, for gambling. Donaghy bet on games that he officiated and tipped off the mob. He won at an 80 percent rate. Although buried deep in a coal mine of corruption, this "canary" never sang.

"I'm alone in this," he said.

For "cooperating," Donaghy was sentenced to only 11 months.

Huh?

How does keeping your mouth shut and taking the rap classify as cooperation? Donaghy never gave anybody up but instead told the FBI that betting on contests he officiated never interfered with his play calling.

* * *

If I wrote 20 years ago what I'm writing now, someone would have put "two behind my ear."

If this tale is true, I couldn't have written it back then, and if the story's a fable, then it's a damn fine fairytale.

* * *

A caricature straight outta "Jersey Shore," came into the Jolly Tinker, an Irish pub where I tended bar.

Frankie had the whole package—gold chains, thin black mustache, and a Brooklyn accent too thick for "Goodfellows."

New Yorkers have a reputation for rudeness. Bronx guys particularly tend to generalize, to categorize and paint with a broad brush. Nothing's sacred.

I figured Frankie for a "Polly-O Mozzarella."

Polly O's a brand name cheese, not the genuine mozzarella sold in good Italian delicatessens. It's a phony, a poor imitation wrapped in plastic and marketed for mass consumption. Irish guys use this idiom to describe bullshit gangsters—"wannabees"—guys who act like they're connected.

A typical sentence from a "wannabee" would be,

"You know who my uncle is?"

A typical Bronx Mick's answer would be,

"Yeah, your father's brother. Now give it a rest."

After knowing Frankie a month, I discover he's a decent guy, a little much with the "wise-guy" shit but an all right guy.

Because I worked in saloons, he asked if I would help him set up a bar that he bought out by Belmont Racetrack. I said sure.

* * *

Two months later,

"Hey Connor. I'm stuck for a bartender this weekend. You think you can do me a solid and fill in?"

"Frankie, I'd help you out, but it's not my kind of joint. I work Irish Pubs. Your place is a wise-guy joint," I said.

"Hey man, I'm really stuck. You gotta bail me out."

* * *

I had a full bar, but because I had set the joint up, I knew my way around and handled the crowd easily. Most of my customers wore suits. Fine-looking women hugged their arms. It was a class joint, so I wore a white shirt and tie, no problem.

A well-dressed guy, as big as a beer truck, walked in and planted himself in the middle of the bar.

I tossed a bev-nap casually in front of him,

"Whatta ya having, pal?"

He decorated the mahogany with a C-note.

"Give me a Dewar's on the rocks with a water side, and give the whole bar a drink. Put whatever's left in your tip cup."

Wow, this guy's a sport, I thought.

Extending my hand, I said,

"My name's Connor. Who should I say the drinks are on?"

He grabbed my mitt and said,

"Tommy."

I built his cocktail and did the honors up and down the bar.

I worked my way down and continually pointed to the hulk sitting in the middle of the bar.

"That's on Tommy. That's on Tommy."

I snatched the hundred and told him the tab was $77.

He said, "I told you, throw the rest in your cup."

"Thanks again, Tommy."

* * *

I had $500 on the Laker game, so as I worked the stick, I kept glancing up at the TV screen.

Tommy noticed.

"Ya got a bet on the game?"

"Yeah, a nickel on the Lakers."

"What's the spread?"

"Four and a half."

"Watch the last two minutes of the game. I guarantee you Magic has the ball in his hands the whole time."

I said, "Yeah, well that's why Johnson gets the big bread. He's the best player on the team."

Tommy said,

"Magic gets the big bread because he does what Jerry Buss wants him to do with the ball in the last two minutes, and he makes it look good."

Buss owned the Lakers and the L.A. Forum. I had seen him play at the World Series of Poker, so I knew he gambled.

Tommy continued, "Buss bets huge on or against the Lakers, and Magic brings it home for him."

I nodded my head politely. But I figured,

What does this guy know?

With the game long over, it was pushing 2 a.m. The bar thinned out, and Tommy had had six healthy pops of top-shelf scotch, which must have loosened his lips.

"Let me tell you a story," he said. "Three years ago, Vegas lost bundles of money on the NBA totals. They got killed by gamblers who bet the over and unders. The casinos demanded that David Stern, the NBA Commissioner, investigate.

"Stern said, 'Nothing's going on.'"

"The casino CEOs said, 'Fine. We're pulling the NBA off the board because something is definitely going on.'"

He leaned closer to me.

"Stern decides to investigate because if Vegas pulls the NBA games, who's gonna watch? They found out someone had gotten to the timekeepers. In six major cities, the timekeepers were quick or slow with the clock depending on whether they wanted to add or subtract minutes from the game. Think about it. There are so many fouls in an NBA game that even a two-second difference on each one could add four or five minutes to the clock."

"How come I never heard anything about that?" I said.

"Why would you? The league doesn't want that getting out," he said,

"What do you do for a living, Tommy?"

"I tend bar."

"You're a bartender. Just like me, so why do you know so much?"

"I just know."

* * *

The next few minutes, I washed glasses and wiped down the remnants of the night.

"So listen, thanks for the splash tonight. I appreciate your patronage. Where do you work? I'll come and make a stop," I said.

"Don't worry about it," he said.

"No man. You came to see me. Let me reciprocate. I want to do the right thing. Where do you tend bar? I'll come and see you."

"Well you really can't. I work in a private club," he said.

"A private club?"

"Yeah, I tend bar in the Ravenite Social Club."

I started laughing, "Good Christ, you work for John Gotti. How the hell did you get that job? You must have to be deaf, dumb and blind."

He laughed, "Just about."

His story suddenly had more credibility. That's exactly how wise guys operate. They don't buy off guys at the top. They wave the money at low-level earners who can be bought.

* * *

Two months later, I was drinking a cup of coffee in a diner and waiting for my eggs. I grabbed a copy of the New York Daily News. Plastered across the front page was a picture of my buddy, Frankie, opening a Cadillac door for John Gotti. He had driven "The Teflon Don" to his trial in Manhattan.

Holy shit. Frankie wasn't a "Polly O." Frankie was on the level, apparently, a lot more on the level than the NBA.

CHAPTER NINE

After Air Force Technical School, I submitted my "dream sheet." Because my brother, Timmy, was stationed in Paris, I asked to be sent overseas.

The personnel department stamped my request, "Worldwide," and I eagerly anticipated my orders.

What exotic continent would launch my odyssey—Europe, South America or Asia?

One month later, I reported to Charleston, South Carolina. A town labeled by my fellow servicemen as "200 years of history unmarred by progress."

Undeterred, I made the best of a weak draw.

I was in town less than four hours, just about long enough to get my 19-year-old ass squared away at the Air Force Base. Like an astronaut ready for launch, I was eager to check out these Southern belles whom I had read so much about. Scarlet, Jezebel and Blanche wait until you get a load of my act.

I was from New York. These goobers down here didn't have nothing on me.

I had already been to two major cities, San Antonio and Wichita Falls. A military man now, I had flown twice, tried blue cheese for the first time, and on leave, I even went "all the way" with a girl. Counting my adolescent grappling, the expected groveling and one or two failures, to my manic mind, I was practically Beau Brummel.

I told the cabby,

"Take me where the action is."

He said,

"That would be down by the navy strip."

He drove down by Charleston Harbor to the seedier section where all the dives and strip joints were and pulled up outside one of the least egregious.

I paid the tab and tipped him liberally adding,

"Here you go, pal. Now you can get that operation you had your eye on."

As I exited the cab, I smugly replayed the line in my head and thought,

What a smooth line.

At the circular bar, I grabbed a stool and ordered a beer. Because I obviously radiated that sophisticated mature military aura, the bartender neglected to proof me.

My cropped haircut and rigidity of carriage tipped off the server that I was a GI. Not one to be bothered with minor incidentals such as proof.

I wasn't halfway through my beer when a knockout slid onto the stool beside me. She asked,

"Would you mind a little company?"

I thought,

Jesus, what a great town this is.

Less than two minutes later, another beauty appeared on my left and gave me the same routine. They prattled on and on about my precious blue eyes and my charming way of talking.

I knew that Bronx accent of mine would carry weight. God, I love women.

Sure enough,

"Sugar, you sound like a gangster," the redhead gushed.

The flattery flowed, and I gobbled it up. This joint was great, but then the bartender interrupted,

"You owe $18 for the drinks."

I looked up surprised.

"Why so stiff? The beer was only two bucks." I casually turned and asked,

"What are you girls drinking?"

"Champagne cocktails." they said in sync.

No matter, I had about $80, and at this rate, I'd have one

of them gift wrapped in short notice. I handed the bartender a $20 and lost myself in my admirers' Southern drawls.

The y'alls and sugar pies continued to fly.

I loved military life.

A few "champagnes" later, I had settled on Sheila. She had suggested a booth. Alone in a dark corner I ran my only move by her, and Sheila responded.

As the night unfolded, we got cozier. Sheila's fingers had the polish and finesse of a three-card Monte dealer. She rubbed my thigh, and her hand occasionally got careless enough to deliver just the right amount of promise.

As the bartender wiped down the bar, and turned the stools up, Sheila confided in me what I had suspected for the last two hours. She worked here, and her job was to make the customers feel welcome.

However, luckily enough, Sheila really liked me. It seemed I wasn't like the other guys that came in here.

I was different.

I wasn't at all surprised. Of course I was different. I was from the big city, New York. Her voice was low and throaty. She let her hand linger a few seconds longer knowing that it was soft and inviting and knowing what it was doing to me.

"I'm not allowed to leave with anyone, or I'll get fired," she husked. "Pay your tab and right down the block is an all-night diner called The Coffee Cup." She rubbed the inside of my thigh and said,

"Go there and wait an hour until I get off, and then we'll go back to my place. This way my boss won't catch on, and I won't get in trouble. Does that sound okay?" She asked the empty space where I once sat.

The moment I heard, "back to my place," my bell-bottoms flapped like flags in a gale. I couldn't have moved any faster, if she had said,

"We found a bomb. You have three seconds before it explodes."

* * *

After eggs, bacon and some horrible concoction that my

eggs raced across called "grits," I got restless.

I passed the hours with two more cups of coffee but still no sign of my "date."

I sauntered toward the Coffee Cup's picture window and glanced up and down the street.

Dead quiet.

I looked around the packed diner and noticed for the first time that the customers were all men. The suckers restlessly checked and rechecked their watches. If not staring at their wrists, they fixated their eyes on the one greasy clock mounted above the cash register. A few, as dumb as me, even looked out the window.

* * *

This humbling episode took some spring from my step, but it also taught me that the geographical parameters of the Bronx streets hindered as well as comforted me.

Growing up in the N.Y., streets wasn't a pat hand.

In life, I'd draw cards from a random deck, a deck not prejudiced by childish beliefs.

The tuition for this particular lesson was $80. More lessons in women and life would follow. But as the years passed, the lesson I paid for in that Charleston diner that night would prove a bargain.

* * *

Realizing "streetwise" might not be the proper adjective to describe my teenage ass. I continued my education. I ran into a tutor in the form of a Greek from Brooklyn.

Jim Ballis worked with me as a data processing machine operator.

"Hey man, you're from N.Y.? Are you hip to the Doors, or The Mother's of Invention? Do you get high? Do you play poker? What part of N.Y.?" He asked.

The barrage of questions didn't faze me. I was familiar with the mindset of the native New Yorker, and Ballis had an A-type personality to boot.

"From the Bronx and yes to all of the above."

Then, I asked, "Where you from?"

For a change, his machine gun mouth produced a single word, "Brooklyn."

I sized up my newfound friend quickly.

This guy was a keeper. He didn't have movie star looks and wouldn't make much of a wingman, but he hit on two of my favorite subjects—drugs and gambling. And he seemed smart as shit.

The dark-haired, wiry Greek continued,

"Yeah, when the Sergeant was showing you the office, the second I heard your voice, I figured I better introduce myself. Me and you are the only New Yorkers."

Jimmy Ballis and I became fast friends. Ballis threw my gambling addiction into high gear and taught me nuances about poker that opened up a whole new world.

I started making money almost as fast as him, and although an Airman Third Class only earned $79 a month, we shared a luxury apartment off base. Jimmy and I ran poker games, and lived a life other GI's could only dream of.

One Sunday afternoon while raping the suckers in our game, Jimmy came home.

"How ya making out?" he asked.

"I'm up about $400," I said.

"Piker," he said, as he tossed $2,000 on the table in front of me.

"Where the hell did you get that?"

"I bet the Giants against Dallas," he said.

"You can gamble on football?" I asked.

My mania shifted into high gear. I thought,

Shit, I know everything about football. I can clean up.

* * *

I had joined the service to see the world. Instead, I was harnessed in Charleston. It was time to take advantage of Air Force privileges. For $2.00, the price of a box lunch, I could hitch a ride on a cargo plane going anywhere that the U.S. had a base.

That meant Europe.

It had been two-long years since I had seen my brother. I

wrote to let Timmy know the good news. Spring would soon lead to summer, expect me in July. No better time to visit.

The glue on my envelope was barely dry, when I tore open his response:

"Connor—

This might not be a good time to visit. Even though I can get the time off, Europe's a little boring this time of year. As much as I'd love to see you, we should figure on a later date. Right now, I have nothing planned. If you reschedule your trip, I could fix up something more definite.

—Timmy"

I couldn't grab a pen and paper fast enough. That son-of-a-bitch, my own brother, and the guy I looked up to all my life. He didn't want me over there. I couldn't believe he didn't want to see me. My mania kicked in. I pulled no punches.

"Tim—

Fuck you. I booked a flight.

I will arrive in Frankfurt on August 1, at 3 p.m. If you're there when I arrive, great. If not, I'll make my way through Europe without you.

Your brother,

Connor"

CHAPTER TEN

It was hotter than crushed red pepper that May in South Carolina.

I gulped a frosty mug of Pabst, winked at my pal Gerry Hannon and goaded the bar's owner,

"Hey Hank, when are you going to start serving blacks in here?"

Hank's steel eyes glared at Hannon and me. Irritated, the stern German sneered, thought and then maliciously spit out,

"As soon as I find someone stupid enough to eat 'em."

His venom stopped me cold.

Three miles from Charleston Air Base, two German racists, Hank and Jim, owned Mueller's. The brothers refused to serve blacks and didn't care much for whites.

It was 1966, racism ruled the South, and being drunk was about to save my life.

* * *

"Why not come to Jacksonville this weekend?" Gerry grinned. "Meet this good old boy Waldo. We'll take you to a joint that makes unbelievable Singapore Slings."

Blessed with teeth like Chiclets, premature-gray hair, and a tall athletic build, Gerry Hannon wowed the women, but I didn't hang with Gerry to bottom feed. I hung with Hannon because he guzzled booze like a man with a month to live.

I hesitated,

"I don't know Gerry. I'm strapped."

"Don't be a pussy. Crash and eat at my house. You only need booze money. Besides, my sister's a piece of ass."

"You're using your sister for bait?"

"Take her to the movies. See how it plays out. She'll like you, man."

* * *

Friday night found me asleep on his parent's couch. A rumble from the kitchen startled me. I opened one eye and spied Gerry's drunken father pissing into the near empty refrigerator . . . so much for eating in.

* * *

In Hannon's promised oasis Saturday night, good old Waldo, Gerry and I sat on stools pounding the famed Singapore Slings.

After four tall ones, I faded fast.

The two Floridians were just warming up.

When closing hour arrived, my two pals poured my unconscious carcass into Waldo's Oldsmobile.

* * *

For the second straight night, a foreign noise awakened me.

Unlike the benign interruption of Gerry's urinating father, this time, a blinding invasive bright light assaulted my eyes.

"This one's alive and moving."

While I struggled to make sense of that sentence, my right palm reflexively searched for my chin. My swollen jaw felt like I caught Muhammad Ali's best right hand. I spat out crumpled pieces of enamel like chunks of sand.

Kneeling on the car's carpet, my head tilted upward toward the Oldsmobile's roof, I uneasily lowered my eyes to the empty space that once held a windshield.

An enormous oak tree climbed from the car's crumpled hood. The Oldsmobile's smashed headlights hugged the oak's splintered trunk. I shifted my eyes left and spied the mangled steering wheel.

Don't move.

Piece it together.

What the hell happened?

What was the last thing Waldo said?

"This old Olds has guts. I got it for a song. Let me show you what it can do."

* * *

Hannon and Waldo were tossed through the windshield like two duffel bags. Paramedics now wrapped their lifeless bodies and hoisted the bloodstained body bags into awaiting ambulances.

I hazily felt each of my limbs: delicately, slowly.

My arms were fine, legs fine, no leakage, no sign of blood.

While the paramedic's cold hands fumbled on my chest, I considered the chaos about me.

How can this be?

Both of my buddies are dead, yet, except for a few broken teeth, I'm unscathed.

When my chin hit the dashboard, my teeth absorbed the full force of the crash and miraculously knocked me cold.

Being dead-drunk saved my life.

The state trooper said,

"Fifteen years on the job, I never saw anyone walk away from a wreck that bad."

I felt awful. Hannon and Waldo got a bad break, the luck of the draw. But between gambling, drinking, and drugging, I had little time for sympathy, too little time, too much to do.

With me, nothing ever changed.

* * *

That same year, Truman Capote's book, "In Cold Blood," vaulted into a National obsession. One chapter chronicled two Kansas killers hitchhiking. Both determined to murder the next Good Samaritan who picked them up.

Perry Smith's unemotional slaughter of the Clutter family haunted my generation's psyche much the way Hitchcock's "Psycho" haunted the previous generation's and "Jaws" would come to haunt a future generation's.

Only days after Gerry's burial, I received another warning.

* * *

After another losing bout with a bottle of Johnny Black, I hitchhiked the short-ride back from Mueller's to the airbase.

It was well past closing time, but cars still stopped along this short-strip for servicemen. So despite the pounding rain, and

Capote's book, I decided to thumb it.

A pickup truck pulled over, and I sprang into the passenger seat. The driver wore a wet, dirty, white trench coat with a raised collar.

"Thanks a lot, man. I really appreciate you stopping."

As my benefactor checked his side mirror for oncoming traffic, my bleary, red eyes sized him up.

He was a powerful man with a large square head under long, black greasy hair. Two huge paws gripped the steering wheel. His knuckles were thick, coffee-colored and round like garlic knots. Dark, broad brows rose outward from twin creases below his forehead and hovered above the unemotional eyes and long hooked beak.

"I was only out there a couple of minutes when you came along. I'm just going up the road to the Airbase," I said.

My silent companion's recessed eyes stared straight-ahead, absolutely motionless.

"I've been in Charleston almost a year, but I'm from New York originally. You from around here?"

Still nothing.

As fog smothered the unlit, deserted road ahead, I began to feel antsy.

Most people pick up hitchhikers for company. Drivers break up the monotony of a long trip, or, as in my case, to help someone out of a jackpot. This guy was different. The indifferent hulk hadn't so much as glanced in my direction.

I fought silence with silence. At least I was out of the rain. Fuck him. It was no skin off my ass. Soon, I'd be back in the barracks.

The stillness didn't last.

As the pickup hugged the curved, slick asphalt road, Frankenstein squinted through the truck's wipers and sang lyrically,

"You really didn't learn a thing from that accident in Jacksonville did you. You're still not on God's path."

What the fuck did he say? Did I hear this guy right? I gotta be fucken drunk . . . Jacksonville? God's path?

"Excuse me? What did you say?"

The monster turned, his face impassive. His cold, black eyes stared through me, but his mouth refused to budge, as if someone had painted the grim sneer on his face.

Now I shivered, shook and felt the thump, thump, thump of my heart. My teeth rattled like two dice. I glanced out the passenger window, clamped my mouth tight and calculated,

If I jump at 55 miles-per-hour, can I survive? When I hit the ground, will I be able to run?

The storm worsened. The curves of the road forced him to slow up, and I thought,

Maybe now's my chance.

But we were less than a mile from the Airbase, so I held on. Seconds later, Capote's novel, the stranger's words, and the night's gloom cast an evil pall over me.

I lost control.

I started to shake and sniffle. The hollow feeling in my chest overwhelmed me. It was a fear I had never experienced before, an obscene feeling, as if soiled steel fingers ruptured my shirt, pierced my breastplate and choked my heart.

The truck mercifully slowed and skidded to a stop outside the Airbase's guard gate. The driver turned, stared, waited what seemed forever and said,

"Nice night for a murder."

That's it. Oh my God.

I sprang the handle on the door and bolted. I never said thanks or even fuck you. I didn't look back nor hear the truck accelerate. I stumbled, tripped and tumbled past the sentry. I felt my lungs tighten, my heart swell, as though oxygen couldn't reach my blood . . . like a vein might pop.

Nice night for a murder?

Was that crazy bastard playing some kind of game?

What was all that stuff about Jacksonville and God? How did he know about Florida?

Who was he?

* * *

My mania forbids lingering.

Good news or bad, my brain hops like a frog on speed.

After contemplating my miraculous survival and the stranger's warning, I dismissed any mystical or spiritual explanations as mindless superstition.

That maniac behind the wheel said Jacksonville taught me nothing. He was right, but I'd learn my lessons soon enough.

The professors ahead would be strict, their curriculum harsh.

CHAPTER ELEVEN

A week before my European trip, Ron pounded on my door. "Wait 'til you try this shit. You won't believe it."

I met Ron Byers here at Charleston AFB, and he figured it was a foregone conclusion that I was going to swallow this shit. Byers knew my weaknesses, but even I was uncharacteristically hesitant.

"I don't know Ron. LSD is an acronym, a warning. 'Look out Super Dope.' You just started smoking pot last week, and already, you're screwing around with this shit?"

Byers wore a pair of tan chinos with a yellow dress shirt peppered with bright red roses. He had it untucked to hide his considerable paunch.

"Exactly, you turned me on to grass, now I'll do you a favor. You'll love it. Come on. It's a beautiful day to trip. You'll thank me for this."

Ron was dead on about the beautiful day, so maybe he was right about the hallucinogenic. It was early summer, and Charleston's famed palmettos sported small, white flowers that blossomed on magnificent, long green leaves. The Spanish moss hung like tinsel from the oaks, and the air was thick with odors that passed for the antebellum South—a perfect day to get walloped.

I examined the small orange keg that Ron handed me. It was no bigger than a rice kernel. How much damage could it do?

We dropped the barrel-acid on the way to a diner. Shortly after breakfast, we were driving in Ron's car, and I felt a funny flavor in my mouth.

An acerbic, lemon drop tang guided my tongue across my teeth. My lips reacted involuntarily and mimicked the sounds crude construction workers make when pretty girls walk by.

When I glanced at Byers, I got my first fright. His head was inflating like a balloon at the Macy's Thanksgiving Day parade.

Multiple waves of exhilaration fluttered through my body. A fatuous smile tattooed my face. Moments ago, I was colorblind, yet now everything was bright, crisp and clear.

Wow, if my eyesight was like this . . .

I tossed a piece of gum in my mouth. It burst with flavor.

Oh my God this gum is fantastic. What is this shit called, Juicy Fruit? Do other people know about this stuff? How do they keep this on the shelves? Is it habit forming?

Sam and Dave blasted from the car radio. "Soul Man's" horns pulsated inside my chest. Vibrations drove through my body.

Then another fright, the radio knobs melted and dripped to the floor mat. Moments later, the radio dissolved completely, but the music still deafened us.

A seismic-shiver started at my heels, crept up my spine and erupted into my brain.

I grasped for a shaky Marlboro and negotiated the cigarette into my mouth, but my Zippo was problematic. A pulsating, throbbing fistful of stainless steel expanded and shrunk in my hand. I couldn't figure out how it opened. Three traffic lights later, I finally torched my smoke.

Then an epiphany, the lunatic behind the wheel was as stoned as I was. How was Ron driving when even tying a shoelace would be a challenge?

Another rush of the acid staggered me. I snuck a cautious peek over at Ron. Thrust from his mouth, like a fat sleek seal, his swollen tongue wagged from side-to-side accentuating two saucer-sized eyes, which glowed in giddy delight.

While Byers squinted to negotiate the road, this prodigious pink protrusion flopped wantonly out of his two massive lips.

"My God, Byers, how in the hell can you drive?"

"I just follow the white line, man. Wherever it goes, I go."

This wisdom placated my twisted brain a moment until I turned and looked out the passenger window. A Ford-Explorer passed with all four wheels facing me. My head pivoted violently side-to-side hoping to correct my vision yet nothing changed.

The Ford's doors hugged the asphalt while it zoomed past me. First the Explorer's front wheels flew by. Its rear wheels lagged way behind. Stretched and elongated like a slinky, the front end patiently waited until the trunk magically scurried to catch up.

I gulped too much air and rasped, "Byers, did you see that car?"

His huge head bobbled.

Thank God.

Byers saw the same hallucination as me. I wasn't crazy. I relaxed a moment until I realized again that he was fucken driving.

What little part of my brain still functioned screamed,

Wake up asshole. This guy has your life in his hands.

"Byers, you can't drive like this. You've got to pull over."

The traffic came to an abrupt halt. Ahead loomed a swing-bridge. The few cars ahead of us stopped to await the go-ahead.

To open, swing-bridges slue on pivot mechanisms.

When the steel turns at a right angle, boats cruise through the newly created void. Utilizing the topography, the engineer ensures that the structure never has to elevate. Instead of opening vertically, like usual drawbridges, the bridge turns 90 degrees.

After the structure swiveled, Byers said,

"Isn't this acid amazing? Doesn't it look like the bridge is rotating?"

"Yeah, holy shit, it does, unbelievable. The steel looks like it's going sideways."

But then a moment of lambent lucidity,

"Wait a minute. If the bridge is not actually turning, why are all the other cars stopping?"

Byers, the man behind the wheel, the man who controls my life thought a moment.

"I got it. Everybody's tripping."

Of course, he was right. Everybody was doing LSD. What was I worried about? The driver had everything under control. Byers' cunning analysis reassured me that I was in competent hands.

After we crossed the bridge, Byers drove to what appeared to be a park, acres and acres of uninhabited land. I was besieged by massive amounts of birds—flocks and flocks of screeching, cawing, squawking pelicans, seagulls, and pigeons.

This is more like it, no stress.

The waves of exhilaration continued while we strolled the glorious acreage, and the colors, sounds and smells were absolutely beautiful, really gorgeous.

Suddenly the movie "Yellow Submarine" made sense. No wonder it was filmed like a cartoon. I felt like I was in one.

Everything was exactly like that movie. I was living in Technicolor. Day tripping, wow far out, I had a new perspective. As the warm sun settled on my face as softly as benediction, the LSD implanted this new insight in my brain. For the first time, I recognized reality.

"Wow, Byers, thanks man. This is the greatest day of my life. Really cool, and this place you brought me to is perfect, really beautiful, all the wildlife, the pelicans, seagulls and pigeons. I mean really exquisite."

"I knew you'd love the acid," Ron said. "But try and keep things in perspective. We're walking through the Charleston City Dump."

Of course, perspective, Ron was right.

But just as he spoke, a seagull rose like the Phoenix from one pile of garbage to settle effortlessly on another. In majestic slow motion, the bird's wings fluttered to a halt and seemed to flap in a magical, poetic cadence, a rhythm that only a musician or spiritualist could appreciate.

Wow man, garbage dump or not, this place was a magnificent paradise. I could stay here forever.

At least until the acid burned off or we found another bridge to drive off.

CHAPTER TWELVE

The C-130 barely touched the Frankfurt runway, when I spied Timmy through the porthole window.
So you showed up. You fuck.
With his arms folded, Tim leaned against a Red Austin-Healy convertible alongside a tubby, balding, short guy who had either neglected to shave for a month or was a Yasser Arafat impressionist.
I was determined to greet him coldly.
But once off the plane, my brother hugged me and said,
"Look at you. You're all grown up. How was I to know? When I left, you were just a kid."
His greeting eliminated any and all resentment that I might have harbored. Because Timmy had been both brother and father to me, I craved his acceptance.
Timmy's companion extended a pudgy paw.
"Hi, I'm Ronnie. Throw your bag in the boot and jump in the back. We're heading up to Belgium for a week or two."
The August day was boiling hot, the air acrid. A smell of fresh tar and dust blew off the paved tarmac.
Because of the weather, I was thrilled Ronnie was driving a convertible, but because it was a two-seater, I was worried if he'd have enough space in his trunk for my massive bag.
I had over two-weeks worth of clothes, yet I was puzzled.
All the Healy's trunk held was two-small gym bags. I said,
"Wow, glad you guys travel light. Sorry for the big bag. I didn't know you were picking me up in a sports car."

* * *

The Autobahn's unlimited speed limit unnerved me.

From the Austin Healy's jump seat, my eyes were glued to the speedometer. I couldn't even enjoy the scenery. Ronnie raced over 100, yet as the sun set behind us, a car astoundingly blinked its lights and looked to pass. Ronnie meekly pulled over to the right hand lane and let a white Ferrari impatiently blow by at 120.

By the time we rolled onto Ostende's streets and parked, it was midnight. Timmy's thirst awaited no mortal. He leapt from the passenger seat, grabbed his gym bag and bolted to the Montmartre district.

I lugged my huge grip behind him.

After a short walk through the teeming streets, Timmy seized an empty stool at the huge U-shaped bar of the Horseshoe Saloon and ordered a Tuborg beer and a shot of Jack Daniels.

I joined him inside and looked around for our accommodations. Not seeing a traditional check-in desk, I pulled up a stool next to him and asked the obvious,

"I'm whipped man. Between the flight and the drive, I need a shower and some sleep. Where we staying? How far's the hotel?"

Crow's legs formed around Tim's eyes.

"What do you mean?"

"Where did you book us?"

"Book us?"

"Yeah. Where do I sleep?"

"Here."

"Here?"

"Yeah. Here," he said.

"But it's a bar."

"So?"

"Where do I sleep?"

"At the bar."

"Where do I take a shower?"

"There are public showers across the street for 25 cents."

"Are you kidding?"

"If we pay for lodging, we'll have no money to drink."

"But what happens when they close?"

"Close?"

Timmy motioned to the entrance. For the first time, I noticed the "Shoe" had no doors. They didn't close. For my dissolute brother, this was paradise found.

"Fall asleep at the bar. No one will bother you."

"What about my bag?"

Timmy yelled to the bartender,

"Donal, throw my brother's bag in the storage room in the back. Would you?"

* * *

After two days of drunken lunacy, Timmy began to disappear in stages, first for a few hours, then for a day, and finally,

"Where the fuck is Timmy?"

On my third day, about 2 a.m., I returned to what passed for my sleeping arrangements. As the bartender brought my Tuborg beer, I noticed a face scrutinizing me from across the bar. Four times his eyes landed on me, but whenever I looked up, he jerked them away.

I tried to ignore him and turn my head. I shielded his glare with my beer bottle, but the stares persisted. Fuck this. Time for a grunt, a stern look, and a questioning head nod in his direction.

From across the bar, the disarmed stranger said,

"Sorry to stare at ya, man. You look exactly like my friend. I've been searching for him for six hours. He told me he'd be here."

"Your friend's name Timmy Kelly?" I asked.

"Yeah, I knew it man, had to be."

He grabbed his beer and change, slid to my side of the bar and parked himself beside me.

I grabbed his mitt.

"I'm Timmy's brother, Connor."

"I'm Roy Silbert. Your brother told me to meet him here."

He laughed and said,

"Where the fuck is that lunatic off to now?"

Roy had an engaging likable smile and bright curious eyes.

"I don't know. I'm getting worried."

"How long is he missing?"

"At least 24 hours."

"Oh, that ain't shit. He's OK."

"What? This ain't strange?"

"I've known Timmy two years. Nothing he does surprises me. Finish your beer. We'll take a walk. Maybe, we'll get lucky."

* * *

The twists and turns of the district's streets transported us past the clubs and the bars of Montmartre. Sounds of Marvin Gaye and the Beatles exploded from narrow doors that led to crammed cellars where sweaty young bodies grinded, rubbed and bumped.

It was the first time I had seen the red-light district at night.

"I've been drunk since I got here. How the fuck do you guys do it, Roy? I'm so hoarse. I can barely talk, and I'm fucken exhausted. What keeps you going?"

He was a powerfully built, medium height man, around 25. Roy wore a tan sweater, loose blue jeans and hiking boots. He reached into the money pocket of his bell-bottoms and grinned. His palm produced at least a dozen black beauties.

"I take these," he said.

For the first time, I noticed that his face had hardened. His cheek had tightened, and the teeth on the right side of his lip were clenched.

Biphetamine.

I had seen and used "black beauties" before in the Bronx, but because of my mania, my tolerance for them was very low. When I took speed, I'd go off the walls. But after two days and nights in Belgium, I needed the boost.

"Well, what the fuck man? Don't hold out. It's about time you clued me in."

I popped one.

"Take two," he said.

"No. I usually only take a half. They seal my jaws. If I take two, I'll have to drink beer though a straw."

"They seal mine too," he said. "That's the perfect name for black beauties, 'the jaws.'"

* * *

Hours passed, inside the clubs or out, no sign of Timmy. One drink inside each dive that we had searched left me well past stewed and ready to surrender.

Just before dawn,

"I've had enough, Roy. Brother or no brother, I'm heading back to the bar and grab some sleep. I might even break down and get a room."

"You're right. For all we know, he could have gotten lucky, and he's lying in a nice warm bed with some piece of ass while we're out here searching for him like two assholes. He might even be back at the Horseshoe waiting for us."

"Let's head back," I said.

The two of us turned around for the short walk back. We turned left at the first corner, and there lying in the gutter head resting firmly on a parked car slept Timmy.

"Holy shit, Roy. He's out cold. Let's pick him up, and get him off of the street."

"Why?"

"What do you mean, why? We can't leave him here."

"Why not?"

"What if someone robs him?"

"Take his wallet. I do it all the time."

"Take his wallet?"

"Yeah, I've tried picking him up and lugging his ass back to the bar. He gets pissed, and I end up breaking my ass for nothing. So now I just take his wallet."

"You mean this happens a lot?"

"All the time."

"All the time? Holy shit. How bad a drunk is he?"

"When your brother's on holiday, he spends it drunk. That's it. That's Timmy. But when he's sober, or getting drunk, he's so much fucken fun that before he steps through the looking glass and turns into a pain in the ass, everybody puts up with his bullshit."

Roy reached into Timmy's back pocket and lifted his wallet. My jaw dropped.

I couldn't believe that only two years in the military had transformed Timmy, my idol, adviser and comforter in adolescence into this slobbering drunk. I was disgusted . . . the fucken Air Force.

Roy read my disappointment and said,

"Hey man, don't get the wrong idea. This is Timmy on holiday. Your brother sober is one of the smartest guys I know, plus he has a social conscience and the heart of a missionary. I almost killed him last year in Paris. We had $5 left to our name, and he gave $3 to a homeless mother to buy milk for her kid. But once he starts drinking . . ."

Roy's not telling me anything I didn't know but still, asleep on the street? I knew that genetically for Tim and I there was a thin line between having a few drinks and full-blown alcoholism. Timmy had already started to erase that line.

* * *

No sooner did we start the short four-block walk back to our "accommodations" than the dawn brought with it a thunderstorm.

Wind kicked up. Black clouds roiled in the sky. In front of one of the clubs, a green-and-white-neon Heineken sign swung menacingly on a metal pole.

Then the sky opened.

Rain clattered on tin shingle roofs. It sluiced out of gutters and formed multiple rivers, which flooded first the streets and then the sewers of Ostende. We had to wade into the bar.

Roy spied two "over-served" German frauleins and started up a conversation.

From the bar's open doorway, I watched the pounding rain dent the massive puddles that flooded Ostende's curbs. My conscience interceded. I walked to Roy,

"We have to go back and get him."

"You go ahead if you want to. I ain't moving."

"You're not going to help me?"

"I ain't moving."

"He might drown."

We debated a few minutes. One blonde took my side.

"You must help your friend. No? You can't leave him out in the rain. In Stuttgart we don't even leave animals out in weather like this. What kind of man are you?"

A bellow from the doorway ended the argument.

"You believe this fucken rain? I saw my life pass in front of me. Quick, Donal pour me a double cognac, neat."

I looked toward the roar. Dripping like a washed puppy, Timmy shook himself at the doorway.

He calmly walked over to Roy.

"You got my wallet?"

"That's it? It's been three months. No hello? No how are you? No glad you made it? Just, you got my wallet?" Roy asked.

"First things first, do you?"

"Yeah, I got it."

"Thank Christ. I was hoping it was you. I didn't think I got mugged."

The bartender poured the cognac. Timmy hugged Roy and then slammed the snifter.

"I don't know how long I was passed out, but when that rain came, it peppered my face like Sugar Ray Leonard's left jab. What a miserable way to wake up."

"You better get into some dry clothes," I said.

"No, I'm cool. Screw pneumonia. A few drinks and a couple of croissants and I'll be back in business."

He turned unperturbed to one of the blondes.

"Hi ya, gorgeous. I'm Timmy. Have a drink with me., and we'll tell anyone who asks or gives a shit that while your beautiful blue eyes watched, I died in your arms."

* * *

Because of the pills that day, I ate next to nothing. At the bar, Roy used a cigarette lighter to heat a can of Campbell's cream of mushroom soup, and we shared it.

Since our ride to Belgium, Ronnie had long since abandoned Timmy for more tranquil and saner activities, so that night found Roy, Timmy and me in one of the hottest clubs in Ostende, Stephano's.

The three of us huddled at the bar and involuntarily gyrated to the sound of Marvin Gaye, which blasted from the DJ booth. Purple and orange lights smacked a disco ball, and prisms of color flooded the dance floor. I saw a stunning young girl dancing with a woman about three decades older.

"Wow, she's a knockout."
Timmy said,
"Ask her to dance."
"She looks a little young."
"Young? What the fuck, you kidding me? You're only 19. You're not in New York. This is Europe. Grow a pair of balls. Ask her to dance. What can she say?"
I gulped my Johnny Black to summon courage.
"Yeah, I will. I will. Don't rush me."
I waited till the dance ended and the two women returned to their table. They joined an older man, probably my target's father. I waited for the next song and decided it was now or never.

She was exquisite, so petite, so lithe that she seemed like she wasn't sitting on her chair but only perched on it.

I had no shot here, but I couldn't look meek in front of my brother. The whiskey steeled my resolve. I stood in front of her, made a pocket of air in my jaw, cleared my throat and sputtered out.

"Excuse me, would you care to dance?"
Innocence lifted her head.
Good Lord, she was stunning. Her coral blue eyes were shy, yet piercing and analytical.

Small, and pliantly thin, she wore two shades of blue. A turquoise mini-skirt and a sparkling, sapphire-sequined blouse, which I can only imagine she carefully selected to match those magnificent enigmatic eyes.

Her lips were full and dark red, which only accentuated the chalk-white teeth that glistened in the crescent created by her timid smile.

"Oui," she whispered.
When she stood, I caught the slightest sparkle in her eyes, which gave me hopes of better things to come. Tied in a bun

atop her head was titian colored hair, which exposed the naked nape of her neck and made her look about 16.

Before grasping my outstretched hand, she spoke two or three quick sentences to her companions in French. I led her to the dance floor to the sound of Otis Redding's, "I've Been Loving You Too Long."

We danced slow and long. She moved gracefully in my arms, and I acted like a gentleman. The next song was a fast '50s classic called "Runaround Sue," and one I liked to dance to.

Dion and the Belmonts were Bronx boys. In the '60s, everyone whom I knew in New York could do a fair Lindy Hop. To this tune I could flat-out dance.

And I did.

I taught her the three or four necessary fundamental moves, and as she twirled, she laughed. When we came together, we both relaxed in each other's arms. She was easy to lead. Her feet were light, the chemistry perfect.

The next song was another Northeast favorite, "Mustang Sally" by the Rascals, another favorite of mine.

A black guy whom I used to hang out with taught me a mean "skate." His lessons came in handy. She was clearly impressed.

Because I was a better dancer than her, it gave me the confidence I needed.

The next song, and I remember every tune and the order in which they were played, was "A Whiter Shade of Pale," another slow dance. We embraced, and two minutes into it, her hair smelled like everything I loved about New York.

Her thighs slid against mine and made me dizzier than the scotch. I unlocked our cheeks and kissed her neck.

My beachhead established, I decided to advance further inland.

I slipped a tongue in her ear, and she pulled back sharply.

She stared at me surprised . . . and then . . . and then . . . her eyes softened and the corners of her mouth slanted upward. She gave me a sisterly kiss and then held up her palm. She left the dance floor, returned to her table, spoke with her parents a few moments and returned.

We moved slowly and barely shifted to the music. I closed my eyes and pulled her hard toward my groin, lost in her arms and the magic of the moment. This was how I had always envisioned Europe, captivated and lost in a beautiful French woman's arms.

When I reopened my eyes, her parents were gone.

Both the table and the night were ours.

We sat and ordered drinks. She spoke little English, so she again held her palm upward to signal wait while she left for the ladies room. When she returned, the bun was gone. Her lovely auburn hair now hung loosely across her shoulders.

She said everything I needed to hear without saying a word. I was ecstatic.

We drank and danced the next three hours in Stephano's until she signaled we should leave.

* * *

The beach was six blocks. But the way I felt, I would've walked with her across Europe. We strolled the sand barefoot, held hands, and struggled to communicate. I spoke no French. Her English was weak to nonexistent.

Clouds crowded the sky and covered the moon, which made the beach as dark as an unlit cellar. When the moonbeams occasionally peeked from behind the clouds, they lit an imaginary path across the English Channel. The breeze was clean, cool and saturated with fresh scents of wet sand and salt.

Monique was from Marseille, 23 and marvelous.

Frustrated with our inability to talk, we just shrugged, laughed and threw ourselves into each other's arms. She had rented an apartment overlooking the beach, and for the next three days, I was glued to her.

We tried to talk and couldn't. Instead, we laughed and made love. At that we succeeded. We made love everywhere and everyway that love could be made.

I had three weeks to spend in Europe. If I had had my way, I'd have spent every moment with Monique. Maybe it was the French mystique, or maybe it was because words couldn't ruin our memories. But to this day those three days remain untarnished.

We used our bodies and eyes to communicate.
We shrugged, laughed and fucked.
Heaven.
When her vacation ended,
Hell.

* * *

In this forgotten age before cell phones, it occurred to me that maybe, just maybe, my brother was worried. He saw me leave with Monique, so I had figured he knew that everything was cool.

While Monique packed, I made her understand that I was stopping at the Horseshoe to tell Timmy and Roy that I was all right.

It was nearly noon when I entered. The sun streaked the streets and cast a shadow through the now all too familiar no-doored opening. The racetrack-shaped bar had few customers. Timmy was half in the bag regaling Roy with a story about his encounter with the blonde German girl.

"I don't remember shit," Tim said. "But this morning, she tosses my clothes out in the street and screams without an accent, 'If you ever come back here again, I'll cut your balls off.' I'm telling you man she sounded like she was from Newark instead of Stuttgart. I mean perfect English and man was she pissed."

Through tears of laughter, Roy asked,

"What da fuck did you do to her?"

"How da fuck do I know? What? You think I stuck around to ask? I'm fond of my balls."

When I approached, neither seemed particularly concerned about my three day absence.

"Hey, here you are. We were thinking about sending out a search party," Roy said. "That little French number you were with was cute. What was she about 16?"

"No, she was 23." I bragged. "And amazing."

"Nice. I figured you spent the last couple of days with her," Tim said. "Welcome to Europe, little brother. You going back there tonight?"

"I wish. She's leaving for Marseille this morning. She's

packing now, but she said she'd stop here on her way out of town."

We had a few beers and compared notes. I was just starting to get comfortable, when Monique appeared. Her dress was too short and too thin. Any curves she had, and although tiny she had plenty, were visible.

I beamed.

Monique nodded civilly to Roy and Timmy, and then her mouth seized mine. When her lips broke our seal, she took one step back. Placing her index finger to her mouth, she kissed the digit and then placed it on my smiling lips and said in perfect English,

"Goodbye, my American."

When she walked out of the bar, the sunlight left with her. Gloom descended.

Timmy and Roy were struck dumb.

But Timmy was never speechless for long. He recovered and said to no one in particular,

"You believe this? Goodbye, my American, I dream of shit like that. I'm in Europe two years. I get, 'Come back again, I'll cut your balls off.' My brother's here less than a week. He gets, 'Goodbye, my American.'"

Drunk, Timmy could be rude, but sober, Timmy always said the right thing.

I glowed.

I could've kissed him.

Perfect, just perfect.

My wanderlust re-enforced, I decided right then and there that even if it meant Vietnam, I was asking for a transfer. I had joined the Air Force to see the world.

I had to get out of South Carolina.

CHAPTER THIRTEEN

I asked for Vietnam, and the Air Force couldn't even get that right. In hindsight, I guess I should have counted my blessings. A lot of lads with lost limbs would have had given more than I could ever have imagined for the safe assignment that I drew, a computer operator on an Air Force base in Northern Thailand. Because of the temperature necessary for the computer to operate properly, I worked in the only air-conditioned building in Nakhon Phanom. Booze was cheap and drugs were everywhere.

"Sith, send one of your boys across the Mekong into Laos. Have him bring back two shopping bags filled with pot," I said.

Sith supervised the Thai civilians who worked the mess hall. He always wore tapered black chinos and a white collared shirt open at the neck. He was sinewy and small, with thick, black hair, which he combed straight back.

In the few months since I had been here, we had become like brothers.

"I send tomorrow, no worry," Sith said.

"Tell him the ferry ride across the Mekong is on me, and I'll pay him $5.00 for his time. Make sure he only cuts the tops of the plants."

In 1969, "Thai sticks" sold for $20 a pound. For a measly $2 a pack, the Thais would even empty the tobacco from American cigarettes and refill them with marijuana.

But I didn't want run of the mill Thai sticks, so I paid $10 for two shopping bags filled with exotic Laotian weed.

With Laotian weed, two hits and I coughed until my

testicles screamed for mercy. When I stopped, the world was a different place.

Amazing.

I could have had Sith's man bring back five or 10 shopping bags for the same price, but why bother? Weed grew everywhere in Southeast Asia. Monsoon season ensured that.

* * *

I sat on the side of my bunk and wondered,

Am I the straight guy or the guy who's high? Wait. Get a grip. That's schizophrenia.

I asked another soldier in the barracks.

"Jose, do you think smoking 20 joints a day is too much?"

"Nah."

"How much do you smoke?" I asked.

"About 40 joints a day. You're all right man."

"Still, given the quality of the weed, 20 joints a day for three straight months might be a bit excessive," I laughed.

But reassured by Jose, I reached for the Marlboro box in my shirt's left pocket, removed a filtered joint and torched it. What the hell, one more nail in my coffin wouldn't matter.

Because of the red line that ran horizontally across my baby blues, the working girls in Nakhon Phanom nicknamed me "Dar Juan." In English, that means "sweet eyes."

Sometimes, especially while high, I wondered why we were even in this strange land of giant bugs, wild weed, and wilder nightclubs. I decided to read a little history about the country that I had been sent to save.

* * *

As early as 1916, Ho Chi Minh had asked Woodrow Wilson for America's help to rid themselves from the yoke of 80 years of French colonialism. Despite his fluency in seven languages, Ho Chi Minh couldn't make Western governments understand that all the Vietnamese wanted was autonomy, so the emaciated, birdlike, wispy-bearded man's plea fell on deaf ears.

Three decades later, in 1945 Saigon, the former pastry chef again proclaimed Vietnam independent. Because the Vietnamese helped America defeat the merciless Japanese during WWII, this time Ho Chi Minh was sure that Harry Truman would support their well-deserved freedom.

The frail little leader opened his petition with words he thought should resonate in the American President's ears.

"All men are created equal and endowed by their Creator with certain inalienable rights, among them life, liberty and the pursuit of happiness."

But Truman couldn't focus on Southeast Asia. He had Stalin, the iron curtain, and a fragile re-election campaign on his plate. So once again, the delicate little Asian man's pleas were ignored within the bureaucracy of 1600 Pennsylvania Avenue.

America was made up mostly of Europeans. French votes might help Truman get re-elected. European voices counted. Asian votes didn't.

Following Mao Zedong's People's Revolution, the Republican Party used China's fall as a political football. The right wing would use any means necessary to regain the power that, thanks to Franklin D. Roosevelt's popularity, Democrats had held for almost two decades. Republicans speciously claimed that Democrats could have prevented the Chinese revolution.

When Truman upset the favored Thomas Dewey for a second term, this ridiculous accusation triggered the final blow to any semblance of civility in American politics. Right-wing extremist, Joe McCarthy, even went so far as to label President Dwight D. Eisenhower a communist.

On the political defensive because of the right wing's propaganda about China, and attacks by the John Birch Society, when Truman was re-elected, his Democratic administration fired all their current Asian diplomats, which included the brilliant John Davies, a man who had lived in and understood Southeast Asia.

Because Truman cleaned house, Eisenhower's Asian advisors were inexperienced and uninformed. Ike's advisors couldn't grasp that Ho Chi Minh was a Nationalist first and a communist second. Communist paranoia of the '50s trumped common sense.

Under the Kennedy and Johnson administrations, 48,000 innocent American boys would pay dearly for the folly of political vindictiveness.

Not this American boy.

I was hardly innocent and wouldn't pay dearly.

But, I wouldn't be on a scholarship either.

* * *

I was thrilled to arrive in Bangkok, "the sin city of Asia." I dreamt of this all my life, at last an exotic land teeming with adventure.

I had a two-night layover before a smaller plane would fly me "in country."

A cabbie procured me some weed, and I hit the nightclubs looking for women.

Beneath disco balls and colored lights, Thai women of every size and shape mobbed the dance floor.

Mama San's system was simple.

Each prostitute had a number. Above the dance floor, an electronic board displayed the numbers 1 through 300. The GI picked a girl and handed Mama San five dollars. That girl's light went off. She was sold.

It was a meat market.

I visited "Thai Heaven" and a few other well-known spots but didn't leap in.

I was no yokel. I was from N.Y. and "sophisticated."

I was only 21. Women in Thailand were, and sadly still are, commodities. Because of the hostilities, every GI knew that the next day could be his last. Although not as immoral as the war itself, we were hardly altar boys.

* * *

Alcoholic and manic, Bangkok hit me the way Alka-Seltzer hits water. A testosterone-loaded, Bronx-Irish Catholic unbridled in a world where most previous taboos were now legal and accessible, I detonated in all directions.

My first night, however, I started slow.

I smoked a joint and slugged a half bottle of Robitussen AC for the codeine. Well-fortified, I headed for a massage parlor.

I lumbered the long stairway, paid Mama San her $2.50, and then tottered down a narrow hallway, which led to an open room that resembled a zoo exhibit. Behind a glass wall, a bevy of young, gorgeous, longhaired Thai women smiled and waved hoping to be selected.

One blew me away, simply stunning.

She held my hand and led me to her spotless cubicle. On the left, clean white linen covered a massage table, to the right sat a bathtub.

She wore Hooters-type shorts and a thin halter. After she undressed me and submerged me into the hot bath, she switched to thin bikini panties with no bra.

Using a sponge, the masseuse scrubbed every inch.

The opal-eyed beauty's expert hands roamed from between my toes to places previously privy to my fingers alone. After the wash, the weed and the codeine, my muscles welcomed her magic.

She towel patted me dry, laid me on the massage table and went to work. She walked on my back, bent me backward and kneaded the stress out of my neck, shoulders and body.

Finished 45 minutes later, she asked, "Chuck wow, duey?"

"OK," I said mystified.

Pleasantly surprised that the phrase meant "happy ending," I watched her rub Vaseline across her fingers and palms to finish me off. She rewashed me with a hot cloth and rubbed me down with talcum powder.

My $2.50 well spent, I could have slid under a closed door.

Massage parlors became a daily routine and a harbinger of an insatiable Asian sexual appetite.

* * *

I received few letters.

My mother faithfully sent a letter once a week. A neighborhood girl wrote once a month. Although 20 years older, her father, Bob, was a friend who was caught up in the swinging '60s phenomena of drugs and rock and roll.

Bob's daughter asked if I might mail some pot to the Bronx.

I thought about it and weighed the dangers. Sending drugs through the U.S. mail constituted a felony. Leavenworth wasn't a pleasant thought.

How could I do it safely?

No return address was a given.
What about dogs smelling the packages?
Mothballs?
How to say camphor in Thai?
It took a week. The camphor cost $25.00, the two kilos of pot $1.50.

I wrapped the pot in plastic bags and then rewrapped the bags with a plastic coating containing the camphor. But what if they busted Bob when he picked up the package?

I scotch-taped a piece of loose-leaf paper to the inside plastic bag. It read,

"I'm sending you a surprise."

With a smart lawyer's help, Bob could plead ignorance.

* * *

After the package went through without trouble, my mania kicked in.

I deliberated starting a business.

I had access to opium, amphetamines, barbiturates and with Sith's help, even heroin. One package of pure heroin could either set me up or put me away for life. But thoughts of a bigger problem than prison scared me straight.

If the package got through, how could a 22-year-old kid sell that much heroin in N.Y. without buying a bullet behind his ear?

* * *

A friend in London wrote that he needed money to get back to the States.

Instead of money, I sent 5 kilos of Laotian weed.

He peddled it by the joint and lived large in Europe for another year.

Laotian weed differed from its Thai counterpart. It tasted milder, almost like smoking a Parliament cigarette.

* * *

Besides Sith, my only real friend in Asia was another GI, a Polish guy from Newark, Richie Malecki. We both spoke Thai but feigned ignorance. We wanted to know what the prostitutes were saying about us when they thought we didn't understand.

One day, we traveled 70-miles north to Sakonnakorn. The

hookers here were not Westernized, little make-up, no miniskirts.

They didn't encounter many Americans. So to attract Orientals, they dressed more traditionally and avoided looking Western like the prostitutes in Bangkok.

Richie and I rented two girls and split a hotel room.

While I carried out my bit of mischief, the girl in the other bed that Richie was with said to her companion,

"Farongs ben yi. Farong mi yi quey duey." Translation, "Foreigners are big. Foreigners must have big dicks too."

The prostitute that I was already screwing turned and said impassionedly,

"Mai, miengun Thai, nitnoy quey."

Translation? "No. This one's the same as a Thai, little dick."

When she stuck a pillow in my mouth to smother the sound of my cawing laugh, she looked confused. Once the working girls realized that I spoke their language, their fees dropped to three dollars, and I negotiated myself into a few bouts of gonorrhea. (I'm not looking for a Purple Heart, but we all serve in different ways).

* * *

After payday, I glued myself to the poker tables. Separating the suckers from their paychecks took four days. Some novices sat in my one dollar to ten dollar game with a chart to indicate whether a flush beat a straight, so I raped them.

A honed gambler, I filled shoeboxes with cash.

As the Italians say, "La Dolce Vida."

I didn't know then that within a month life wouldn't be quite so sweet . . . and that I would end up gambling with my life.

CHAPTER FOURTEEN

Like many gamblers, I liked to vacation in Vegas.
Compulsions don't allow holidays.
The stickman wore a string tie, a white shirt and his emotionless face seemed like he wanted to be anywhere but here. Even his thin brows couldn't make his eyes seem interested. Double sixes tumbled to "ahs" of disappointment.
"Box cars, craps, he didn't come to do it. He won't do it again," the croupier sang.
I slid $1,000 worth of chips into the table's grooved wood and grinned at the savvy houseman's jargon as he worked the hot table.
"Craps, the danger's over," he sang as his stick flicked the dice back to the player.
"Double up, and catch up."
I liked the lingo of craps and the pleas of desperation from the wild-eyed, desperate gamblers who crammed the table.
In short, I loved the juice.
I glimpsed to my left at the middle-aged, fat man deluding himself with the high-priced bimbo attached to his arm.
"Blow on these baby. I need a hard eight."
He wore a gray leisure suit with a yellow silk shirt opened too far to the waist exposing a thick matt of curly chest hair. The cowboy hat was blacker then his chest hair and probably a Stetson. The diamond on his pudgy-left pinky told me that this high roller would never wear imitation anything.
His sweaty palm massaged the six dice against the soft green felt. He coaxed and charmed them with a soft certainty before

his right fist selected two of the six ivory puzzles and shook them. His hand climbed to his ear, and he asked,

"Come on dice. What did the monkey do to the banana?"

Before he flung them against the far end of the table, the squat gambler answered his own rhetorical question.

"He ate it."

The dice caromed off the table's embankment and tumbled to a halt. Two magical fours faced upward to a table full of happy faces.

"Eight. Pay the point. Pay the eight. Pay the line. Pay the hard eight," the stickman recited.

Bones are fun and fast, but the more obvious the bets on a craps table—big 6, big 8, the field, the hard ways—the higher the house percentage.

The "free odds," the ones that benefit the player, are less conspicuous. You have to ask the stickman to get down on those.

I placed $50 on the pass line. The hot shooter threw a five. I backed up my bet with another $50 to take the free odds. The house laid me $90 to $50 that the shooter wouldn't roll his point. I already needed the five for even money. Backing up my bet at almost two to one just made sense.

* * *

I played a little blackjack too.

As a second picture card flopped atop my first, the dealer saw the two queens and mechanically chanted, "Siegfried and Roy." He wore the same outfit as the casino's stickman, and his pun about the two gay performers wasn't lost on the full table. The players chuckled their approval.

I didn't laugh.

I never do.

That second queen gave me a solid 20. The other six players at the table grinned and cheered me on. Two even raised their thumbs.

The five black "cheques" I had stacked behind the two queens earned their encouragement. Each black chip was worth $100. Because I had been betting the minimum $10 a card for the past 30 minutes, all eyes shot to my sudden and dramatic wager increase.

Seconds later, their cheers would turn to jeers. My solid "third base" play was about to change. My next move was going to be unorthodox, and the other gamblers wouldn't approve. I didn't give two shits about the other six players at the table. I wasn't in Vegas to make friends. I was there to make money. These chumps didn't pay my rent.

The reason I sat immediately to the dealer's right had nothing to do with them. The last seat before the dealer, "third base," gave me a better view of the table, more time to count cards, and insured that no idiot screwed me up by doing exactly what I was about to do—something stupid like splitting 10s and possibly taking the dealer's bust-card on a misplay.

The dealer showed a six. My frozen 20 made my $500 bet golden. When the dealer got to me, I split the two queens and pushed another $500 on the table. The players at the table acted like I just pulled out my prick.

One yelled,

"What are you an asshole? You don't split picture cards."

I didn't look up. I never do.

The dealer crossed my first Queen with a five. The five gave me a 15. Although I didn't show it, I was ecstatic. By my calculations, there weren't many low cards left in that deck. If I had stayed good with my 20, and the dealer's down card was a 10, as I suspected, that five he just hit me with would had given him 21.

The dealer flipped a jack across my second queen. That gave me a solid 20. I stayed stoic, but my heart raced. I watched as the dealer turned his hole card. Both bets rode on his hidden card.

Bingo, he flipped a king. He had sixteen, and I had him by the shorthairs. I knew the deck was loaded with 10s and aces. As long as his next card wasn't an ace, I stood to win both bets. He took his mandatory hit and turned a seven. Twenty-two, dealer busted, no losers at the table. The derision turned back to "way to go" and the loudmouth said,

"That was lucky. You're never supposed to split picture cards."

I still didn't look up. I never do.

My "count" was at plus nine. The deck was still "rich," and I had a window of opportunity.

A deck that's rich is top-heavy or overloaded with tens and aces. Every 52-card deck in a dealer's shoe has 16 cards that equal 10 and four aces. Those 20 cards and the four fives are the most significant cards to a card counter.

To screw up card counters, most blackjack shoes use six decks, not always, some use eight, some four. To card count, you have to be aware of where the deck cut indicator lies in the shoe. You have to know the amount of decks being used and guesstimate the number of aces and tens left in the deck.

Sounds incredibly complicated doesn't it? It isn't. With practice, it's easy. But that was before the rule change.

When "wise guys" ran Vegas, casinos made money, but at least they greased the pan so the cookies didn't stick. They gave us suckers a shot.

Now that the corporate boys run the town, you have as much chance of a square deal as you do of a politician fulfilling his promises. In Vegas, the corporate shysters made two simple, but insidious, rule changes at the blackjack tables.

Dealer must hit soft 17 and blackjack pays 6 to 5. Before the corporations ruined Vegas, the dealer had to stay on all 17s, and blackjack paid 6 to 4.

This gives the house another 5 percent advantage, which ensures that even the best card counters will lose.

Remember, these MIT boys and their ilk are the same guys that invented derivatives on Wall Street. You're not beating these guys.

* * *

Gobbo and I loved to gamble, but we weren't dopes. We were careful about what games we played. Red liked to gamble too but had less patience. Red would play slots, keno, video poker, and anything else built electronically. Gobbo and I wouldn't.

Gamblers must walk through armies of slots before they get to the gaming tables for a reason. Slots are sucker plays.

Gobbo favored the ponies. He'd dope out the morning line, study the paddock before he bet and generally held his own. I preferred high stakes poker. Both of us were excellent card players.

But Red had no patience for cards. He liked his action fast and loose, crap tables and $100 slots. Red couldn't even be bothered to wait for a football game to end before he plunked down another bet. He bet football by quarters.

He was the sickest one of the three of us. He even bet on Jai Alai.

Jai Alai was fast all right, but only Red would bet on a game where all the players came from the same town in Spain and probably were related to one another.

Eyes determined, chins defiant, the players posed their mugs like Mussolini and then marched out and pretended to play for their honor. If you gambled on this nonsense, you might as well have had put your money in a pile, doused it with kerosene and lit it.

* * *

You're not beating Jai Alai, but you're not beating sports either.

Despite Damon Runyan's warning,
"Never bet on anything that can talk."

All three of us were addicted to sports wagering. Our sports betting compulsion was why Gobbo, Red and me got in the bookmaking racket to begin with.

Despite pocketing mountains of cash our first year bookmaking, we really didn't know what the hell we were doing. In 1988, we were worried that everyone would load up on Joe Gibbs's Redskins against John Elway's Denver Broncos in Super Bowl XXII, and we would get buried on the game.

Bookmakers shouldn't have opinions. Bookies should never lay off any of their customers' wagers. The old adage about opinions and assholes was dead on. Bookies should eat bets like Pac Man. The players will go broke eventually. Why give your customers' money to another bookie?

But we were novices. We thought we'd get hurt. We didn't want to give our entire seasons' winnings back on one game.

Because Internet betting was still only a gleam in the

corporate eye, my two partners, Gobbo and Red, decided that as soon as the NFC Championship game was finished, I would fly out to Vegas and bet the favored Redskins.

If we could get a bet down two weeks before Super Bowl on the early line, when the line went up, we could sell the game at a higher price and protect ourselves if (when?) Washington won.

Or the three of us could get real lucky and middle our customers. By middle, I mean if we bet the game at three, and the general public bet the favored Redskins up to five, the game could fall on four. In which case, we'd win our bet with Vegas and also beat our customers.

After the NFC Championship Game, the Super Bowl line opened with Washington as a three-point favorite. I remember that because not only was 1988 our first year in business, but with a stinking $10 grand, I changed a Super Bowl line.

* * *

After the Redskins beat the Vikings 17 to 10 for the NFC championship game, the sports book at Caesar's Palace posted Washington a three-point favorite over Denver. Two minutes after the line was posted, I walked up to the window.

"I want to bet $25,000 on the Redskins."

"Whoa, $25 large? Slow down. Take it easy. Don't get caught speeding. I'll let you have $5,000."

The clerk was a powerfully built, medium height man. Probably around 40 but he looked 10 years older.

"Why only $5,000? I thought this was Las Vegas. I want 25 dimes."

"You can't walk in off the street and bet $25, 000. You want the $5,000 or not?"

He had a broad pleasantly ugly, pockmarked face, under not much hair of any particular color.

"Yeah, I want the $5,000."

He punched a ticket, and the computer went into "2001 Space Odyssey" mode. The lights flickered as the five-dime bet traveled to every casino in Vegas.

Seconds later, he handed me the ticket.

I started to walk away.

"Hey."

"Yeah?"

"You want another $5,000 at three?"

I turned and shoveled $5,000 more through the cage.

Same routine, again he punched the computer and handed me the ticket.

"The line's now three and a half," he said.

On Super Bowl Sunday, changing a line would take an incalculable amount of money, but with only $10,000, I changed a Super Bowl line.

Vegas won't allow the public to outsmart the house.

* * *

When I was a kid in New York, I'd root for the Giants. But once I started taking action, the only team that interested me was the green team, and I don't mean the Jets. I mean cash.

If I didn't bet $5,000 on a game, it was as dull as watching grass grow.

Some plays still haunt me—Franco Harris's "Immaculate Reception." In 1982s NFC Championship Game, "The Catch," where Joe Montana hit Dwight Clark with 51 seconds left to beat Dallas. Philadelphia's Chuck Bednarik's crushing hit on Giants' Frank Gifford, in 1960.

But when gambling became my new mistress, I lost my love for football. Gambling's action, her juice and rush proved too hard to resist.

* * *

I'm a poker player, and like I said before, a damn good one. Poker is work. If you play cards for fun, or play to make friends, you've lost already.

You want a friend? Buy a dog.

Poker stayed lucrative for me but gambling didn't.

Like all compulsions, gambling narrows the world. Nothing else interested me. I only hung out with other gamblers. I abandoned all interests that didn't jackhammer my jugular or tighten my intestines.

Everything but gambling bored me.

But it was much easier to find a phone than to drive all over New York to find a poker game.

My gambling progressed from a calling to a compulsion. The more I fed it, the hungrier it got. My family life suffered. I missed family dinners, communions and birthdays, because I was totally self-absorbed in my lust for action.

Each year my downward financial spiral continued. I borrowed to gamble. I banged out credit cards, postponed paying bills, and scrambled for cash to satisfy my insatiable habit.

Despite the nightmare, I couldn't find the strength to abandon my compulsion.

Finally, I bottomed out. I owed money to every bookmaker I knew. (And I knew plenty.) In desperation, I hit upon a plan. No surprise that since I was enslaved by my addiction, my solution would exacerbate the problem.

I planned to make my compulsion work for me. I'd take action instead of betting.

I'd become a bookie.

While a bookie for the next five years, I learned that it wasn't just the three of us, myself and my two partners, who lost.

No one wins—no one.

As a former bookie, a good friend once asked me for football handicapping advice.

"Throw all the specialty bets out the window—teasers, reverses, if bets, parlays, forget them. Bookies don't even keep track of how much the suckers wager on them," I said.

"Wait a minute. Let me get a pen. I want to write this down," he said.

"Like poker, you can be a winner or a player. If you play for enjoyment, if you play every hand, you'll lose. The more games you bet, the worse your chances of winning," I said, "So limit your bets."

"Talk slower. Let me get all of this down," he said.

"Pay attention to the opening line on Monday. Make a note on what lines you think are too low or too high. Try and guess which way the smart money will change the line on Tuesday.

Wise guys, the pros, bet early. The general public doesn't bet until game day. So Tuesday's lines are critical."

"Wait," he said. "Slow up. Let me write. Got it," he said. "Tuesday's lines are critical."

"Right. Now look for the lines that go against your instinct. If a line goes down from four to three, but you think it should be moving up ask yourself why? If the line movement goes against all logic, that's the game you want. Bet with the bookmaker's move. Bet against the general public."

"Wow," he said. "That's great advice. So find one game, and bet against the grain."

"Exactly."

"Thanks so much, Connor. I really appreciate it. I'll try it for a couple of weeks. I'll call you and let you know how I do."

"Oh no man, don't bother to call me. I know how you're going to do. You're going to lose. You're not listening. Everybody loses. This way, you won't lose as fast, or as much, but you're still going to lose."

"So what the fuck? Don't bet?"

"Exactly, now you got it."

* * *

John Timoney, former Police Chief of two cities, and Commissioner of a third published a memoir, "A Tale of Three Cities."

John shared a yarn with me over a pint.

On December 29, 1968, Timoney, then a rookie cop, was leaving his precinct house at 8 a.m. when he spotted Joe Namath.

After what was obviously a rough night, "Broadway Joe" was exiting the side entrance of the Summit Hotel. Namath's famed right arm was draped around the shoulder of a charming young creature in go-go boots. The Dublin-born Timoney recognized a hangover when he saw one.

Timoney had coveted inside information. In just five hours, the Jets would play Oakland for the AFC Championship at Shea Stadium. Timoney scrambled to a pay phone.

He pressed his brother to "send it in" on Oakland.

In the most physical game Namath ever played, he led the Jets past the Raiders and into the Super Bowl 27-23.

The rookie cop blew his rent money.

* * *

My ex-partner Red's still a bookmaker.

These days' computers take all the action. Many of Red's Wall Street customers subscribe to high-priced betting services. Before games, Red checks his computer to see what teams he needs and for how much.

Because he sees his customers' bets, Red has free access to all his player's sports handicapping services. Not one expensive betting service, but four, for free, yet even he can't make money gambling.

That's the bottom line—inside information, both sides of the law, both losers.

If people behind betting services could predict winners, they wouldn't sell information or write columns. They'd do as you or I would. They'd sit in bed all day with cell phones and high-priced company sipping champagne.

When Wilson manufactures square footballs, when rubber no longer bounces, then "experts" will pick winners. Until then, clutch your cash in your hands, and keep those hands deep in your pockets.

CHAPTER FIFTEEN

With a Marlboro sandwiched between two fingers, I sat on my bunk's army-brown blanket and stared through the propped-open wooden-shutter at the torrential rain. It gushed from the fronds that blanketed my hooch in Thailand and swam down the palm's lean trunks in multiple rivulets before emptying into milky brown puddles, which the arid soil sucked dry.

For the thirsty cracked earth, monsoon season was here at last.

The other five bunks in my hooch were empty. After making a deposit in our small latrine, Jose, one of my hooch mates, came back to my bed and took a Marlboro from my pack. He placed it between his teeth and continued our conversation.

"Downtown, I'll tell you where to go."

Jose didn't look like a military man, or much of a man at all, actually. Unkempt, unshaven and overweight, his pig-faced jowls made it easy for him to slobber his speech, and his psoriasis-laden hair looked like he combed it with a firecracker.

"Opium, Jose?" I said. "No shit. What's it like?"

"Try it. It's only two fucken baht."

Fifty cents to try a new drug experience that no one in the old neighborhood had ever tried? I had never heard another GI talk about opium either. A guaranteed source of pleasure for a half a buck seemed like a bargain. Why the hell not?

My "mentor," Jose, was the guy who told me that smoking 20 joints a day wasn't too bad. He smoked 40. I was always glad to see Jose.

Knowing that he was in worse shape than me gave me solace. I was like the alcoholic who drank a quart a day but delighted in watching the poor soul next to him guzzle two quarts.

But I had to be careful. Everything was too easy over here, too accessible. I told myself that I'd just smoke opium on special occasions, like weekends. At half a buck a pop, the last thing that I needed was an opium habit. My brain was fried enough from Laotian weed and cheap Mekong whiskey.

To top it off, my Jersey friend Richie told me that, just like Bangkok, we could cop codeine and downs in any downtown Nakhon Phanom drugstore without a prescription. Of course, I should have known. If they'd sell pills and cough medicine in Bangkok, they'd sell it in country, but right now opium was on my mind.

Jose said,

"You can't miss it. The hut sits on stilts about a 100 yards from the jungle's edge."

* * *

Nakhon Phanom, where I was stationed, resembled a wildcat town in a Hollywood Western, one of those boom and bust oil towns that the heroes tamed so respectable citizens could stroll the streets.

The sidewalks were temporary wood platforms that separated dusty, unpaved streets from the dilapidated structures that the Thai carpetbaggers had hastily built on them.

The bars and massage parlors got the bulk of the action.

The Thais reserved concrete block construction for the jewelry stores, teak shops and other money pits that they deemed more valuable than women and whiskey.

Teakwood didn't interest me. The U.S. had forests aplenty.

Thailand had wide-open drugs, women and booze.

In the downtown cab, I smoked a fat joint of Laotian weed and reached into my back pocket to read a letter from my brother. The letters I received were few and far between. Once in a while Bob's daughter wrote, and once a week, without fail, I'd get a letter from Mom.

But Mom's letters were short and predictable. She'd tell me mundane news about the family and end them by saying she was praying for me. Tim's letters were rare, so I read them over and over.

"Connor—

I stopped by the old apartment yesterday. Not much has changed at home. Dad is still drinking and working, and Mom's just working.

Write me more often.

I want to know what Southeast Asia's like. Tell me about the people, the women and what you think of this whole Vietnam War thing. I just read a book called "The Best and the Brightest" by David Halberstam. If you're not familiar with his work, you should be. This guy seems like the only journalist who's telling the truth.

Are we losing? Should we be there? What's our ultimate objective? Are you in any danger where you are?

It seems to me that the Democratic system we knew as kids is slowly disappearing. America doesn't have elections anymore. We have auctions. Over 90 percent of the time, whatever candidate spends the most money wins. This disturbing trend worries me and doesn't bode well for our country's future. It's frustrating. Nixon campaigned on a promise to end the war, yet now we're invading Cambodia.

As you know, I got discharged a few months ago, and now I'm working as a welder a couple of blocks from the old apartment. So here I am back in the old neighborhood, but I gotta get out of here. Nothing's the same, or maybe, I'm not the same. Funny, Thomas Wolfe was right after all. "You can't go home again."

You remember Roy?

He wrote me a letter that he's doing a radio gig in New Orleans. I might go down there for a few weeks and check it out. He said it was a real live-wire town, similar to Europe.

Write me you little fuck. Let me know what you're up to, and let me know what you think about this fucken war. Read Halberstam's book, and tell me what you think. I haven't seen

you since Europe. Come home safe. I love you.
—Timmy
P.S. Have you heard the Beatles' new album? As always, it's amazing. Everybody's digging 'Abbey Road.'"

It was nice to get a bit of relevant news from the States. Good old Timmy. Without his letters, I think I'd lose my mind. Knowing that I'd read this letter at least a dozen more times, I carefully refolded it and placed it back in my rear pocket.

I reflected on Tim's letter and stared out the cab's window. The cab's shadow streaked the ground slightly ahead of me just past the swollen rice paddies and the flooded earthen dikes and fields. My cab zoomed past the samlots and bicyclists that sprinkled the muddy-dirt road.

Once the taxi pulled into town, I had the driver let me off by the main cabstand.

Unsure of Jose's directions, I decided to hoof it to the opium hut, but the farther I walked from the reassuring presence of other GI's, the more paranoid I began to feel.

A leathery, emaciated old woman passed and smiled a toothless grin. Her twitching stick thumped a yak's rump with a lazy rhythm.

I watched her trudge slowly by. Sometimes I felt like I was in a fucken movie.

Where was this hut? I was stoned and alone, and this dusty, dirt path kept luring me farther and farther from civilization. I almost turned back, but then I spotted the stilted, circular hut that Jose described. Its entrance had stairs, not planks—high-class for Northern Thailand.

It was the "swinging sixties" stateside and only the young and hip got high while Thailand was the opposite. The young abstained. The ancients smoked.

Too old to contribute to the economic structure of his family, Papa San squatted in his hut and sold pot or opium. He brought in a few baht and eased the pain of whatever ailments he might have accumulated over his long life—an efficient, cheap retirement system.

I climbed the steps of the two-room hooch and found a

bare-chested toothless old man sitting cross-legged like Gandhi. He had a high, shiny forehead, and dull, glossy recessed eyes with two tiny black dots pretending to be pupils. A smooth head covered his lean and leathery face. One hand motioned me to sit.

I told him in Thai, "Pom ow soop fin."

He gave a knowing nod, smiled and held out his hand.

I greased his palm with the two-baht tariff. A young girl in a sarong entered, bowed twice, snatched the money and came back with a bamboo bong.

Papa San took a small ball of aluminum foil from inside a box of kitchen matches. With worn, gnarled, broken hands, he unwrapped a black orb the size of a ping-pong ball.

Using a machete, he sliced two thin pieces off the black tar and chopped it like garlic. He pinched a small portion into the bong's bowl and fired it up.

Wrapping his lips around the pipe, he sucked deeply. His neck tightened from the strain of holding down the smoke. He passed the bong to me. I parked the kitchen match over the bowl and inhaled. The smoke flooded my lungs.

After three or four bong passes, my stomach tightened and my lips, face and body became numb. I felt like I could slide through a postal slot. I needed to lie down. Waving away the bong, I sprawled on the floor of the hut.

I sealed my eyes and dreamt. I wanted the full impact of the drug. I wanted to compare it to hashish, marijuana, mescaline, LSD, and all the other drugs I had experienced.

So far, it was no big deal, like washing down a sleeping pill with a bottle of cough medicine. It was not like sex or my first roller coaster ride. Satisfying but nothing I couldn't live without, so I started to relax, just another high, nothing dramatic.

I let the drug work its magic.

I dreamt and drifted.

It was satisfying, easy to handle. I got this.

After what seemed like days instead of hours, I popped up, and Papa San offered me another hit. I figured for the road, why not?

I crossed my legs and faced him. As he relit the pipe, he took a hard hit, held what he had inhaled for a few seconds and released it. Only a wisp of smoke escaped.

Something was wrong.

He lit the pipe again.

The opium overcame me again. Now all I wanted was to lie back down.

But I didn't want to get trapped in another nap because while lying on the hooch floor, I had an idea.

After I was finished here, I'd take the short walk back to town and get a bath and a massage. Lying naked on a table while a pretty girl massaged me from head to toe and all places in between had to be a good way to wait out the effects of opium.

If I fell asleep, so what? I'd give her five bucks instead of the $2.50 it usually costs for the hour. She'd wake me when the massage was over with a "happy ending," rub talc over my body and open me a cold beer.

Papa San still fiddled with the front end of the pipe, trying to draw through it again. His persistence tried my patience.

I thought,

Come on old man pass the fucking pipe. Let me get out of here and into town.

I watched his antics with the bong. Everything he did seemed slow, contrived and exaggerated.

He lashed the kitchen match at the bong's bowl again and inhaled like a pensioner at his six-month checkup . . . yet, when he exhaled . . . still barely a puff of smoke.

Papa San's patience finally exhausted, he raised the bamboo pipe shoulder high and slammed it loudly on the hut's wood floor. Like a plunger that had unclogged a toilet, thousands of giant red ants cascaded out of the pipe's end and stampeded across the floorboards.

The red devils ran up the legs of my pants and swarmed across my feet and sandals. I leapt up screaming. Like prickly heat, 1,000s of pins stuck me at once. I was dancing over hot burning coals.

I tried franticly to brush the bastards off.

The stoic old man stared at me like I was nuts. For him this seemed to be just another day at work, as if the office copier had sprung a leak. His quixotic stare screamed volumes.

Stupid foreigner afraid of ants.

The bastards ran up my pants, onto my legs and up under my shirt, yet the more I screamed, the more he laughed.

I ripped off my t-shirt and sprinted down the steps. As I raked off my tormentors outside the hut, my hands rattled like cocktail shakers. Relieved that they were off of me, I settled down to start the short walk back to town.

I thought,

Was Papa San laughing because of the opium, or was that crazy fucker laughing at me? Or was he laughing at how absurd we Americans are? Terrified of ants yet willing to send half a million soldiers to conquer a country of millions of people who'll fight to the death to keep it.

On the dirt trail back to the massage parlor, my mind segued from the ants to Asian bugs in general. Never had I seen so many types and sizes. Nine months of heat followed by three months of rain acted like Miracle Grow to bugs.

Rice bugs resembled the great American cockroach. But our roaches looked like sprinkles next to these behemoths. If you wanted to kill one of these mothers, you put a knife in your teeth and swung aboard like a pirate. You straddled his back like a rodeo rider, and let the bug have it like Anthony Perkins in "Psycho." If the knife didn't work, you'd call in heavy artillery.

These were big fucken bugs.

Centipedes were the size and shape of Cuban cigars, and the ants that covered me were as big as grapes. Yet the old man never moved . . . so cool, so stoic.

The sun snapped me back to reality.

It sat high and white and lashed me with hot-heavy beams. Drops of sweat dripped down my face. This sucked. Less than a mile to town, yet my legs felt like I had just crossed the Himalayas.

My head throbbed.

I made a mental note to myself. From now on, never smoke opium and walk in the sun. The peasants I passed seemed oblivious to my discomfort, or even their own. They appeared almost insouciant, like what they did didn't matter. Life just went by.

In the States, everyone was running from point to point and determined to make a difference. The Thai's never bounced when they walked. Less animated, like zombies, they were resigned to a hopeless shuffle. As if nothing they did would make a difference.

A woman wearing Thai pajamas scurried past me. Her skin was as tough and colorful as the rooster she chased, her few teeth as yellow and spotted as an overripe banana. The opium drove me to fixate on the small irregular ridges that dented her severe face.

I felt like an artist had painted me into this strange landscape.

I gotta focus on the massage parlor. Focus. If I miss the turn for town, I could walk down this endless road for the rest of my life. The town should be right at the end of this street. When I turn left at the end of this road, I should see it. But wait. What if it's not there? Who knows that I came downtown? Who'll find me in the jungle? I could die on this road. Jesus, it's hot. My head is killing me. This was a big mistake. The sun is brutal.

My skin felt chafed and as dry as paper, my palms were stiff and hard to close.

I thought,

There's a samlot. Maybe I should hail it and ride to town. Relax stupid. Town is less than a few hundred yards.

My legs feel like lead, I should have worn a hat. Where the fuck is this town? I should have grabbed that samlot. What if I don't see another one? Just a few more steps, focus, concentrate.

Don't miss the turn. Be there. Be there. I hope I didn't walk the wrong way. If I do, I'll never find this fucken town. I'll just walk and walk, until I die.

There it is. Thank Christ it's there.
Calm down.
Calm down, asshole. You've been high before. Relax. Relax. Any massage parlor will do. Just up this flight of stairs. All will be well.
Get a cold beer and spend some time indoors. I'll be fine. Calm down, just up this flight of stairs.

When I opened the door, relief smacked me like a surfer's wave.

Fans pushed stale air around the five or six couches that the girls lounged on.

Thank God I made it.

I said, "Mama San, nung cang Sing Hai lao lao."

I had to have a beer quick.

Sitting on the leather sofa and slugging the Sing Hai, I was starting to settle down.

Wow, I was so out of control. Was it the opium, the heat, a combination of both? Relax, relax, breathe deep . . . scared to death of a short walk . . . those fucking ants started me off on a bummer . . . never again, sun and opium . . . fucking Jose should have warned me to only go at night or stay in the hut after I smoked . . . never again with this shit.

"Mama san Sing Hai, cop con mak."

Grab another beer. Calm down. I'll be fine now.

I picked a thin, pretty girl named Song and left for her cubicle. She held my hand and led me down the corridor. Still walloped, I cradled my beer like a security blanket, but I was OK now.

Song opened the door to an 8' by 6' room containing a massage table, a bathtub and a small table with a wooden hook above it. While she filled the tub, I hung my clothes on the hook.

Within minutes, Song rubbed the soapy sponge across my body. Her hands combined with the warm water made me drowsy and secure. Song's educated fingers massaged my scalp. I closed my eyes and sank deeper into the pool of soapy warm water.

I could handle this shit. Opium was no big deal.

Thoroughly cosseted and lying naked in the hot water, I reflected on the last couple of hours. Examining my feet, legs and hands, I was mystified. No welts, no bites, no marks of any kind from my misadventure with the ants, as smooth as a marble statue.

Wow, maybe this opium is a much bigger deal than I thought? How do you say lightweight in Thai?

CHAPTER SIXTEEN

Richie's thumb and index finger pressed the roach to his lips. Before inhaling, my best buddy in Nakhon Phanom said,
"This is what Dang would have wanted."
I shot the traitor a cold look and gagged. This prick would have said the same thing had Dang's cold, lifeless carcass been mine.
But the five of us pretended nothing had happened. We shared whiskey, passed the joint, and just stared into the fire.
I've rehashed that tragic day a million times. Dang's washed-up, bloated body haunts me still.

* * *

As soon as we arrived at the Mekong, I yelled at Richie.
"Didn't I screw your mother on this sandbar?"
Richie answered in Thai.
"At least I have a mother, cock breath."
All four Asians understood our rudimentary Thai, but of the four Thais, the three Thai-Air Force guys were confused. We two round-eyed white men were supposedly friends. While one of the three baffled soldiers passed me the joint and the pint bottle, the other Thai, my pal Sith, the only civilian, explained in Thai,
"Foreigners are crazy. When they're good friends, they insult each other. Their friendship's so strong that words mean nothing."
Sith was right. Richie and I were East Coast inner city guys. Neighborhood blocks created permanent bonds. Color and nationality meant nothing. We stuck together, especially against outsiders.

* * *

In Southeast Asia, the heat clung, burdened and finally exhausted you. The white-hot debilitating sun, now at its zenith, made the cool, yellow-green water cascading around the sandbar irresistible.

The Mekong River divided, Thailand, an American ally, from unfriendly Laos.

The Thai side provided our Air Base with the ideal location to monitor the Ho Chi Minh trail, which was a major conduit of supplies and communication vital to the North Vietnamese war effort.

A calm Mekong awaited us at that morning.

Just another day in Nakhon Phanom, and the marijuana stench that wafted along the sandbar was as natural to us two Americans as our meat-eating body odor was to our Thai companions.

Wanting to learn the Thai language motivated Richie and I to spend more time with the Thais than the other GI's. We became their friends, not guests. The Thais thought Richie and I were wacky, yet a welcome contrast to the sterile stereotypes turned out by U.S. government sensitivity training.

The American government taught us not to point the bottom of our feet at the Thais. They said that the Thai culture was so sensitive that even a benign body-language miscue like that would insult them, yet Richie and I spewed non-stop verbal abuse in Thai about our mothers, their mothers and both our countries. Nothing was off limits.

And they loved us for it.

Similar to the Friar's Club of professional comics, insults showed your friends that you loved them. The Thais found this hip and happily joined in.

The empty bottles and cans strewn about the sandbar meant a lot of time had passed. It also meant that time no longer mattered.

Some life experiences you never sort out. Time gets fuzzy, like the memory itself. What you do remember plays back through a cracked lens. What happened next was like that.

* * *

Because the six of us were walloped on whiskey and weed, we were unconcerned that the infamous Ho Chi Minh Trail was less than a mile away, so the raging river's unpredictable current wasn't even on our radar. That was before I heard the yells and commotion,

"Chuey, Chuey, Chuey."

Screams in Thai, "Help, help, help."

Dang was in trouble. He was drowning.

I looked around.

All heads inexplicably turned away.

Even stoned, this didn't make sense. Like being at a boxing match where the audience stood and turned its back on the ring.

Screw this.

Maybe it was a chance to prove my manhood, or just a feeling of indestructibility that made me do what I did. Or maybe, it was just because I was still a kid and didn't realize how precious a gift that life was.

I didn't stop to analyze it.

Instinct told me that when a man was drowning, another man was supposed to do something.

So with the same ineffable, mystifying recklessness that causes a kid to charge a cannon, leap on a grenade, or volunteer for combat, I sprang into the water.

As soon as the rapids hit me, I knew I had made a mistake. The current was stronger than I thought. The harder I pulled through the water, the less headway I made.

As I wrestled for air, I could barely make out Dang's body disappearing below the Mekong's surface. Scared sober, thoughts galloped across my brain.

Do bodies sink three times? Do victim's lives pass before them?

I had no idea how far I had swum, or how much headway I had made, until Dang's head punctured the surface only yards away.

I tried to bridge the gap between us, but a series of eddies held me back. Like running on a treadmill, the harder I swam, the less ground I gained.

When I got closer, Dang's cold, panicked eyes reminded me that he was not the only one who could drown here. Overcome with desperation, thrashing wildly, screaming unintelligibly, Dang, his face stretched tight with fear, lunged at me for salvation. His face was contorted and appeared to have aged years in seconds.

He grasped, guttered and choked . . .

Like a fish hopelessly flopping on dry land, he already had the stink of death.

Fear climbed from the depths of my bowels.

If I grabbed him, I'd go down with him.

I wanted to save him, not pay the tab for his mistake.

Less than a foot from me, the hysterical, wild-eyed man disappeared for the second time. I dove below the surface but saw nothing.

Like a shard of glass, panic speared fear into my chest.

I was in big trouble.

Even without the burden of Dang's dead weight, my arms shook like a weightlifter on his last repetition. It took every ounce of my strength to do what had come so easily only moments ago.

Dang surfaced.

As his desperate eyes locked on mine, a strange moment of recognition swam through his pupils. Like he knew that his entire life had been reduced to a contest that had already been played. No fight, no screams, no thrashes, just a lifeless stare trapped in his bulging eyes.

His palm waved a calm goodbye.

Adrenalin drove me the last necessary few yards. Too late . . . Dang sunk into a murky grave. Because it was my life . . . and only my life that worried me now, when he disappeared, I felt shamefully relieved.

Terrified, I swam for safety. The faster my hands windmilled, the less ground I gained. The sandbar wasn't getting any closer. It was over. Tears ran down my face. I wouldn't make it. My mind raced . . .

Thoughts popped like firecrackers. Vignettes rifled my

brain—drill instructors, my brother, Big Tom's rants, drunken brawls, my mom's battered face, egg creams, Asian women, stickball, and the song a "Whiter Shade of Pale."

Richie screamed, "Swim," but his voice sounded slow and exaggerated, and the sandbar was no closer.

"Swim, Connor. Keep swimming. Keep swimming, Connor."

It was as if someone ripped the hands off a clock.

It was clear now. This was the last chapter, nothing more, the not so grand finale.

Here, 12,000 miles from everything that I loved, was where it would end. Here, in the mother of all rivers, a place that I had never even heard of one short year ago. Here, among people I hardly knew, I would be dealt my last hand.

Richie yelled to keep swimming.

Why wasn't he in the water? Why wasn't Richie trying to save me, like I had tried to save Dang?

No one was in the water. No one was coming. Richie was safe on the sandbar with the other quislings.

"Swim Connor, swim."

Resentment changed to hate.

I wasted my last precious breaths,

"Help. I can't make it. Jump in the water. Help, help, I'm drowning."

Nothing.

I slipped below the surface. The water raged and churned above me. The current tumbled my inert body like a sock in a washing machine. When my dark raging assassin finally hurled me to the surface, the sandbar seemed closer, yet hazy like a distant cloud.

Chants from the sandbar sound vague, muffled, and almost melodic. It was all a foggy dream.

An improbable calm replaced my panic. My arms no longer hurt.

Nothing hurt.

With the calm came noble echoes.

"It's a far, far better place I go to than I have ever known;"

"One for all and all for one;" "When a man's partner dies, a man's supposed to do something."

Along with these fictional words and phrases, President Kennedy's voice rang clear through a sudden hole in the dimension buried deep in my psyche.

"The torch has been passed to a new generation of Americans . . . a generation who will pay any price, bear any burden."

As I sank deeper into the muddy Mekong, these words seemed as distant as the Bronx.

And all these noble words sounded like total bullshit.

* * *

During WWII and the post-war years, Hollywood churned out movies depicting altruistic acts of bravery where protagonists sacrificed everything for the common good.

Kids my age were riveted by these "Beau Gestes."

These "grand gestures" had strong influences on our characters.

Even our institutions indoctrinated us.

For didn't the Boy Scout oath necessitate reciting the expected virtues of duty to God and country, over and over, until it could be regurgitated verbatim by any loyal child wearing brown short-pants and a red kerchief?

Oaths, great novels, an immigrant's debt, Hollywood idealism, plus an insatiable hunger for foreign adventure all drove me to this watery grave.

What a fucken moron I am.

My face was hot, my ears pinged and pressure drove thousands of pins into the back of my head.

Still my mind drifted.

My ancestors were from an island country, sailors, nomads, curious about other lands and distant places.

I was curious too. My hungry, Irish wanderlust demanded to be fed.

Soldiers in foreign lands were presumed men, yet I still felt like a boy. But I knew, no, I was cocksure that exotic locales, women and war's rite of passage would make me a man.

A boy soldier finds it easy to confuse experience with

maturity. I sampled all things forbidden. I searched everywhere, went anywhere, and kicked over anything that might have held what I was looking for. I didn't want to taste life. I wanted to run it over in a stolen car.

But I looked in the wrong places.

Plato was right. I should have looked within.

As long as my search remained external, I was vigilant. But I wasn't interested in looking in the dark places where the roaches were hiding. If I flipped on the lights within, it would be nasty, messy, scary.

Some men go to greater lengths than others, searching for the happiness they didn't have as a child. They substitute superficialities like sex, drugs and alcohol to hide feelings of worthlessness. I was one of them.

I thought the happy place I sought was out beyond the horizon.

But the earth is round, horizons only illusions.

* * *

Screams from the shore snatched me back.

My "friends" mouthed something new.

The current's roar and the distance, made their voices garbled. They weren't shouting, "Swim, Connor, swim."

It was something else.

I heard their voices, as if I were in a trance . . . the same distant, unintelligible phrase over and over, like a mantra.

"Behind you, Connor, behind you. Connor, behind you."

As I struggled to decipher their message, a boatman's powerful hand came out of nowhere and grabbed my shoulders.

He deposited my limp, exhausted body on the sandbar's warm, wet sand.

I melted face down and slept a sleep only familiar to the near dead.

* * *

I didn't know how long I was unconscious. I knew that the sun had burnt my skin, as though I had bathed in acid. I knew that my arms felt like I was 70 years old, and that I still couldn't collect enough air into my lungs.

Hours later, we found Dang's cold, repulsive corpse miles downstream.

Staring at this strange, bloated-blue hulk, I felt less than nothing.

Hours before, I had risked everything for this lifeless mass. What made me do it? Why risk everything for someone I barely knew? Was it an error of judgment, an impulse, a reflex action?

While the sand crabs blanketed Dang's corpse, I eyeballed Richie with contempt. No written law said my best friend should have jumped in the water, but in my neighborhood, loyalty was chiseled into our souls.

A stand-up guy doesn't stand by and watch a friend die.

* * *

I inhaled the joint, swallowed the harsh whiskey and stared into the fire. But tonight, the whiskey didn't relieve the overwhelming sudden, misplaced, internal grief that I felt.

Not for Dang's death, nor Richie's betrayal, but because despite all that had happened, I still felt like a boy.

Inside, nothing had changed.

I still wasn't a man.

* * *

To the Thai Air Force however, I was a hero. While their countrymen watched, I tried to rescue one of their own. They were both astonished and grateful. Sith spread the word of my heroism. To the Thais, this unlikely tale was tantamount to Simon Legree risking his life to rescue a black slave.

* * *

To reward me weeks later, the Thai Air Force treated me to a no-frills whorehouse that they frequented. Loaded on Singha beer, weed and Mekong whiskey, I crossed a shaky plank deep in the jungle. From my tenuous perch, I flinched. Below me a living, horrifying, breathing, gray-river of rats writhed and squirmed atop each other's backs. I leapt terrified into the thatched hut.

Seven unattractive women waited.

Each costs 50 cents.

One skinny virgin, about 12-years old, sold for five dollars.

I bolted back outside and vomited into the slimy, slithering mass of vermin that overran the ravine.

* * *

In my neighborhood, we didn't watch men drown, nor sell children. In Thailand, at 21, I'm a man at last.

It makes me sick.

CHAPTER SEVENTEEN

After Dang's incident, the airbase curfew of 11 p.m. no longer applied to me. I came and went when I wanted. If I was downtown after curfew, I merely flagged down a Thai Air Force truck and jumped inside its enclosed back. Because of international courtesy, American military police were forbidden to search the Thai military trucks.

One moonless night, well after curfew, I walked along a downtown dirt road stoned as usual. I heard a nearby gunshot, and then another followed by a deafening barrage.

I jumped into a clump of dense high grass.

My mind rattled.

Holy shit, now I've done it. I was too cute for my own boots. The Vietcong have overrun the town, and I'm trapped outside the base. I'm fucked.

The next few hours my mind jumped from puddle to puddle of manic overreaction. I visualized myself as James Clavell's character, King Rat, running a Vietnamese internment camp. I saw myself finally getting moral comeuppance for my lust and moral transgressions in Asia. I saw an angry, vengeful Catholic God sending my corpse back in a pine box. I did what most atheists and nonbelievers did in times of dire need. I prayed.

Please God, if you're truly up there, forgive me my trespasses.

I followed with numerous Our Fathers, Hail Mary's and other prayers programmed into my brain since childhood.

When the gunfire stopped, still stoned and frightened, I stayed hidden in the high grass. Now the thought of scorpions, crate snakes and centipedes tormented me.

What if I'm poisoned? What if I die here in the elephant grass? Who will find me? Will they find me?

When the sun finally peeked through the jungle foliage and shown a welcome light on a passing Thai Air Force Truck, I decided to chance it. I hurdled out, hailed the driver down, and jumped inside the back of the truck. On the ride back to the base, a sergeant explained that I was alarmed for nothing. A gunfight broke out between the Thai military police and the Thai civilian police.

Worried for nothing?

Even the authorities exacerbated the fragile nature of life in Southeast Asia.

* * *

So there I was, an Irish kid from the Bronx, over 12 thousand miles from home and stationed in a remote Thai/Laotian village on the Mekong River.

Now more than four-decades later, I look back at that strangest of years, in that strangest of places and still wonder what it was all about. The sentence that sums it up, and I guess applies to most wars in other lands, is:

What a tragic fucken waste.

* * *

A 22- hour plane ride had initially landed me in Thailand. From there, a cloth harness seat attached to the skeleton-metal perimeter of a C-130 took me "in country."

I rumbled and bounced for two more uncomfortable hours until the camouflaged aircraft settled softly onto Nakhon Phanom's tarmac runway.

My first day in town seems surreal now.

I walked a dirt road and gaped at a toothless old woman in a sarong prodding a yak. When I turned a corner, I met throngs of swollen bellies huddled on the side of the road begging. I remember vividly the nausea that sight churned in my own well-fed stomach.

Attached to these swollen bellies were emaciated bodies with extended twig-like arms. Their voices begged for money to buy food, to make the pain of hunger go away.

Because of gambling, I had lots of money, but not enough for their needs, not all of them.

Do I give all I have? I thought.

How else could I claim to be human, but what about tomorrow? There won't be any less of them tomorrow.

When I signed my enlistment paper at 18, I had no idea that one year later on a dusty, dirt trail in a remote village that I had never heard of was where I would collide head-on with my humanity. A young man shouldn't have to make decisions this monumental.

I loved my country in a way that maybe only an immigrant can. I felt I owed it everything. And when my country led me to believe that I was needed to stop communist aggression, I was more than happy to settle my debt.

* * *

The jungle heat was heavy, and like a spoiled overweight child, it insisted on being carried everywhere. We Americans couldn't put it down for a second. The heat wore us out and beat us up. When it went away after nine tedious, arid months, the jungle handed the baton to another thug to finish us off.

The thug that grabbed the baton was called monsoon, and it brought a never-ending torrent of rain every day and night for three months. Monsoon transformed the jungle into a gigantic sponge, which sopped up every drop of water from the forest's canopy and turned the arid, cracked soil into a sea of mud.

Mud was everywhere, not just midst the mangroves, but also in the hootches where we slept, in the showers where we washed, and even in our clothes and shaving gear. Mud was in parts of our body almost as foreign as the jungle itself. The mud mixed with relentless humidity, which gave it a texture more permanent and penetrating, like cement.

Not surprisingly, my enlistment brochures didn't contain glossy photographs of the dirt and muck, nor of the thousands of poor American boys being shipped home inside body bags.

I saw too many of those dirty, wet boys when they were clean and dry, but I couldn't identify them. Coffins covered what was left of their faces. We loaded the parades of pine boxes on cargo planes, so what was left of these kids could be buried back home. These young patriots believed their sacrifice was necessary, so the Vietnamese could be free to make their own choices.

To ensure free choices for the Vietnamese, eager boys in men's uniforms would in President Kennedy's words, ". . . pay any price, and bear any burden."

The price these dead boys paid was the ultimate one.

* * *

But in the book Timmy told me to read, "The Best and the Brightest," I found out that much of what our government said about the war was lies. I confirmed this by reading other books by other real journalists besides Davis Halberstam, journalists like Tim O'Brien and Neil Sheehan.

The young patriots who paid this exorbitant price were swindled. They weren't shown U.S. intelligence reports declaring that if there were free elections in Viet Nam, Ho Chi Min and his Communist Party would have won overwhelmingly.

So there would be no free elections.

Instead America installed Diem, a Christian puppet, friendly to our government. President Johnson borrowed a line from F.D.R. to describe Diem:

"He's a son-of-a-bitch but he's our son-of-a-bitch."

Installing Diem was only one of many deceitful actions the U.S. government took during the war. President Johnson told Congress and the American people that North Vietnamese forces had fired on the U.S.S. Maddox.

This "attack" in international waters led to a direct and massive build-up of American forces in the region. Many years after the Gulf of Tonkin resolution was passed, however, President Johnson said,

"For all I know, their Navy was shooting at whales out there."

The dead soldiers that we loaded on those cargo planes weren't privy to those remarks.

My generation trusted authority. We thought that because people in power were experienced, they usually knew best. We were hopeful and idealistic and believed in our country.

We were told that freedom had a price, and that our country stood for democracy around the globe. We also believed, as we now know erroneously, that our government was committed to that paradigm.

Age has not blessed me with wisdom. But I know that old men make wars, and I sincerely believe that they feel truth is just a game to play with young idealistic boys. Old men have little time left so they hold life dear. Powerful men, who manufacture the wars, are both old and rich. They hold life dearer still.

Old men start wars, but they don't fight them.

Congressmen who start wars are too important to fight, too important and much too busy. Too busy lobbying, too busy collecting the lucrative pensions they have allocated themselves, and too busy assigning defense contracts to companies who will line their pockets after their tenure in Congress.

Combat is for children who have mountains of time and for whom years mean nothing. These young men may have felt immortal, but body bags didn't leave room for such delusions.

Reality registers quickly in combat, and options have to be weighed. A soldier can't desert. All that's out there is the enemy and the jungle. If a disgruntled patriot prefers the stockade to death, he'll abandon his brothers and his honor.

Young soldiers hold both their honor and their peers' approval priceless, so once on the battlefield, kids commence to kill.

The perpetual conundrum for old men who start wars is how to con guileless boys to commit to combat. The manipulators solve it by selling soldiers on a catch-all word, freedom.

Somehow all of America's recent wars are about freedom.

Whether they ensure freedom, or make the world safe for it, or because other countries allegedly hate us for having it.

Men who spin these yarns preach that the only way to ensure freedom is to "liberate" villages, towns and cities. Our Marines and infantry did that in Nam.

* * *

After patrols, I saw many troops wash away the nightmarish collaterals of liberation with tumblers of scotch or rye. Back at our base, scores of soldiers silenced their nightmares in a community lean-to appropriately christened, "Bombs for Peace."

One night, while guzzling a pitcher of Manhattans, I looked up at the television and heard President Nixon making an urgent address to the nation.

His words were clear, concise and complete bullshit.

"We are not now, nor have we ever, bombed the country of Laos."

I finished my drink and rolled a nice, fat joint. It was 7:45 now, so I went outside to torch it. After dark was when the Air Force usually started napalming Laos. I didn't want to miss the fireworks.

After all, how many people get to see bombs that don't exist?

When my year in Southeast Asia was up, like every other GI, I boarded my plane home. On the long journey, I sat and reflected on what my year in Asia was all about. I realized that I too was sold, in Neil Sheehan's words, "A Bright Shining Lie."

One thought resonated . . . What a tragic fucken waste.

CHAPTER EIGHTEEN

Back in the States only a few months, a friend tightened me up with a job working for Jimmy Hoffa's teamsters.

I was thrilled.

I grew up with these guys. Thanks to our union, we earned decent pay. In 1970, no one dared cross a teamster's picket line. We earned $12 an hour. Cops and firefighters only earned $8.

* * *

Of course, the boys from my Bronx neighborhood knew how to supplement their income. A product of 12 years of Catholic School, and naive, I still thought everything was on the level.

You would have thought that after Vietnam's moral insane asylum, and after hearing firsthand from my old acid buddy, Ron Byers, that South Carolina's senior Senator, Mendel Rivers, shook down local pimps for kickbacks that I would have known better. But no, I still thought the country was legit.

Yet, I grew more cynical daily.

My pals and I delivered appliances and televisions.

At least once a week, something "fell" off the back of the truck. If the stolen piece sold in stores for $600, we'd charge $300.

My neighborhood's tenements appeared dreary, gray and grim from the outside, but inside the squalor, new appliances helped make life bearable. Our parent's kitchens and living rooms looked like Sears' showrooms—everything was brand spanking new.

We made a buck, and Sears could handle it, I justified.

I felt like Robin Hood.

* * *

"Then we gotta do what we gotta do," said the "Murph."

My driver today was the biggest thief on the job.

A tough prick, Murphy weighed 270 and liked to throw his hands around.

Murph was one of those guys who had five o'clock shadow at noon. He probably started shaving in the sixth grade.

"The shop steward wants to see you two in his office," a coworker told us.

I gave an inquisitive glance.

"Did he say why?"

"No. Just see Joey before you pull out of the lot."

We walked into the shop steward's small office aside the garage.

"Listen, Murphy, you've been submitting 'not on truck' slips every day for a month. Sears isn't stupid."

Joey was an athletic, dark, medium-aged, no-nonsense kind of guy, broad through the shoulders, narrow through the hips.

"This shit has to stop. You're lucky I'm the steward and not someone else. You should be fired. Shit, you should be in jail," Joey said.

"If Sears can prove I stole something, let them. Until then, don't break my fucken balls," Murph said.

My eyes got saucer wide. I would have begged for forgiveness and thanked Joey for the heads-up.

"I shouldn't tell you this. It could mean my job, but Sears has two spotters following you today." Joey warned. "For God's sake, don't steal anything."

* * *

The sun had only begun to paint the morning clouds with its hazy humid brush, yet already my forehead oozed sweat from Joey's warning. My nerves pushed the droplets over my eyebrows and clouded my eyes until my sleeve made them a memory.

I vaulted into the helper's side of the truck, slammed the door and lit up a nervous Marlboro. As the calming nicotine rushed down my throat, I reached to lower the radio's volume.

"Thank God Joey told us about those spotters, huh Murph?"

"Whatta ya mean?"

Murph wore a gray Sears' shirt with cutoff sleeves, which emphasized the size of his considerable arms. He topped off the outfit with blue work pants and black motorcycle boots. He had a red bandanna tied around his forehead to keep the hair out of his hazel eyes.

"I mean, shit, if Joey hadn't warned us, we could have gotten busted," I said.

"I've already sold a TV. We gotta make the drop."

I almost pissed my pants.

"What about the spotters?"

"I'll figure out something."

"But what if they bust us?"

"Then we gotta do what we gotta do," said the Murph.

"What does that mean? I'm not killing anybody. What the fuck do you mean by that?"

"Don't worry. You won't have to do anything. I'll take care of it."

I searched the money pocket of my jeans, and my straight Irish Catholic ass popped a Valium.

* * *

We made the first few deliveries as scheduled. Murph pulled from the curb and checked the rearview.

"I see the spotters."

I needed a drink.

Murph said, "Don't sweat it. I got this."

"What are you gonna do?" I asked.

"Don't worry. I got it figured out."

He drove a few blocks, made two hard rights and landed us in front of the 44th precinct. He said,

"Stay with the truck. I'll be right back."

* * *

Murphy tore into the police station. My eyes followed him. The steep rounded slope of his shoulders seemed too wide for his tapered back. His legs were stumpy, yet strong, like two fire hydrants.

Parked alongside me, a green Toyota wanted to pull out. I signaled to the driver that I'd check my rearview and wave her out when the traffic cleared.

She carefully pulled from the tight spot and crept up the street to the stop sign. I watched her pull out onto the main drag just as Murph bounded down the precinct steps stifling a laugh.

"How'd it go?" I asked.

Murph grinned, "I told them that I'm a Sears' driver. I'm carrying COD s, and I think someone's following me."

"Holy shit. Are you crazy? What did they say?"

"The cop at the desk said don't worry. Go back to your truck. Keep making deliveries. We'll take care of it."

* * *

Two deliveries later, Murph again checked the rearview mirror and said,

"The cops are shadowing the spotters."

Murphy was hysterical now.

"You believe this? This is like something out of the Keystone Cops."

We delivered a dishwasher and a dryer. I tossed our dolly and moving strap into the truck's back box. I started to lock the pull-down gate, when I heard the whrrr whrrr whrrr of a police siren.

I spun a quick 180 degrees. The cops, guns drawn, pulled over the spotters.

"Quick, jump in the cab. Let's go drop that TV," Murph laughed.

I blessed myself and said a silent prayer.

* * *

The next day, Lenny and I cruised down Park Avenue after an air conditioner delivery. My driver Lenny weighed at least 250 pounds. His belly overhung his belt, which left only the thinnest of space between his gut and the steering wheel.

I said, "Lenny, you ever work with Yak Yak?"

Lenny had dense, dull eyes and carelessly shaved dark jowls. He was chatty enough but always talked out of the side of his mouth.

"Yeah, Yak never shuts up, a real pain in the ass, but the cocksucker's a hell of a worker."

We stopped for a light. Lenny asked,

"You getting hungry?"

Not waiting for my reply, he spotted a wafer-thin pedestrian standing on the broad, tree-lined divide that separated north and south and asked one short question.

"Say pal. You got the time?"

"You got the place?" came the effeminate reply.

Taken aback, I pivoted my head, laughed and said,

"A gay guy huh? Only in fucken New York."

Lenny shrugged, whipped his head back to the street and calmly said,

"Back of the truck."

Stunned, I said,

"Lenny, what are you crazy? That's a guy."

"A hit's a hit," he said stoically.

I can't believe it. I was comfortable enough with my manhood that I could withstand a failure or two, but I drew the line at sex with men or animals. Holy shit, Lenny acted like he lived in ancient Rome.

I nervously took a Seconal from the money pocket of my dungarees. I pierced the plastic coating with a pin. The faster this down hit me the better.

* * *

Another guy I worked with was Patty.

Patty sported a thick, black, handlebar mustache turned down at the corners like a Mexican bandit, and I couldn't argue with the impeccable logic that just flowed from the wise lips beneath the brush.

"He seems like a good kid, Patty. Why don't you like your daughter's boyfriend?"

I stared into the sincere, green eyes of the most streetwise guy on the job and waited for some Teamster logic.

"I saw him in a bathing suit. His prick's too big. I don't want him putting that weapon in my little girl," he said.

Just then, a tall, lean black man shot his head through

Patty's rolled-down passenger window and interrupted our conversation.

"Hey, you guys wanna buy two bottles of Dewar's?"

Patty drank scotch and didn't hesitate.

"How much ya want?"

"Fifteen dollars for both bottles."

"Fuck you. You boosted them anyway. I'll give you $10," Patty said.

"Twelve," said the thief.

"All right. You win," Patty said.

The boost pushed the bottles through the passenger window, and we pulled from the curb.

I sat silently between Patty and Lenny.

Five minutes later, Patty talked past me to the behemoth behind the wheel.

"Lenny, I have plenty of scotch at home. The holidays are coming up. You want these two bottles?"

"Sure," said Lenny. "If you really don't want them."

Lenny forked over the $12 and put the bag behind the driver's seat.

After our next delivery, while Lenny was still inside collecting the COD, Patty and I slid the dolly back on to the truck's cab.

"You drink Dewar's, Patty. That shit doesn't go bad. Why'd you sell the scotch to Lenny?"

"After I paid the shine, I looked through the rearview mirror and saw him running away. I figured it must be iced tea. Better Lenny gets stuck than me."

I was impressed.

Here was a guy who wouldn't know a book from a bayonet, but on the street,

Patty was slicker than oil on ice, almost as slick as his brother, Vinny.

* * *

"You want to make some money today? I got an idea," Patty said.

"Whatta ya got in mind?"

"We'll stop at Cousin's novelty store on Fordham Road and buy some cheap handcuffs. We'll fake a hold-up."

My first thought?

Shit, I forgot to bring my Valium.

Recovering,

"How ya wanna do this?"

"First, we make all our deliveries. Do a full day. Get all the CODs. Then we'll have Gene meet us later, and we'll hand him all the cash. After that, we handcuff ourselves to a stairwell banister, and tell the cops we got held up."

"Won't the cops suspect it was us?" I asked.

"You've been watching too many Colombo's. City cops couldn't find a thief in prison."

* * *

"Oh my God, what happened?" the matronly woman asked.

"Lady, call the cops. We're Sears' deliverymen. We've been robbed."

An hour later, two boys in blue arrived.

As one hack sawed the cheap handcuffs, the other said,

"Tell us what happened?"

"We just finished making a delivery to apt 3A when two black guys came out from under the stairwell with guns. They handcuffed us to the banister and robbed us. They even took our wallets," Patty said.

"What did they look like?'

"They had black curly hair, broad flat noses and they were wearing sneakers," Patty deadpanned.

Our interrogator, incredibly, made a notation of Patty's description, then said,

"What surprises me is that this is a pretty good neighborhood."

Too nervous to speak, I let Patty handle things.

"We started out in Harlem," my driver said.

"I bet the guys who robbed you followed you all day," Sherlock said.

Now, I relaxed. Patty had this covered.

"Wow. I never thought of that." Patty smirked. "You might

want to write that in your report. You might make detective."

* * *

Besides our pay and the added income from our innovative activities, we earned tips. Not a lot, usually just enough for lunch and a few beers.

Counter intuitively, the tips came not from the rich, nor the upper class, but from those least able to afford them.

If we had to lug a refrigerator up five-urine-drenched flights in the Harlem slums, the occupant of the roach-infested apartment would often offer a soda or a beer and toss us a few singles to say thanks.

By contrast, in the butlered, marble-laden co-ops of Park Avenue, we were admitted through the service entrance. No matter how high the humidity, or how hard we labored, not only would we get skunked, we would seldom be offered even a glass of water.

We stopped asking if we could use the toilets of the rich long ago.

True enough, they didn't want deliverymen defecating on their porcelain, but the extremely rich didn't really despise us. It was just that the working class simply wasn't on their radar.

* * *

Here's an anecdote a good friend of mine told me that illustrates how the rich hang onto every dime they have.

Pete was one of those "can do" guys. So capable, so curious, that if he came across an oil burner, he'd take it apart and reassemble it just to see how it worked.

He was meticulous. Anything he did had to be perfect. You know the type, a guy who got out of the shower to piss just because it was the right thing to do.

One day, Pete painted a kitchen on Sutton Place for one of the Vanderbilts. He walked in, plugged in his radio, taped, patched, primed and painted the considerable surface.

As usual, his work was impeccable. Pete could paint in a tuxedo.

Next day, Pete's boss called and told him that Mrs. Vanderbilt complained.

He screamed,

"Are you fucken kidding me? What could she complain about? I left that place immaculate."

His boss said, "Mrs. Vanderbilt complained that when you plugged in your radio, you stole her electricity."

* * *

We'd occasionally spend our tips on diversions other than beers.

If we wanted a quick $5 blowjob, we'd grab a Hunts Point streetwalker and use the back of the truck. I wondered what the customers would say if they knew that an hour before their delivery, a prostitute had used their new couch, or divan, to service their deliverymen.

But sometimes on paydays, we'd skip lunch and treat ourselves to a "high-class" whore.

* * *

The coffee truck pulled up outside the Sears' pad, and we Teamsters crowded around it to grab some breakfast before the shop steward dished out our delivery locations for the day. While we waited on line, Paulie Sica, Frankie Chas and Joey Tripps were telling me a story.

Paulie began with a wide grin separating his chipmunk jowls. "We stopped at Rivington Street yesterday. They had a blonde there that blew my brains out. Man she really knew what the fuck she was doing."

When Sica raved about Rivington Street, a mob-run whorehouse in lower Manhattan, he got animated, excited, almost as if he was still experiencing an orgasm.

A clean, cheap and convenient oasis, we younger teamsters stopped at the brownstone periodically to break the tedium of lugging double-doored refrigerators up stairs. After my year of debauchery in Vietnam, I had no qualms about exchanging money for sex and was eager for the details.

"She was unbelievable, tits that could resurface the Titanic and an ass that could crack a walnut, unreal."

Sica extended his thumb and pinky and vibrated his hand for emphasis.

"Plus, she was one hell of a worker."

Sica, the bearded, overweight horn-dog currently rambling on about the stunning Nordic 6'2" sword swallower who worked at Rivington had looks that would turn off a nymphomaniac. What surprised me about his slovenly appearance was that his sister, Lorraine, was as neat as a Pez dispenser, a living doll that I had been trying to ask out for a month. But without whorehouses, Lorraine's brother, Paulie, would have been shit outta luck.

He said, "Madonna mia, Frankie, Joey and me parked outside the brownstone and locked our truck. You've been there, right Connor?" He ripped the cover off his coffee. "Out of the four buzzers, ya gotta ring the one marked spa."

He sipped from a Styrofoam cup and said,

"Anyway, the madam takes our $14 and tells us she has three girls working. When the three show up, they're all knockouts. But one of them," he said, "looks like Ms. Sweden. I nearly shit. I lunged from my seat, grabbed her hand and disappeared."

Frankie chimed in.

"Yeah, the other whores were nice too, but they couldn't hold a candle to the blonde. So me and Joey told the other two girls that we'd wait."

Frankie looked at Paulie and said,

"So after 20 minutes, this fat bastard comes out grinning, so then Joey jumps up and disappears with the blonde. Gracie, I think her name was, right Joey?"

"Yeah Gracie," Joey said. "After one glimpse of her, man, I felt like I was gonna explode. I couldn't get in there fast enough."

Frankie interrupted. "Me too. I almost came before I even got in the room. Don't forget, I had to sit and wait until these two cocksuckas were finished. Waiting made me want her twice as much. I needed to get in there. The next 20 minutes was fucken torture," Frankie said.

"Finally, Joey blows out of the hallway grinning, so I grab the blonde's hand and disappear."

Frankie tore the cellophane off of a Danish, took a bite, but didn't bother to swallow, then said between chews,

"All that's in there is a massage table, a sink and a nightstand. I know the routine, so I take off my pants, take the washbasin, and the washcloth from the sink and hold it underneath my balls."

Frankie wore a tight blue T-shirt stretched across his massive arms and chest. His bright brown eyes were laced with mischief.

"She takes off her flimsy negligee, and all she has on is this thin, pink g-string. And man she had a body exactly like Paulie said. While she's scrubbing me down, she's polishing, and playing with my knob."

Frankie was engrossed in his tale, but took the time to wolf another bite of his Danish.

"After she dries me, she stands and pushes me onto the white-linen, covered massage table, but she still had my cock in her hand. She tears a Trojan wrapper with her teeth and her thumb, and sticks the condom in her mouth. She put the rubber on my prick with her mouth."

Frankie's black, curly coiffure looked like it could withstand a gale. He never had a hair out of place.

"While she was exploring me with her tongue, I was thinking, *'Oh my God, this chick could empty the cargo hold of an oil tanker with a soda fountain straw.'* Her mouth felt like she had gargled with crazy glue."

Frankie grabbed his coffee from the fender of the truck.

"So now as I'm loving the blowjob, she pulls a fast one. I've been to a 100 whorehouses. I don't kiss prostitutes. I'm not there to show them a good time. I'm the one that's paying."

Frankie sipped his coffee.

"She slides off her g-string, and while she's still blowing me, she takes one of her perfectly formed legs and straddles my neck. She pushes both feet from the floor and mounts me in the 69-position. I'm lying there with my mouth about an inch from her pussy. I swear to God I started talking to myself." He started laughing.

"The devil in me said,
"*Go ahead. Eat it. You know you want to.*
"I said to myself,
"*No way. I can't eat that. I don't even kiss whores. No way I can do this.*"
Frankie's hands became so animated that he looked like a conductor for the philharmonic.
"But man, Connor, she felt so good. She was so beautiful—beyond beautiful, perfect. Her mouth moved so slowly, and her pussy had this amazing light-blond heart-shaped patch. So fuck it. I broke down and gave it a quick postage stamp lick . . . and fuck it. You know what? I didn't die. The ceiling didn't collapse."
Between sips of his coffee, and the way he told the story, Frankie laughed so hard that he could hardly speak.
"This time, I gave her pussy a long ice-cream cone lick.
"Still . . .
Still nothing. The cops didn't show up. I didn't die. Fuck it. I went after it the way a wolf goes after a pork chop."
Frankie put down the coffee, his two hands grabbed his stomach, and he bent over in convulsive laughter.
I cracked up and said incredulously,
"You crazy fuck. You ate out a hooker?"
"You would have too, man. She was amazing," he said.
"And wait, wait, this is the best part. You ain't heard nothing, yet. Shut up. Shut up." He held up and extended palm. "When I went downstairs, these two crazy fucks were waiting for me in the truck."
He nodded toward Paulie and Joey who both had tears in their eyes from Frankie's tale and urged him to get to the punch line.
"So Paulie pulls from the curb, drives about a block and stops at the red light. He turns to Joey and me and says, 'Hell of a worker huh?' Jimmy and I both say, 'Oh yeah, hell of a worker.' So when the light changes, Sica shifts the truck into first gear and says, 'so, did you eat her?'"
Now Paulie's hugging his stomach in laughter and Joey's

jumping up and down, stomping his feet laughing. I'm dying too, but I'm urging Frankie to finish the story.

"Come on ya cocksucka. What did ya say? Did ya confess?" I said.

"Fuck no. I didn't," Frankie said. "Whatta ya think I was gonna own up to that?"

"Tell him. Tell Connor what you said" said Paulie.

"What do you think I am, a fucken idiot? I've been to hundreds of these joints," I told Paulie. "I'd never eat a whore," I said. "I'd have to be out of my fucking mind to eat a prostitute. Besides, you two slime balls went ahead of me."

Joey jumped in.

"Come on Frankie tell him. Tell him what happened."

"Shut the fuck up. Will ya, Joey? Let me tell the fucken story."

Frankie slowed his pace a bit and said,

"Joey here says, 'Frankie's right. No one in their right fucking mind would eat a prostitute.' So Paulie turns onto First Avenue heading south. Three straight blocks of nothing but silence before Paulie turns again and says, 'so, did you eat her?' and cracks up laughing."

Frankie shoves Paulie now and says,

"So I start laughing and says to this fat fuck, yeah. I ate her. What the fuck? That shit ain't like tires. Pussies don't wear out. I cracked up because then Joey says, holy shit. I ate her too."

Paulie said, "Wait, wait. This is the best, Connor."

He put his hand on my shoulder and pulled me closer while convulsing with laughter.

"And instead of being ashamed, we all high-fived. I tell ya it was a pissa. The broad was amazing."

"You fucken guys are crazy," I said.

"Tell him. Tell him what you said next Paulie. Tell him," said Joey.

"I said, ain't it something how pussy makes us crazy? Think about it." Paulie said. "Pussy killed King Kong, man. Planes didn't kill that giant gorilla. Blonde pussy drove that fucken monkey crazy."

I couldn't argue with Paulie's Teamster logic. "Pussy killed King Kong," fucken screwballs. But the more I thought about it, the more I realized that they didn't eat that prostitute because they went crazy. She was just one hell of a worker.

CHAPTER NINETEEN

Delivering Sears' appliances for Hoffa's Teamsters earned me a good buck, but I gambled.

I was compulsive, so naturally, I overdid it.

I owed three bookmakers.

I needed more outlets to bet, so Patty, my co-worker, hooked me up with his brother.

Vinny was the real deal.

Vinny did a stretch for a big wise guy from Arthur Avenue, an Italian enclave near the Bronx Zoo.

In the Bronx, Angelo was "boss of bosses," so all bookies kicked back cash to Angelo.

Vinny did a "bit" for Angelo.

After his five-year stretch was over, Angelo hooked him up with three "numbers shops" in Harlem, so he could "earn." He also bought Vinny a $200,000 house in Westchester. In 1971, $200 large was real money.

Vinny and Angelo were understandably tight.

I settled up with Vinny weekly. As Angelo's "runner," he got 50 percent of my losses. (Runners bring in business for bookmakers and work off percentage).

Besides being a Bronx Don, Angelo owned a neighborhood restaurant, Michael's, and a huge discothèque in New Rochelle.

Another of Angelo's runners, Joe, lived above the restaurant. To make ends meet, he played guitar in Michael's on Friday and Saturday nights. He strolled, strummed and serenaded diners with Italian songs.

One Saturday night before the restaurant got busy, Angelo,

Joe and Vinny ate pasta at the round roped-off booth reserved for the boss. The waiter said,

"Hey Joe, you got a phone call."

Joe wiped the white cloth napkin across his mouth and walked to answer the phone.

"What are you some kind of asshole? Up in your mother's xxxx," he screamed and slammed the receiver onto the cradle.

He returned to his meal steaming.

"What the hell was that all about?" Angelo asked.

"Some fucken asshole telling me he's Robert Deniro, and he wants to put me in a movie. Like I ain't got enough fucken problems without this prick breaking my balls."

Joe returned his napkin to his lap and barely re-gripped his fork when the waiter said,

"Joe, phone call again,"

"Jesus Christ. I can't believe this shit. I've gotta work tonight, and I can't even eat in peace."

Joe retraced his steps to the upside down receiver,

"What are you some kind of a sick bastard? I swear to Christ if you were here in front of me. I'd rip your fucken throat out. What did I tell you before? Up in your mother's xxxx."

Down slammed the phone again as Joe returned to the table.

"What a fucken asshole. Can you believe this guy? Did you two guys put this prick up to this shit? Bobby Deniro, my cock. I'm up to my ass in debt, working two jobs trying to earn, trying to keep my head above water and this fuck has got nothing better to do than break my fucken balls."

Angelo and Vinny raised their wineglasses and laughed, then toasted,

"Salute, Joe Pesci, movie star."

* * *

Thirty minutes later, the door opened and in walked Robert Deniro. Celebrated smirk chiseled firmly in place, he approached Joe's table and extended his hand.

"Hey, I'm Bobby Deniro. I know we had a misunderstanding on the phone, but I really do want you in a movie I'm making."

Angelo ignored Joe,

"Oh my God, Bobby Deniro. Sit down, mangia, mangia. Hey Mario, bring a plate for Mr. Deniro."

With Rolexed wrist and diamond-ringed fingers, Angelo patted the red-velvet seat next to him,

"Sit here, Bobby. Have a little vino."

Deniro explained that he saw a movie that Pesci shot with Danny Aiello. Although Pesci had a small role, Deniro thought he'd be perfect for a bit part in his latest film, "Raging Bull."

Deniro was shooting the film in the Italian neighborhood's Mt. Carmel Gym where Jake LaMotta, who the story was based on, trained.

After dinner and drinks, Angelo insisted the four visit his discothèque, "Rings."

After midnight, they arrived in New Rochelle and grabbed four stools at one of the three circular bars.

After a few belts, Deniro stared out at the crowded dance floor. A pretty young blond gyrated beneath the strobe lights. He told Angelo that the girl was a dead-ringer for young Vikki LaMotta, Jake's wife.

Angelo told Vinny,

"Have the young lady join us at the bar."

The 17-year-old girl, Cathy Moriarity, got a break.

She went on to stardom in Scorsese's monumental masterpiece "Raging Bull."

* * *

Pesci devoured the script and convinced Deniro and Scorsese to let him play the major role of LaMotta's brother, Joey.

As Sam Spade said when he stared wistfully at the Maltese Falcon, "This is the stuff that dreams are made of."

When Raging Bull was released in 1980, Joe Pesci skyrocketed from "wanna be wise guy" to film legend in movies such as, "Casino," "Goodfellows," and "My Cousin Vinny."

Primarily, Pesci played himself, or guys he had admired all his life.

One caveat, once you worked for Angelo, you always worked for Angelo.

Angelo relocated to Hollywood to protect his "investment."

He partnered a production company with Walter Matthau who, fortunately for Angelo, and unfortunately for Matthau, was an avid gambler.

* * *

Vinny told me years later,

"Angelo's making a fortune. He never uses his own money to produce a film. This way whatever happens at the box office they come out ahead. It's legitimate stealing. The sweetest racket he has ever had."

But, before he left for Hollywood, I had a run in with Angelo that scared the shit out of me.

* * *

"Yeah, that'll help me out, Vin, thanks."

I owed Vinny six large. Not much by today's standards, but I only took home $350 a week working at Sears.

"At least, it'll help you get out of the hole," Vinny said and shook my hand.

Vinny had just given me a quarter sheet. If I brought in players, I'd get 25 percent of their losses. If they won, his boss, Angelo, would pay, but then I'd go in the red, the minus side of the ledger. Provided I was on the plus side of the ledger, the black, I'd get one quarter of my player's losses. If I were in the red, I wouldn't earn anything until after my players lost enough to get me back in the black.

For a few months all was well. I had knocked $3,000 off my debt, but of course I was still chipping on sports, nothing serious, a few hundred a game every night.

I was also spending a lot of time with Paulie's sister. She was a great gal, but dangerous, Italian and family orientated. I couldn't stand it when I wasn't with her, but I was smart enough to know that I wasn't marriage material, too selfish, and too fond of partying and gambling. Nevertheless, Lorraine had me roped in pretty good.

* * *

I picked up a new player, a big one, a "whale."

First week, he crushed the office.

Matt won $22,000.

I paid him, or more precisely Vinny's boss, Angelo, paid him.
Second week, Matt got paid $33,000.
Third week, he lost $41,000 and never showed up at the collection site.
I was anxious but not frantic . . . yet.
I called Matt, no answer.
I left a delicately phrased message on his machine.
I sweated blood waiting for his callback.
Nothing.
I drove to his apartment in the South Bronx and knocked on the door.
Nothing.
I leaned on the bell.
Nothing.
I was fucked.
I headed to the roof.
Across the tarpaper, I spotted the fire escape and descended carefully.
Two stories from the roof, I came to his window and looked in.
Jesus, Mary and Joseph—empty.
Not a stick of furniture, nothing.
I was really fucked.

* * *

"Hey Vinny. I've got a big problem."

"If you got a problem, I've got a problem," Vinny said.

"This guy Silvera, the guy who has been pounding the office, he never showed."

"What? Let's go to his house."

"I did. He's gone."

"Gone? What the fuck do you mean gone? How much does he owe?"

"Forty one, large."

"Are you fucken kidding, $41,000? We gotta find this prick and fast. I'll call Angelo and give him the bad news. Expect a phone call."

My stomach cartwheeled; Angelo was boss of bosses. I was in deep shit.

Ten minutes later, Vinny called.

"I'll pick you up. Angelo wants to see you."

"When?"

"When? When the fuck do you think? Now."

My stomach problems escalated.

* * *

Considering I recommended this guy, Silvera, Angelo acted like a gentleman. I was just a kid and he could have buffaloed me, but he was a businessman. He wanted to get paid.

"You sure you don't want a drink, kid, some whiskey, some espresso?"

Pinky extended, Angelo lifted his cup and nodded toward it.

"No. I'm fine. I just want to straighten this out," I stammered.

"Look kid . . . Connor, you said your name was, right? Look, Connor, Vinny said you're all right, but look at this from my point of view. How do I know there is a guy named Silvera? How do I know that you're not robbing me?"

"Angelo, I'm no fool. I wouldn't rob you. Shit, I wouldn't have the balls."

"Maybe, maybe not, but I need to have a body. You said this guy's gone. Gone where? It's simple. Find me him, or someone related to him; otherwise, you're on the hook."

"I'll do my best. I can't pay that kind of money," I said.

"Do better than your best, kid," Angelo said business like, reasonably, coolly.

Now my Catholic upbringing spurred an error in judgment. I said, "If I find him, what are you gonna do to him?"

Angelo shot me a hard glance.

"What the fuck did you just ask me?" He sipped his espresso calmly. "What am I gonna do to him?"

Angelo hit the ceiling. He stood and slammed his fist on the table.

"What am I gonna do to him?" Yelling now, "This cocksucka robbed me. He got paid, and then as soon as he lost . . . he took off. He had no intention of ever paying me."

He turned to the seven or eight sycophants in the social club and said,

"You believe this little Irish punk? He wants to know what I'm gonna do," and laughed. "Doesn't know how to mind his own fucken business."

Then he turned back to me, eyes bulging, veins throbbing, screaming now,

"Did he give a fuck what I was gonna do to you, when he took off? Well, did he?

Fuck no. I'm gonna beat his fucken brains in. Just get his ass down here, and then you're off the hook. Otherwise, I want my fucken money. Meeting's over."

* * *

I asked around Silvera's neighborhood and discovered his older brother owned a florist.

Bingo.

Thank God, a body.

I told Vinny.

He said, "Good job. I'll take care of it. We'll pay his brother a little visit."

Next morning, I got a phone call.

"It's me, Matt Silvera."

My heart jumped into my throat.

Relieved, I could barely talk.

"Where the hell are you?"

"California."

"California? Listen man, you've got to come back and straighten this out."

"What are they gonna do to me?"

"They just want to get paid man. They aren't gonna do nothing. They just want their money."

I needed him back and quick.

"They threatened my family," he said.

"That was just to make you surface. They just want you to work something out. Come back to N.Y. Straighten this out. Everything will be fine." I lied.

* * *

One week later the day of reckoning, I brought Matt to Angelo's social club.

The two of us took the short walk through the familiar, seasoned sidewalks. The smells that would normally make my mouth water saturated the street. From the many restaurants, sauces seasoned with seafood or pork, and from the numerous bakeries, the sweet smells of cannolis, cookies and bread.

But I couldn't think about food, about Lorraine, or anything else but my problem.

Last night, I knocked off a quart of scotch with little effect. As I lay in bed, my ears rang. My legs felt funny. My eyes kept staring at the dark, and my mind kept pounding on my dilemma.

What am I gonna do? What if they kill him?

I was scared, couldn't sleep or eat.

Shit, I couldn't even get drunk.

The two of us rang the bell of the rolled-up security-gated storefront. A Luca Brasi type character opened the door and managed a grunt. Matt and I started in when Luca's tennis racket sized hand swatted my chest.

"Not you. The boss said just him."

I looked at Matt encouragingly.

"Stay cool. Everything will be fine," I lied again. "I'll meet you in the bar down the block. I need a drink."

I jogged to the local gin mill to pound a few triple scotches. The further I got from the crime scene, the better I felt.

If they kill this prick, am I an accessory to murder? I set him up. I could be in major trouble, I thought.

Then, my manic mind skipped.

How many people know that he skipped out on his debt? Who would drop a dime and give me up?

I was only on my second tumbler of scotch when through the door came Matt Silvera.

"What the fuck? You're back already? How'd it go?"

"It went great."

"What happened?"

"Angelo said he didn't want the money. Forget about the debt."

"What? What the fuck are you talking about? Tell me exactly how this went down."

"I told him I had blown the money, but I was willing to pay him $100 a week, until we were square. He just started laughing. He got up from the table and said,

'Don't worry about the money. You don't owe me anything. It's OK Forget about the whole thing.'"

"So, I left."

"Are you fucken crazy? You can't leave it like this. You gotta go back."

"Why? He said I was off the hook."

"Yeah, you're off the hook, and soon you're gonna be off the planet."

I drained my scotch. Rivers of caution dented my forehead.

"Trust me, Matt. Go back. Straighten this out right now while you still can."

"You think so?"

"I know so. Go back. I'll wait here."

He slugged out the door and back to Angelo's social club.

"Bartender, take the air out of this glass. I need another triple."

This wouldn't be my last encounter with the wise guys, nor their cousins, "the wannabes."

What I didn't realize then was that soon enough I'd be on the other side of the fence using Angelo's methods to collect gambling debts myself.

Right now I just wanted this nightmare to end.

I needed a break from the "Gumbas." I even needed a break from my Italian girlfriend, Lorraine. I needed to think things out. Put things in perspective. I knew just the place.

Timmy told me that where he lived now, New Orleans, reminded him of Europe.

I needed that.

I needed a few laughs.

I needed my brother.

CHAPTER TWENTY

In 1972 New Orleans, a nickel still bought a dial tone. I listened to Timmy's answering service spew a banal taped message.

"Tim Kelly is not home at the moment; however, he may be reached at the following establishments—Sid's Dream Lounge, The Mouse Trap, Pat O'Brien's or Johnny White's Saloon."

I should have known. The last time I saw my brother in Ostende, Belgium, my salient memory was of Timmy passed out drunk against a parked car.

I glanced again at the phone number he gave me, and all I could do was laugh, answering service my ass, fucking Timmy.

Now, I got to track this lunatic down.

I told him I'd be in town tonight. You'd think he'd stick around. His unreliability was such a pain in the ass. Well, that's Timmy. I just wish I could describe the intangibles that made him so magnetic.

I guess it's because anyone who was around Timmy suddenly had more fun. He had so much size. Even in New Orleans, a town that personifies partying, he was bigger than life.

I had given the Teamsters my leave of absence letter. I hoped I hadn't made a mistake. If I ever found my fucken brother, I guess I'd find out.

* * *

I hustled the three car lengths from the pay phone to my convertible.

Back from Vietnam less than a year, I had bought my white Austin Healy "hot" in the Bronx for a $1,000.

Vinny warned me.

"Don't drive it in Riverdale."

When he delivered the car, it still had wires dangling from the ignition switch. In the days before sophisticated computers, a pro like Vinny supplied the registration along with the car. Here in the Deep South, I was a long way from Riverdale.

I turned right on Canal and crawled up Bourbon just as the neon lights launched the town to life.

Although annoyed, my left cheek puffed and pressured the skin at the corner of my mouth, which forced a smirk. When used in the same sentence, Timmy and Sid's Dream Lounge were as natural as red beans and rice.

From the open club doors, the hot and lively sounds of jazz, blues and rock flooded the narrow crammed streets, action everywhere. As my sports car crept up the crammed streets, vendors hawking hot dogs, corned dogs and roast corn haunted the intersections. At a stoplight, I heard a sidewalk barker promise—girls, girls, girls and more inside.

The shill confirmed what I already suspected. The French Quarter wouldn't disappoint.

The light changed.

I brought the engine to life and eased toward Duquesne Street where I sighted the most perfect set of tits my young eyes had ever seen. Two exquisitely shaped breasts were barely hidden behind a T-shirt tied at the waist and a full foot of defined flesh exposed above a pair of skimpy Daisy Duke's.

Her T-shirt read,

"If God didn't want us to eat it, he wouldn't have made it look like a hot dog."

No. New Orleans wouldn't disappoint.

* * *

On Rampart Street, just outside the Quarter, I found a rare parking spot and decided to hoof it. I walked with purpose, yet occasionally lingered to gaze up at the ornate wrought-iron balconies heavy with ferns and potted plants that clung to the Vieux Carre's pastel buildings.

I hadn't eaten since morning. To escape the bouquets of baked bread and gumbo, I turned off Decatur Street and onto St.

Philip. Like the rest of the Quarter, plenty of bars were up this street as well. I had to find Timmy.

I finally stumbled into a crowded, no-frills joint called The Mousetrap. I scanned the oval bar from the entrance and focused on the barman who was pulling a frosty mug from the cooler in front of me. He filled it until foam ran over the lip.

Directly in front of the bartender, with his back to me and surrounded by a four-girl laughing entourage, an obviously intoxicated Timmy held court.

I listened to a cumbersome goateed man with a Cajun accent interrupt my brother's monologue.

"Timmy, I just walked past your car padner. Ya left your headlights on."

Timmy had an unkempt mop of brown curly hair, broad shoulders and thin hips. He calmly dragged on a cigarette, swigged a shot, sipped his beer and shrugged,

"It's cool, man. I've got jumper cables."

"But your car's right up the block, just shut off the lights," the local said.

"Hey Luke, man, don't be a pain in the ass. Thanks, but I'm busy now."

From the swinging doors, I shook my head and smiled. Timmy pulled one of the girls towards his lap and nonchalantly continued. I interrupted.

"Here you are, Jesus, I hit five bars before this one. Every bartender in town knows you. You knew I was coming today. I thought you were going to stay home."

Ignoring my rant, Timmy leapt from his stool and hugged me.

"Connor," he screamed.

He barely finished putting his arms around me when he segued.

"Girls, if you think I'm crazy, wait until you meet my wacky brother."

Timmy yelled to the bartender.

"Hey, Don. What's the name of this desert? Get my little brother a drink will ya? Connor say hello to Shane and Misty.

They strip in the joint around the corner. Great gals, you're going to love them."

Then Timmy turned to the two other girls.

"Sorry girls, I forgot your names. Introduce yourself to my brother."

I extended my hand, but Timmy's whisper detoured me.

"Don't waste too much time with them. They're tourists. We'll have another drink here, and then we'll head back to Shane and Misty's apartment. They're big time into S&M. We might have to take a few whacks, but what the fuck? We'll have lots of laughs."

My head pivoted between the two strippers like I was watching a tennis match on speed. This was why I drove 25 hours.

Let the games begin.

* * *

Overlooking a crowded Royal Street, Kyle, an overweight friend of the girls', mixed drinks. Below the strippers' balcony, tourists gathered and tossed money into a street musician's hat.

Timmy had a muscular arm around Shane while Misty filled my lap.

"We'll make sure you two have a good time, but Kyle pays half the rent. Do you mind if he joins us?" asked Misty.

"What do you mean, join us?" I said. "I'm no prude, but I draw the line with men or animals."

"Oh, you don't have to do anything sexual with Kyle. He just likes a good whipping," Misty said.

Kyle wore tailored khaki pants, a bright yellow shirt tattooed with red parrots and expensive brown-tasseled loafers without socks. The smile on his bloated face seemed forced-frozen.

"As long as it ain't me on the receiving end," Timmy laughed. "I'll beat him to within an inch of his life."

As Kyle's pudgy fingers handed Timmy his gin and tonic, his frozen smile morphed to nervous concern.

"If you really want to get this party started, I have a few hits of acid," Shane said.

"Acid? You gotta be shitting me, acid?" I said. "Well, in for a penny, in for a pound. What the hell, I ain't going anywhere for the next six or seven hours."

* * *

Once the acid kicked in, my eyes traced the scrolled-iron decorative work that lined the balcony over and over. The weight of potted roses, bougainvillea, chrysanthemums and geraniums sagged the balcony's center and made the metal terrace appear malleable, Gumbyish. A slight breeze blew through the plants and made the air smell like damp, bruised spearmint. The potted flowers spun and twirled and made me dizzy, so I averted my eyes and stared into the streets below and roared senseless laughter into a kaleidoscope of color.

Misty reached around and rubbed my zipper.

"I love sex, when I'm tripping. I'm peaking my ass off. Come inside off the balcony," she said.

The feel of her hand titillated me, but the blood-red bougainvillea plants that saturated her balcony had me hypnotized. I was fascinated by their pin-wheeled swirls.

But lust trumped any newfound fondness for fauna. Inside the apartment, whips, manacles and even a spiked mace decorated their walls.

"Wait here. I'll be right back," Misty said.

From a back bedroom, she returned in boots, leather underwear and mask. We entwined, fondled and kissed before she shoved me onto the bed.

Now the acid started playing games.

A small mole on Misty's left shoulder fixated me. Not her outfit, not her body, not the fact that she had my cock firmly in her hand but a Goddamn mole. I wanted to ignore it, but I couldn't. This fucken-dancing mole kept pulsating, expanding and shrinking.

I ripped my eyes off it. Timmy, Kyle and Shane had progressed well past my dalliance.

In full punishment regalia, Shane had her fat friend handcuffed to the bottom bedpost. Kyle's pants puddled the floor. Shane teased his bare ass with light smacks of a riding crop. Far from sexy, the sight drove me to a fit of uncontrollable laughter.

I gasped for breath. Caws flooded the apartment. Misty tried to stick a towel in my mouth, but it was fruitless. Timmy heard my laugh and decided screw sex. He doubled down on the memories.

He leapt at Shane and tore the riding crop from her hand.

"I'll show you how to whip that fat bastard," Timmy said.

He lashed Kyle's rump as if he were a jockey two-lengths behind at the Kentucky Derby.

A panicked Kyle squealed.

"What the fuck do you think you're doing?"

"What? She beat you, and you didn't say shit," Timmy managed to spit out amid streams of laughter.

"But she knows what she's doing. You fucking hurt."

My stomach ached from convulsive laughter exacerbated by the acid.

Meanwhile, Misty had me pinned across her knee. Her arm pressed the small of my back, and her left leg imprisoned my thighs. In an attempt to arouse me, she smacked, caressed, whacked and caressed.

Arouse me?

This poor prick, Kyle, was handcuffed and trying to convince my crazy brother, who was on acid, to stop making me laugh?

Not bloody likely. Just the thought of Timmy with a whip drove me to more hysterics. All thoughts of orgasm disappeared.

* * *

Later that night, the jukebox played Louie Armstrong's "What a Wonderful World." Maudlin drunk, Timmy and I sat in Johnny White's and reminisced over shots and beers.

"You know when the old man finally crapped out, I don't remember a minute of his funeral. I must be a shrink's wet dream," I said.

"He drank himself to death. Your mind sheltered you from the pain," Tim said.

"Pain? That ain't it. I hated what he did to us. He kept the whole house in turmoil. Without mom, we all would've starved. The old man only thought about where his next drink was coming from. He was too proud to admit he was an alcoholic. You were more of a father to me than he ever was. You told me what to read, taught me about life. I could never go to him for help or advice."

I lifted another shot, drained it, winced and then,

"You know, I'm not sure that's a good thing. You're way wackier than I am."

He laughed. "That's debatable. I knew what was happening at home. Someone had to shelter you from that lunatic, so I took most of the heat. Whenever he was pissed, I always said it was my fault."

Timmy threw back his shot.

"Any big brother would had done that . . . But, I always felt bad for Mom, trapped in that Irish Catholic philosophical prison. 'Never leave your husband no matter what.' The fucken Catholic Church has ruled and ruined Ireland from the beginning. Kept the people ignorant and backward, yet still we Irish produced some of the world's greatest literature. I guess to make sweet wine first you must crush the grapes. Just ask the Russians."

He ordered another round and said,

"Fucken Irish, it's a blessing and a curse. . . You know, when I'm drinking, I get to a point that if I take one more shot, I won't remember a thing. I know exactly what point that is. So I order a double and throw it back. Powerless."

"You can't get away with that shit forever. Remember when we were kids? We both swore we'd never be drunks like the old man."

I paused to chug my beer, then smiled,

"I guess we got no bitch. He fed us and clothed us. I'm sure he had his own issues. A blue-collar guy didn't have the benefit of a psychiatrist in those days." A redhead in tight shorts walked passed, and my head turned to watch her ass.

"Tim, remember how mom always said if we drank alcohol when we were young, we wouldn't drink when we got older?" I laughed, "Another myth exploded."

"Talk about myths, some guy told me if I bit lemons when I drank tequila, it would keep me sober." Tim said. "That same night I woke up in a bar with about 15 lemon slices stuck to my head."

He smiled and lifted his beer.

"The difference between you and me little brother is small. You're having a good time on this drunk, but I know that right here, right now, it's as good as it gets. You'll look back and remember this night as something special. I know that now, right here. I savor the moment. I won't need to reminisce."

"Either you're crazy or a Zen philosopher or both. By the way, how come you moved again? Every time you send me an address, you live somewhere else."

He spit his beer across the bar through crazed hysterical laughter.

"Usually I'm one step ahead of next month's rent, but this time was different. You remember that address out by City Park? Well, I was lying on the couch one day yanking my crank when I see some guy on the porch looking at me through the window. I was only wearing a towel, so I got up to see what he wanted." Timmy lit a Marlboro.

"The towel looked like a pup tent covering my hard-on. I opened the door and saw this mousy little parasite. I said, 'Who the fuck are you?' He said, 'I'm the landlord. You're two weeks late with the rent.' I said, 'Oh, sorry, man.' To act civilized, I go to shake his hand. He jumped back like a cobra bit him on the prick. You should have seen the look of horror on his face. So I wiped my hand on the towel and extended it again. Naturally, he still wouldn't shake it."

"You're a pisser. You just don't give a fuck," I said.

"Fuck him. What guy hasn't jerked off? In the big scheme of things, we're all just dots on the universe. We don't amount to shit. We're all here for a short ride man."

"You've got part of it right. It's a short ride. You should make the most of it and curtail the booze a bit. No sense in making the ride shorter."

"Funny, when I'm offshore, that's when I'm happiest. I can't get to the booze. I work out and read. I try to knock off a book a day," he said.

"You don't have to isolate yourself to be that person. It's like you use your job to protect you from yourself. You're one of the smartest guys I know, Timmy, and not just because you're my brother. You really are. You've been giving me advice all my life."

I called to the bartender to replenish our drinks. I poured the bottle of Heineken he served into a cold glass and watched it settle.

"I need some advice now," I said. "Something has been driving me crazy."

"What took you so long to bring it up? You know I'm always here for you."

"I'm in a bit of a moral dilemma."

"What's going on?" Tim said.

"I met this girl. I'm crazy about her. Can't get her out of my mind."

"So what's the problem? Good for you."

"This chick, Lorraine, is the real deal. Not the kind of girl you fool around with and dump. She's real family orientated, a keeper. She has the whole package, looks, personality, brains, the whole deal."

"Good for you. I still don't see the problem," Tim said.

"Come on, man. I'm like you. I drink and party too much. I'm not ready to get married."

Timmy smirked and lifted his glass. A long swallow later, he pushed his nose an inch from mine and said softly,

"You're not a drunk. You're young, and you like to laugh. So what? That's what you're supposed to do when you're young and single. No one's like me, not anymore than anyone's like you. Don't be a poor imitation of me. Be yourself. I wish I could be more like you. Tell me something. Does she love you?"

"Yeah, she's crazy about me," I said.

"You said she was smart. Do you think she'd toss her life away on a drunk? Don't be so hard on yourself. You know all about that low self-esteem thing that children of drunks have, right?

"Yeah, I know all about that. We hate ourselves or some

other kind of horseshit. But she doesn't know me the way you do. Besides the drinking, there's the gambling and the whoring. I just don't want to grow up."

"Think about it. Besides Mom and me, how many people genuinely love you? Are you so rich in love that you can afford to tell someone who loves you to get lost?"

"No, of course not, but . . ."

* * *

Hungover again, I hit every bar in the Quarter looking for Timmy. I started where I had left him last night at 4 a.m.

I finally entered a random saloon and spotted him.

I felt like I sighted Sasquatch. I needed a drink.

Copious small circles chained the mahogany bar in front of Timmy. He chatted to a woman. From the back, she was blonde and broad. I saddled up in the stool alongside the two. As soon as I got a closer look at the woman, I started laughing like a hyena. I struggled to catch my breath.

I overheard Timmy say,

"So what do you say, sweetheart? You want to seal the deal or what?"

The woman ignored Timmy and focused on me.

"What's so funny?"

Ignoring her question, I said,

"Jesus Christ, Timmy. That's a guy. You're talking to a transvestite."

Timmy slurred,

"How da hell do you know she's a transvestite?"

"How do I know?"

I gaped at the least convincing transvestite in history. Her peroxide-blonde wig sat askew on an enormous head and jaw. The bad hairpiece only highlighted her five-o'clock shadow and smeared red lipstick.

Still laughing, I grabbed Timmy's money off the bar.

"Come on, Tim. Call it a night. You'll see her again. Things will be clearer after you've had some sleep. Let's get you a bite to eat."

We walked down St. Philip, turned right past St. Louis

Cathedral, through Jackson Square and strolled to the Café du Monde. The square seemed out of place in the 20th century. In front of the cathedral, street bands, mimes, jugglers and unicyclists performed as if it were the Middle Ages.

I gorged myself on beignets and poured three cups of chicory coffee with heated milk into Timmy to make him a bit more manageable.

I walked him home and decided to explore some of the town. It was my first weekend in "The Big Easy," and I hadn't drawn a sober breath yet.

Despite the coffee, and the overdose of powdered sugar from the beignets, my hangover was killing me. I slipped off Royal Street and darted into The Ivanhoe Bar for a cure. My hands shook and the vodka wouldn't go down. The alcoholic whispered,

Bloody beer—half draught, half tomato juice. If you keep three down, you can switch to screwdrivers. Four or five should put you right.

I was alone at the bar.

A band began to tune up from a small stage adjacent to the huge, ornate green doors, which swung out to crowded Royal Street.

Despite my hangover, I welcomed the live music.

The emcee said,

"There's a band opening for 'Humble Pie' at the Warehouse tonight. They call themselves 'The Faces.' Their lead singer, Rod Stewart, is in the house and wants to sing a few songs."

Cool. Whomever this guy was I was 20' from the stage with a prime seat.

This rooster-strutting pipe cleaner of a man exploded onto the stage. He grabbed the mike, swaggered up and down and started to rip up Sam Cooke songs.

He was hypnotic.

Sidewalk passersby stopped, listened and finally started cramming The Ivanhoe—dribs at first, then drabs, then finally throngs.

Within minutes, I was hemmed in.

Stewart sang eight songs. When he was finished, I fled home.

"Timmy, we gotta go see this guy tonight. You won't believe this fucken guy. Fucken amazing."

After a few hours sleep, Timmy was hardly sober and held out for perks.

"Get some acid, and I'll go. Otherwise, I'm staying in."

"I'm telling you, you won't believe this guy."

"Get the acid."

* * *

The acid hit me hard, and we had two long miles to traipse to the Warehouse. We passed by the Café DuMonde, and the beignets' bouquet beckoned. I was suddenly hungry but way too wasted to handle the straights.

I staggered on. Everything solid formed before me, evaporated and then reformed. Wow. The pink-threaded clouds above me were like strips of Christmas ribbons, which floated above a blue wrapper of light that cloaked the magnificent Mississippi. Above all these colors, a red sun hovered and seemed to smile.

I squinted through the exaggerated heat wave patterns. Cartoon cars crawled by. Their hoods elongated. Their trunks scurried slinky-like to catch up.

By some miracle, we reached the Warehouse.

We stood among a sea of elbows that rested on the dominating stage. The emcee, missing from my memory, must have introduced "The Faces" because the next thing I knew the doors blew off.

Holy Fuck. Stewart raised his mike and let us have it.

Every note he rasped, I heard in Technicolor. His hoarse voice was gumbo, cold beer and oysters, all the magic of "The Big Easy." Visuals were vivid at first, clear and deep, then they dissipated, distorted and faded into delusions.

When Stewart's indelible performance ended, Timmy and I shuffled out crooning, "Cut across, Shorty, cut across." We didn't even stay for "Humble Pie."

The acid fluttered in my stomach. Its exhilarating waves buckled my knees, then an impulse,

"Timmy, what does sex feel like on this shit? The last time

I was tripping, you had me laughing so hard I couldn't screw." Timmy said,
"I'll call Shane and Misty. You can give it another try." Timmy managed to dial their number.
Here we go again, I thought.

* * *

The next day was a rough one. I was hungover so bad my mouth felt like the Polish Army had marched in it without socks on. On the outside steps leading to Johnny White's, I drained a beer. Shane and Misty pulled up in a convertible with two other strippers.

"Connor, can you do us a favor?"

"After last night? Anything for you, honey. Just name it."

"We've been arguing over who gives the best head. Would you judge a blowjob contest?"

The question defined rhetorical. I had arrived from New York with intentions to stay two weeks, but Lorraine or no Lorraine, I wasn't going anywhere.

CHAPTER TWENTY-ONE

When we first started taking action, Carmine, Steve and I laid off some big bets to other bookies. Because we had a small bankroll, I suggested that we hold no more than $5,000 a game.

Back then, I didn't get it.

Nobody wins.

Nobody ever wins.

Most gamblers know about vigorish. The "vig" is the 10 percent bookies skim off the top of a loser's bet to ensure the occupation stays profitable. Gamblers bet $110 to win a $100, or $1,100 to win a $1,000.

The "all-knowing" Wikipedia defines vig:

"Bookmakers use this concept to make money on wagers regardless of the outcome . . . It ensures bookmakers have no interest which side wins. They're interested in having equal action on both sides, so they always collect a small commission called vigorish . . . Bookmakers adjust the lines to attract equal action on each side of an event."

To summarize: "Joe bets $100 on the Giants; Frank bets $100 on Dallas. The bookmaker lays them off against each other and snares $10 for his trouble."

Bullshit.

In today's computerized world, most bookies operate over the Internet via offshore casinos, so they don't have individual control to adjust a line and balance their books. Offshore services charge standard fees to take action for bookies worldwide. The bookmaker checks a weekly printout and then pays out or collects.

Here's how the system really works.

The first Sunday of the 2014 NFL season, 13 games were played. Of those, only five or six would have meant a lot to a bookie.

For a Miami bookie, the Buffalo-Miami game, for a New York bookie, the Giant-Dallas game, or whatever game CBS showed as their match-up of the week. All those games would have been loaded with action.

Sunday night's game is always significant because it's a gamblers last chance to bailout or break even for the week. The other seven or eight games would normally have minimal money spread across the board.

So for argument's sake, let's say five games are top heavy with money. Because of the "juice," the vig, the 10-percent, all the bookie has to do is win two out of those five games, and he breaks even. In any occupation besides bookmaking, when you're right only 40 percent of the time, you're broke.

The bookie also provides "specialty bets," such as parlays, teasers, reverse bets and other novelties. "Sucker bets" help bookies balance their sheet and usually involve what we call, "double juice," or 20 percent vig.

If the bookie wins three of his crucial five games, he wins big. If he wins four of those five games, he crushes. To beat the bookie, betters must win four out of those five top-heavy games. That might happen twice a season. The bookie cleans the players' clocks the rest of the schedule.

Our first year in business, Carmine, (Gobbo) Steve (Red), and I (Mars) had 100 customers. I asked my two partners how many winners they thought we'd have by seasons end.

Gobbo paused, reflected, and said 12.

Red didn't stutter and shot back eight.

When the football season ended, we had no winners. Next season—200 customers, no winners. The third season—300 customers, no winners. We didn't count money. We measured stacks of cash by inches.

If bookmakers ran the Treasury, there'd be a budget surplus every year. Their lines are laser accurate.

Study the football lines and pick a team you like. Take your money out of your left-hand pocket. Count it. Count it again, then fold your money, and place it back in the same pocket.

Don't bet on sports.

Spend it on something productive, like a hooker and an eight ball.

If you're compelled to wager, make a "mind bet." If you lose, all you'll have lost is your mind.

CHAPTER TWENTY-TWO

Just past noon Saturday and after a quick couple of games of hoop, it was time to grab a squirt at my new French Quarter local, The Mousetrap.

I vaulted the two outside steps and slid into a stool.

"Allan, how about a beer?"

With the doors wide open on this beautiful, sunny day in the French Quarter, I took two short strides to the entrance, swigged my beer, and watched the scenery stroll by in shorts and halters.

Today was exceptional.

On the weekends that LSU played a home game, troops of women flocked to town to party, crash and screw.

Tonight LSU played Alabama. The town was packed.

It seemed like most gals I met in the South were married at 17 and divorced at 20. These Southern gals partied hard, and they came to New Orleans to do it.

In New Orleans, you got to drink 24 hours a day, an alcoholic's Utopia. Provided you poured your drink into a plastic cup, you could even carry your cocktail from bar to bar.

Allan, the owner, slid the mug in front of me and spit out one of the most beautiful sentences in a gambler's world.

"Connor, do you play cards?"

"What kind of cards?"

"Poker. I have a game tonight upstairs. Do you play?"

"I dabble a bit. What limit?"

"We start at $1 to $5, but it usually grows," Allan said.

"Sure. God hates a coward." I said. "What time?"

* * *

The game broke up at 5 a.m.

After a few hours sleep, I was back in the Mousetrap by noon.

Allan skated me a frosty mug.

"So you were the only winner?" he asked.

"I guess so. I didn't ask."

"How much did you win?"

"About $850," I said.

"You're a pretty smart guy. Ever thought of tending bar?" He asked.

"I used to tend bar in the Bronx, but at the moment, I'm working as a computer operator at Maison Blanche. I gotta be there every morning at 8 a.m. That's tough in this town. Most nights I don't get home until 2 a.m. It costs me half of my paycheck for diet pills or speed just to get through the day. You offering me a job?"

"You want to jump behind the bar, and give it a try? It doesn't get busy till around 5 p.m."

"I've been behind the stick before," I said. "I've hung out in bars since I was six-years old. Sure. Why not? I'll give it a shot."

* * *

Tending bar in the Vieux Carre was a drunkard's wet dream. My thick N.Y. accent was catnip for the Southern belles that flocked to sin city. Because it was slow offshore, my brother tended bar in the Mousetrap as well. Timmy and I shared an apartment around the corner. No need to chase women. They came to us.

"Connor, two chicks from Mississippi walked in about a half hour ago. Get your ass down here. They're dying to meet you," Tim said.

In the time it took to place the phone back in its cradle, I was on my way. It worked both ways.

"Tim, I sent two gals over to the house to smoke a joint. I get off in an hour. Keep them entertained."

Life was sweet. No surprise that my two-week trip to New Orleans lasted two years.

* * *

I developed a good reputation as a barkeep in town. Smooth and fluid, my mania made the essential bartender's trait of multitasking instinctive. I ended up in the premier joint in town, Pat O'Brien's.

In Pat's all new bartenders started by mixing drinks for the waiters at the patio bar. A manager sat by the register, and when a waiter barked a typical order like,

"I need two Heinekens, three hurricanes, a pousse café, and a squall,"

I'd toss the beers at the waiter, shovel ice into the premixed hurricanes, and then await the manager's instructions.

"Take the squall glass, two ounces of rum, one part grenadine, one part Collin's mix, shake and pour."

After a few nights mixing cocktails at this volume, a novice soon learned how to make every drink in the joint.

Within a week, I moved to the side bar where I dealt with customers, not just waiters. Once proficient there, the next step was the piano bar and so on until I reached the bartender's golden ring, the main bar.

I vaulted the hierarchy easily enough, and the perks in the main bar proved worth the effort.

Besides earning a good buck, celebrities visiting town always stopped into Pat's. And the women, ahh the women . . .

Life was better than good.

Then I got fired.

* * *

At the end of my shift, a blue-coated manager told me,

"We're cutting back on staff. Don't come in until you get a phone call."

I couldn't believe it.

I had hurdled their pecking order faster than any previous bartender.

Don't come in until you hear from us? Cutting back on staff?

Business had never been better. Pat's did $1 million a year just selling souvenir glasses.

Devastated, I did a little investigating.

After weeks of prodding, and well-lubed by a half bottle of

bourbon, one of my coworkers spilled the beans.

One of the managers noticed an increase in the collective tip cup whenever I worked, so he assumed I was stealing.

He was dead wrong. I had stolen before at Sears but always lived by the street adage, "Never steal anything small."

Why would I steal to split with three other bartenders?

* * *

A bartender was only as good as his reputation. Mine was demolished. New Orleans was a big town, but the Quarter wasn't.

I was through in this town.

No harm I guess. Things happen for a reason. Although innocent of thievery this time, I was no Boy Scout. This could be divine payback, and I needed a geographical cure anyway.

Only 25-years-old, alcohol-related red veins started to appear in my face, and I felt an unusual pain in my stomach fairly close to where I suspected my liver was located.

Besides, although separated by 1400 miles, Lorraine was never far from my mind.

I decided to head back to N.Y. to get sober, a dubious decision at best. My plan was to take my newfound knowledge of the bartending trade to supplement my income and use the GI Bill for school.

The geographical cure didn't work in Asia, and it wouldn't work in N.Y. Ahead was a roller coaster more turbulent than the one I rode now, and I would selfishly drag Lorraine into the front seat with me.

CHAPTER TWENTY-THREE

The burly, off-duty Bronx firefighter behind the bar grabbed the phone.

"Hello, Jolly Tinker, how can I help you?"

Brian listened a moment and said,

"Which Bob? We got six."

"Crazy Bob," the caller said.

Brian laughed,

"Are you kidding? Which crazy Bob? We've got three."

Brian had curly black hair, a spotted complexion, and a quick tongue.

"Oh, that Bob? No, Menderhoffer's not here."

Brian roared laughter.

"Call back in about six months. He's doing a bit."

Translation, Bob's a guest of the N.Y. State Penitentiary.

After Brian hung up, he told All Day Ray," who earned his nickname by pounding vodka from sunrise to sundown,

"I never thought about it, but how many joints boast three crazy Bobs?"

Brian poured a Fleischman's straight up to "Mac," another Jolly Tinker morning fixture.

The rye drinker wore an old army fatigue coat and a blue turtleneck sweatshirt. One of Mac's cheeks seemed swollen, the other clawed. He had a flat, broad nose, and his hatless head was a tangled mess of auburn hair.

As he attempted to spill a shot glass of whiskey into his toothless mouth, Mac's wrist shook like an epileptic crapshooter.

Above the bar to Mac's left, the "Mike Douglas Show"

blared from the TV. Mr. Douglas introduced a six-year-old blind, black boy who will play a Mozart sonata.

Mac grinned like a satyr.

"Big fucken deal." He swallowed his shot and chuckled, "Show me a blind spear-chucker who can't play the piano."

Hearing this, Brian's eyes winced. His thin, black mustache snuggled the tip of his nose. Shrugging off the hardly unexpected remark, he pivoted his head and lifted the cellar's trap door.

"Tinker, we're out of Johnny Walker Black."

No answer, so he yelled again,

"Mike. We need scotch."

Mac snickered, sneered and then muttered cynically,

"The Tinker's downstairs? Johnny Walker my ass, the last time real Johnny Walker was delivered to this joint, it was in the back of a covered wagon."

Brian laughed, "Even money says that any minute now, the Tinker will be asking me to send down the empty Black bottles . . . but ya gotta admit, Mike's the best . . . one of a kind."

"The Tinker" owned the oldest bar in the Bronx, yet after more than 40 years, no one had ever said a bad word about Mike the Tinker. No better man had ever laced a shoe.

* * *

Eight hours later, I parked my white Healy outside the pizza shop next door to the Jolly Tinker. It would be safe enough while I trotted inside to practice a little larceny.

Tomorrow, Super Sunday would finish off the football season, so tonight would be the next-to-last week that I dropped off and picked up envelopes.

Since the Silvera mess with Angelo was straightened out, the quarter sheet that Vinny gave me had been fairly lucrative. I had 40 players, so I "earned" about $5,000 a month. So did Vinny.

He was on a half sheet.

Vinny gave me 25 percent of whatever I brought in on his sheet. He made the same as me and did nothing. Although that sounded unfair, I had no risk. I didn't pay the winners. Angelo did. Vinny had always been square with me.

Because of the playoffs, this week's collections were lean.

Next week, the week after the Super Bowl, would be even less lucrative. The fewer choices the suckers had, the less money we made.

After football season, I only had about five degenerates left who would bet hockey and baskets. I'd just give them Vinny's number and take a much-needed respite.

* * *

The Tinker was the first stop of a long Saturday night. I did a quick inventory— Marlboros in top left shirt pocket, vial of coke in the small change pocket of my jeans, stack of $20s in my left-front pocket, small notebook in back left, envelopes in back right, yeah, I was ready for work.

I traipsed through the familiar door.

My old man started drinking here in 1953, when I was five years old. I knew this gin mill like my own reflection.

I entered to a chorus of hellos, bellied up to the bar, and tossed three crisp $20s across the mahogany. I stood amid four or five regulars and The Tinker himself. Without looking up, I yelled one of my standard bar lines.

"Hey, this would be a nice place to open a bar. Any chance of getting a drink around here?"

Usually, the bartender was an off-duty fireman, a Fordham University student, or just a neighborhood screwball down on his luck. I was pleasantly surprised. The bright emerald eyes that greeted me belonged to a wild-haired gypsy beauty straight from the mists of Irish mythology.

I altered my tone.

"Sorry honey, I wasn't expecting a lady. Could you build me a pint of Guinness and do the honors up and down the bar please."

Her tongue played a silent tune, but her eyes sparkled a smile.

She strolled the bar's length and mechanically placed cardboard coasters in front of glasses already filled. She changed tempo only to remove the air from the glasses that were empty. As her striking figure shook, sashayed and bent, I glued my eyes to her.

"Who's the new talent?" I asked.

"What?" The Tinker seemed incredulous.

"Shuh, you must know her. Colleen's been working Saturday days for the past three weeks."

With his thick Waterford brogue, Mike said,

"Shuh, what's the matta with ya?"

I smiled and said, "No, I don't know her, but I'd like to."

Some things take root in the brain and just grow. I lifted my pint and thought,

Gambling, drinking and drugging are full-time vices and don't nurture relationships. I don't need a girlfriend. I don't even know what to do about Lorraine. But man this Colleen's really something.

Like cement, Colleen's image poured into my brain and solidified.

* * *

A week after Super Sunday, I was back in the bar and no longer collecting for Angelo. Financially scarred, I needed revenue. After a couple of stiff belts, I had an epiphany.

"Anyone want to open a bar?"

One skeptic averted his eyes, hoisted his highball to his mouth and muttered,

"With your history, that's the last thing you need. A bar? Are you crazy?"

I shot doubting Thomas a stern look and thought,

I'm Irish, a drunk and a womanizer. A bar's exactly what I need, ever-flowing beer taps that no one but me can shut off, an oasis where women float through my front door? I'm single, not too bad looking. What better way to meet women?

I was too lazy to learn to play guitar.

When I tended bar on Bourbon Street, I learned to build fancy drinks, from Hurricanes to Pousse Café's, so I was a bona fide mixologist.

I persisted, "No, really. Who has a pair of balls and wants to take a shot? In New Orleans, I worked in the busiest bar in the world, Pat O'Brien's. I can do this."

Mike, the witty Waterford rapscallion who owned The Tinker, loved action. If roaches raced, the Tinker would bet on the outcome. Mike abruptly perked up.

"Where are you thinking about opening?"

"In Queens, not far from where Buffalo tends bar."

"Can we get Buffalo involved?"

"Do we want Buffalo involved?"

Tinker said, "Jesus, maybe you're right. We'll discuss this properly."

Mike called for a drink. While he got Colleen's attention, I glanced at the wall behind the bar. Front pages of past Daily News issues hung in dusty frames: "Bobby Sands Dead," "Nixon, I Won't Resign,'" "Man Lands on Moon."

The headlines testified to the Tinker's stability. Mike was as dependable as gravity. Despite the madness he created and thrived on, the "Tinker" was an unpretentious, generous giant of a man who could recite pages of "Paradise Lost" effortlessly. If he was aboard, I couldn't miss.

We discussed Buffalo.

The "Fat Man" came with enormous baggage, but those trunks were packed with talent, a 320-pound gentle giant so smooth that he wouldn't leave footprints in snow.

Buffalo personified the Irish adage,

"He can tell a man to go to hell in a way that he looks forward to the trip."

When the "Fat Man" tossed troublemakers through doors, they tipped him on the way out.

* * *

Opening a bar sounded impulsive, but the horses in my head had already left the gate. My mania assured me that my credentials were impeccable. I was an excellent bartender. This was my best shot to earn and still have fun. Plus, I could stay loaded. Imagine, never having to hear last call . . .

The voices won. I shot for a big joint. Better to sink in 100 feet of water than two.

* * *

The old cliché states that the three most important things in the bar or restaurant business are location, location, location. The adage, like most aphorisms, is an oversimplification, but it has merit.

I had to carefully consider this crucial factor.

For years, old Irish pub owners opened bars next to funeral homes. The dead unintentionally provided the living with a steady stream of transient business.

Anyone who had ever attended a wake knew that after an hour or so the "Sorry for your troubles" had all been said, and the grave's breath would drive anyone, whether insensitive or hypersensitive, to drink.

Funerals forced distant families to spend time together, and a few drinks in the saloon next door diminished the discomforts of extended family intimacy.

But a bar's location had other considerations.

A corner, crossroads, main drag, or neighborhood where you were well-known all helped your chances. Corporations did surveys before they set up shop. Taco Bell, McDonalds and Kentucky Fried Chicken all knew how many people pushed their Florsheims across their pavements before they built.

Once I found the right location, I'd try to land a job tending bar in that area. This would let me get the feel of the neighborhood, and help me gauge what the traffic would bear as far as prices. Also, I'd build up a clientele. All while being paid.

If after a few months I felt I had the wrong location, I still hadn't lost shit. I'd have had been paid for my time and more importantly still not invested any money.

The more I thought about opening a bar, the more it made sense. The big problem would be the financing. I was always broke, but if I borrowed 10 large from four close friends and got Mike as a partner, maybe I could pull this off.

* * *

I even had the name for my joint. I'd call it P.O.E.T.S. The acronym would stand for Piss On Everything Tomorrow's Saturday, and it would provide free word of mouth advertising. Once I told a few people what the initials stood for, they'd feel like they were in the know. Impressed with their own importance, they'd spread the news.

"Do you know what the initials of that new joint stands for?"

I'd throw loads of old books around, sprinkle a few great literary quotes, and do this on the cheap.

If I could make this happen, with or without gambling . . . I'd be where I wanted to be, in constant action. This was no problem. I had this.

My path clear, one non-business decision still disturbed me.

What to do about this pesky love thing? That problem wouldn't go away. I didn't want to live with Lorraine or anybody else.

But could I live without her?

CHAPTER TWENTY-FOUR

Mike and I opened P.O.E.T.S. in Flushing, Queens a year later. By that time Lorraine had left New York and moved to Oregon. I'd get over her. It was tough to think about one woman, no matter how special, while staring at another.

With prosperity around the corner, her timing couldn't have been better. Even limited success fueled my mania. When money wasn't a problem, drugs, alcohol, gambling and sex galloped like the four horseman of the apocalypse through my delusional brain, so freedom was better.

When you build a bar, you make a 1,000 decisions. One I had forgotten was the first liquor delivery was C.O.D. Mike and I were out of money. I decided to reach out on the street.

Vinny said, "You need $10 large? The normal rate is three points. For you, ya Irish cocksucka, I'll give it to ya for two."

The night before we opened, my partner, the Tinker, added stress,

"Maybe we built the place too big."

My jaws tightened. The veins in my neck and forehead throbbed. I sure hoped not. I thought I had this covered.

The bar looked like a million bucks. We hired three of the best bartenders in the Bronx. All of them certified lunatics with huge followings. The last month I tossed money around like a lottery winner, so every bartender in Queens owed me a stop. If they didn't come for me, they'd come out to see the new joint or to see one of the screwballs behind the bar.

My experience at Pat O'Brien's had paid off.

Since Pat's was the busiest bar in the world, I knew how to

set up to pour volume. If we packed the joint, I was ready.

Another detail I had forgotten was I never thought about the music. The Tinker wouldn't know a jazz trumpet from a tractor, so when he asked me who was performing tonight, I realized that it was on me to magically materialize music.

The plan was to open a jazz joint with a little class. We figured that kind of music would keep kids out, and older people had money to spend. So I needed jazz fast.

I tore through the Village Voice to grab a last minute band. After three calls, and three responses of,

"Are you kidding? We're booked."

I booked "John Abram's Flutes and Saxes" because they were available on short notice. The big night arrived. As expected, the place packed out, but the 300 people could as well have been attending my wedding.

I knew everybody.

All bar people from the Bronx and Queens, all friends here to spend as much money as possible, and all anxious to get me off to a good start.

Everybody was buying rounds for the bar.

Bear in mind, the bar was 60' long and three patrons deep. No one cared about the music. No one wanted something for nothing. Everybody was in the joint to drink, spend cash, and spread good will.

About nine o'clock, my partner said we had a situation. I stop stuffing the registers with cash and asked,

"What's up?"

"The band showed up. They're unloading at the back door."

"Great, show them where the stage is."

Mike said, "But they're all black."

I said, "They're playing jazz. What did you expect, five guys in kilts?"

* * *

From the first minute of the first song in the first set, I knew I was in trouble. Mr. Abrams and his group were progressive musicians. They were all about rifts and idiosyncratic horn blasts, anathema for laymen, especially here.

I had a Bronx-Irish crowd.

Twice, I pleaded with Abrams to play something recognizable. I was desperate. For Chrissakes, play the National Anthem, anything. He nodded, said no problem but drifted back into abstract jazz. By the middle of the first set, I stood in front of the stage waving money.

"Hey man, I'm not a fan. You want the cash? I'm the one paying you. Play something somebody has heard of."

Of course, this was all my fault. I forgot all about booking the music. Any band that can play on a weekend with a day's notice couldn't be any good. After the first set, I paid them in full and fed the jukebox.

But I learned a valuable lesson.

* * *

The remainder of the night went swimmingly. Everybody had a great time, and I made a ton of cash. Saturday night another 300 people showed up, and this time I only knew half of them.

New faces abounded. Vinny showed up. I paid him his juice. He threw it on the bar, added $500 to it and said, "Keep buying everybody drinks until this runs out." He grabbed me by the back of my neck and gave me a Sicilian Kiss. "Good luck, ya wise-ass Irish prick."

Sunday night, we were mobbed. I looked around and didn't know a soul.

Mike said, "Christ, Connor, we didn't build the place big enough."

In Flushing, Queens, P.O.E.T.S. was a huge hit.

* * *

The Romans had an adage.

"Whomever the Gods would destroy, they make successful young."

I respond to success with excess. I acted like I had been elected Governor. I started screwing everything in sight. I loved the notoriety and figured I'd never see another dry day.

My priorities were to get laid and drunk. I wasn't in this for the money. I just wanted to party and continue to do what I had been doing my entire "adult" life.

I worked hard and practically lived in the joint. I was there five hours during the day and every night till closing...because I loved my "work."

I was particularly fond of interviewing girls that trotted through the door looking for waitress jobs or barmaid positions, and I also loved not having anyone able to shut off the beer spigot on me. Most nights I locked the door at 4 a.m. and continued to party, and I was seldom alone.

I paid for a want ad in the Queens' papers three months prior to opening. "Wanted bartenders, barmaids, waitresses, cocktail waitresses for new bar and restaurant in Queens. Please apply in person."

Already fully staffed, I wasn't hiring anybody. I just figured that anyone out of work in this business would read the want ads and pay more attention to those three lines than they would a half page of advertising.

Another angle was that whoever read the want ads probably owed money. They would hold off their creditors by letting them know they might be getting hired at this new place on Northern Blvd.

This cheap, effective advertising costs $35 a week and added to the buzz.

And to the women . . .

I used to spend a couple of hundred a night in bars to meet them. Now chicks danced through the door in a conga line. They all wanted to meet the boss, and they all wanted something from me. I know this is offensive and sexist, but I was young. My hormones were raging, and I looked at spending time with women the way Douglas Macarthur looked at combat:

"No substitute for victory."

* * *

Getting drunk and spending money came easy. I had a talent for chasing women from saloon to saloon. I genuinely loved women and not just the carnal aspect. I loved everything about them. Their rhythmic walk, their aroma, the nape of their neck with their hair up, everything about them.

When not meeting women in P.O.E.T.S., I bounced around

town doing "promo." This involved hitting the smaller gin mills within a five-mile radius to spread good will. Buying drinks, leaving large tips and of course, taking bows for my joint's success.

I had an even better talent for this.

My favorite part of this exercise was the whispers. Every bar I bounced into, I ordered a Black on the rocks and added,

"Give the bar a squirt."

As the bartender placed the drinks in front of the customers, he'd lean over and say,

"That's with Connor Kelly. He owns P.O.E.T.S."

The patrons immediately hoisted their glasses in my direction and then turned and whispered to whomever was next to them something like,

"That's the young guy who owns that new nightclub on Northern."

This bit of news traveled like a wave along the bar, and it always got the attention of whatever young ladies might be in attendance. I knew the more women I had in my place, the more successful I'd be.

I had instructed my bartenders to buy any unescorted girls at the bar their first drink, and to do it with flair,

"You girls are too pretty to have to pay for your drinks. This round is on P.O.E.T.S."

They enthusiastically followed my instructions.

I knew this would come back tenfold. In bars, most guys who spotted good-looking women needed four or five belts to fortify themselves before they grew the balls to make a move. Unescorted women at a bar were "found money." I bought women rounds at other joints and persuaded women to defect to mine.

The whispers were especially gratifying when girls took time to leave their stools to thank me for their cocktails.

All girls wanted to know the owner, especially if he was relatively young and the spot was hot. I routinely gave out my business card with "free admission" handwritten on the back and my signature - more marketing.

If the gals could get in free, it was likely that they'd check out the bands in my place before anyone else's. If the band couldn't hold them maybe the alcohol, my bartenders or my self-assessed charm might.

Because the Tinker and I were from the Bronx, we had one major problem.

Every stool-fool and punching bag that had been banned from every other bucket of blood in Queens knew that they had a clean slate in my place. Until they screwed up, I had no idea whom the assholes were.

Thank God, I had Buffalo working the gate. The first three months we tossed so many troublemakers I needed a revolving door.

My bartenders had all been around the block. If a beef broke out, we got the trouble under control quickly. Whoever threw the first punch, we banned for life.

The Tinker and I weeded out the palookas. In short order the place filled with women and emptied of undesirables.

And now I had a handle on the bands.

As I said earlier, I learned a valuable lesson with the jazz. People who liked jazz got high, but they didn't drink. They nursed a glass of wine, but they didn't get banged up. Only three kinds of music really sold booze: Irish, country, and rock and roll.

Irish music was my bag. But it was expensive, and it might not sell in Flushing, Queens. Because Travolta just made "Urban Cowboy," country music was huge, but country, like disco, was ephemeral. I decided on rock and roll.

The same kids we once kept out now lined up and paid $10 for admission. I sold space. The door's receipts paid for my band, my security and before I ever poured a drink put $600 a night in my pocket.

What a great fucken country!

The only thing pissing me off was that someone kept punching holes in the sheetrock of the men's bathroom. I was making money, so I replaced the walls. But I broke my ass to build this place, and I wasn't happy watching my efforts torn asunder.

I know how to handle this.

Monday morning, I told the carpenter replacing the usual disaster to take all the sheetrock down and place ten-penny nails facing outward indiscriminately throughout the studs and then replace the sheet rock.

The next prick who punched my wall would get a surprise.

* * *

I hate violence. I'm not a tough guy. In fights tough guys are calm, precise and dangerous. I weigh 170 and feel more comfortable at 165. My hands are small.

Watch a professional fighter in the ring.

When the good ones get hurt, they hold. Only the amateurs retaliate wildly. That's why novices get knocked out. I have a bad temper, especially after a couple of cocktails, but if someone gets me mad enough to fight, I know he must be an asshole.

Once I lose my temper, I can be treacherous, but I can get hurt. I'm not calm in fights. I'm a lunatic. Besides, I pay $300 worth of muscle a night to protect my joint. If a fight breaks out, I shouldn't be the one throwing punches.

* * *

One Thursday night above the band's deafening sound, a loud wail escaped the men's room. I charged toward the sound of the pain.

Some unlucky bastard blew out of my men's room bent over and holding his bleeding hand. I saw he had me by four inches. I answered his cries with six months of pent-up frustration.

"You rotten son of a bitch. I'll kill your ass," I screamed.

I took a running punch and launched my right hand to his throat. When his hands clutched his Adam's apple, I balanced myself, threw my legs in motion, and hit him with two savage left hooks.

His blood splattered the bathroom wall, and he thudded to the deck. Once this prick was on the hard tile floor, I drove three or four more rights into his splattered nose. Next, I dragged him by the hair through the stunned crowd and out the front door.

Even my employees were puzzled. No one knew why I was so furious. Everybody watched flabbergasted while I pummeled an injured man. Once on the street,

"If I ever see your ass back here again, I'll kill you ... You rotten bastard ..."

Once I regained control, I turned. The crowd parted like the Red Sea.

Head up and striding through the throng's corridor, someone whispered, "Crazy, the son-of-a-bitch is crazy." Another bystander whispered, "That guy's really fucking nuts."

I knew a bar fight didn't last long, two minutes maybe. The first punch thrown had better be good. A big guy hit in the jaw by my small hands might not go down, so I always aimed for the throat.

Years later, long after P.O.E.T.S. demise, I would again hear whispers. They would loom from a far more perilous place than a Queens' sidewalk.

And the voices would be trying to save my life.

CHAPTER TWENTY-FIVE

"How many floors to this pussy palace?" I laughed.

The manager behind the posh lobby's marble desk bowed Oriental to us and then said politely, but firmly,

"Please, you no say pussy palace, this gentlemen's club. You no act right, we ask you leave."

He wore a light tan summer suit with a striped red and green tie and $800 brown-tasseled loafers. He dressed like a sales representative from Saks Fifth Avenue.

"I'm sorry pal. I didn't mean to insult you. Believe me. I'm thrilled to be here. I've never seen anything like this in my life, and I've been around the block."

* * *

Once the bar had kicked into high gear, money poured in. What to do with it? I could have saved it, but I wasn't the Christmas club type. My mania met the challenge. Enamored with exotic locales all my life, I began an odyssey to explore the brothels of the world. Without much objection, I convinced my gambling buddy, Steve, to share my adventures. Steve and I decided on Hong Kong for a week's holiday. Naturally that week included whorehouses and drugs.

"Our place very unusual. You not member?" Our host asked.

"No, a friend recommended me. I'm only in town for a week. How big is this joint?"

"Seven floors big, many different women."

"Seven floors?" I asked.

"Once you join, I give you menu."

"I was told every floor has a different nationality."

"Once you join, once you pay, I give you menu."

"What's the tariff?" I asked.

"You pay $200 now. Then you talk with beautiful ladies. They tell you."

"Just to get in, $200? That's kind of steep. What are the average prices once inside?"

"Me no can say. You talk with beautiful ladies."

"Give me a ballpark figure."

"Sorry, me no understand?"

"The average cost, once I'm inside?"

"Sometimes $200, sometimes less, sometimes more, you talk with beautiful ladies. With membership, you come all month."

"That doesn't do us much good. We're only in Hong Kong until the weekend."

"You no worry. You pay $200 now. I show you menu."

I turned to Steve. "Whatta ya think? I heard good things about this place."

"This place is high class. We bet thousands on a football game. Who gives a fuck? We can spend all day in there for all I care. I'm not coming this far and not going in."

From the roll of '50s, inches thick and rubber banded in my pocket, I peeled eight crisp ones.

"It ain't the money. I hate getting ripped off." I said and handed the little gentleman my cash. "OK brother. You got a bet. Show us a menu."

* * *

The menu shocked even a licentious, intemperate pagan like myself. Holy shit. What a grab bag.

Each floor had a receptionist. The menu broke down sections by nationality: Scandinavian, Italian, Greek, Japanese, Thai, well you get the idea.

Once on the preferred floor, the room was categorized again to straight, bondage, gay, even bestiality. Good God, what a sin parlor.

I smiled and turned to Steve,

"Holy shit, we thought we were wacky. People are nuts, man. How about a blonde or a redhead?"

"I love Greek girls."

"You love Greek girls or you love Greek, ya cocksucka?"

"A little bit of both," he grinned.

In the elevator, I decided to opt for a darker complexioned beauty than I had wanted originally. Sated with Orientals after Thailand and Laos, an Asian girl would have been out of the question. I would have selected a Swede, but I deferred to Steve.

Hungry for the experience, I anxiously punched the button for the fourth floor.

"Steve, did you know that the Greeks invented sex?"

"What the fuck are you talking about?"

"Well, granted, it was the Romans who introduced it to women," I grinned.

Steve gave me an obligatory smirk and said,

"Asshole." His face turned serious.

"Thank God they had a tram to get up to Victoria Peak this morning. I can't believe that the Brits were able to build anything on the side of this mountain." He shook his head for emphasis. "I've never seen a city so vertical. How do people live here? Shit man, three or four escalators just to get home from shopping? It was crazy looking out that tram's window and seeing sideways buildings against the trees."

The elevator door opened to a huge, carpeted office. Couches bordered each side of a coffin-sized desk occupied by a gorgeous, black-haired woman, and I mean a knockout.

I had seen hookers, lots of them.

I had seen whores with faces that would convince you they were saints, but with bodies that told you that their faces were lying. I once saw a prostitute in Atlantic City so beautiful that she stopped a red-hot crap game. Shit, I had blown money on hookers that I could look at all day.

But this one had something more.

She wasn't stacked, wasn't lush. She didn't have a face like Selma Hayek's.

But she had "it."

She was about five-foot-five and 115 pounds, tightly packed. And from the black, strapless floor-length gown slit from her ankle to mid-thigh, to the bright, clear-ice smile that she greeted us with when we walked in, she had "it."

"Welcome gentlemen, welcome. Would you care for a cocktail while you're waiting to see the girls?"

"See the girls? I'll take you," I laughed.

"Aren't you sweet," she said. "No. I'm out of that line of work now, but you'll be more than satisfied with what we have to offer."

"My friend has his heart set on a Greek," I said.

"Well, he's in the right place. All the girls on this floor are Southern Mediterranean."

"Italians too, honey?"

"Yes, Italians too, honey," she grinned. "Did you boys see a menu?"

"We glanced at it," I said, "But, like I said, my friend has his heart set on a Greek."

"Well, why don't you boys sit? I'll fix you a couple of drinks, and we'll see what we can do about your friend's heart. What will it be?

"I'll have Johnny Black on the rocks," I said.

"I'll have an Absolut martini shaken not stirred," Steve said.

I sent him another smirk.

"Who da hell do you think you are, James Bond?"

The doll laughed.

"I'm Tiffany. While I fix your drinks, you two sit over here, and I'll have some of the girls come out and say hello."

We sat as told. Within minutes, the girls entered, one bombshell after another, all in high heels and lingerie, all dark and bronzed, all with bodies that would stop sermons, and all, and all . . . amazing.

Tiffany returned with the drinks. I was stupefied.

She said, "Enjoy your cocktails. No rush, take as much time as you'd like. Before you select a companion, get to know the girls. Your membership is good for the month. Come as often as you like. Remember, they're here to make you happy. If you have any special requests, ask the young lady before you choose. And don't be shy. They've heard it all before."

My first thought was,
I'd like to request another prick. I'd like to make love to them all.

Steve took his time. I didn't.

The goddess I chose, Annette, was long and lean with butt-length black hair. She wore a black garter belt, fishnet nylons and a gold Teddy. She had a woman's body, but a girl's face, innocent, wide eyed with a come-hither confident smile, which said I'm the best piece of ass in the building, and I know it.

She led me to her cubicle. Her hair fell over her shoulders in snaky curls.

She looked liked the illegitimate daughter of every gorgeous hooker in the world. My devils were going to get their money's worth today.

Before she even cut the lights, my arms were around her.

When I kissed her breasts, her eyes shown down at me like two green stars. It was like being in church on Christmas Eve. But women are better than Christmas.

Hell could have opened for me then, and it wouldn't have made any difference.

I had to have her. If she cost a million, I had to have her.

Even if I hung for it, I had to have her.

And I had her. And it cost me plenty.

And she was worth every dollar.

CHAPTER TWENTY-SIX

An old joke tells of a horny man in the female-barren Klondike who needed sex. He asked his co-worker, Clem, what to do. Clem pointed to a barrel in the corner of the saloon.

"Put your prick in the hole in that barrel," Clem said.

Once a week for the next two months, the horny man followed the same satisfying routine. One night, he placed his prick through the barrel's hole and nothing happened. He turned to Clem and asked, "What's wrong?" Clem said, "It's your turn in the barrel."

* * *

Tending bar in P.O.E.T.S. the Thursday night before Christmas, my tired feet screamed close. It was 3 a.m. and I was down to three customers. Following modus operandi, I poured myself a mug of Johnny Black on the rocks and headed for the phone. On the other end, a familiar voice answered,

"Black Bart's."

"Fat Man," I yelled. "How many customers you got?"

"About 10," he said.

"I've got three." I said. "Your turn in the barrel. See you in 30 minutes."

"Take your fastest horse," he said.

Buffalo worked for me on weekends, but to supplement his income, he tended bar weekday nights in another Queen's bar.

I returned behind the bar, shouted last call, and by way of apology said,

"Here's the deal. I'm closing early, but if any of you want to hang out, I'm heading for Black Bart's down on Bell Boulevard to have a few jars. My partner's tending bar, and he's staying late."

One perplexed customer asked, "You have a partner?"

"No, not really, but we're closer than friends, so we call each other partner. A friend is just a friend, but a partner? A partner will go out and get two blowjobs on a Saturday Night and come back and give you one."

The customer laughed, and he and his buddy said they were in. So I counted the till, wiped down the bar and locked the doors.

A half-hour later, I was parked in front of the saloon where the Fat Man worked the stick.

I garnished the mahogany with three $20s.

"Partner, give me a Black on the rocks and do the honors."

At the sound of my voice, a nebulous glow burst across Buffalo's veined face.

His cheeks flushed, his eyes gleamed, and as he reached for the vodka bottle, his words filled the room.

"Partner, about time you sprang for a drink. How long has it been since those $20s saw the light of day? I'll get mine first, then yours. Your posse is next, and then I'll get around to the rest of these hooples."

Buffalo was a lit explosive in a room full of damp firecrackers. Big in any direction you measured, and none of him was fat. Not an ounce of malice marred 320 pounds of muscle, constant sarcasm, and cutting staccato humor.

He had five customers, so counting the two guys with me he now had the ingredients for a nice little after-hours crowd.

People draw people.

I was getting real comfortable. Buffalo was in the barrel, and the night was still young. I didn't realize how young.

The next few hours proved routine. Some stragglers came and went. The whiskey fulfilled the distiller's intentions, so the usual laughs and ball breaking permeated the saloon. After everyone left, the two of us reminisced, and when I got the Christmas blues, I unintentionally lit the Fat Man's fuse.

Maudlin, I told Buffalo,

"I feel like getting on a plane and heading down to New Orleans. My brother lives down there. It has been too long since I've been drunk in that town."

Buff said, "I've never been to New Orleans."

"You've never been to New Orleans? Oh man, whatta town, 24 hours. Get a drink anytime of the night or day. You can even drink on the streets."

He lit up, "You can drink on the streets?"

"Yeah, as long you keep your cocktail in a plastic cup, no problem. You walk into a bar and buy a drink. If the bar is dead, just tell the bartender you want a "go cup." Then you head for the next joint. There's a bar every few yards in the French Quarter."

He said, "You got any money?"

"I got around $500 in cash and a credit card. Why? You can't go. If you're not home for Christmas, your wife will kill you. You got three kids."

He said, "Janet has a great sense of humor. Let me check last night's receipts. I hope the boss has as good a sense of humor as my wife."

The Fat Man had the balls of a blind burglar, but even for him, the next move was over the top. He counted the register and told me he rang $1100. But he left the cloth bag reserved for the receipts empty except for the cash register's ribbon and this note:

"Gone fishing. Borrowed last night's receipts, be back by next Saturday night
—Buffalo."

"Are you crazy? Black Bart will fire you for this," I said.

"Fire me? I'm taking $1100. That's job security. If he fires me, he's out the money. No, he'll take a $100 a week out of my pay until he's even. If he's still pissed after 11 weeks, then he'll fire me."

We both roared with laughter.

* * *

The flight from LaGuardia put us on a connecting plane in Atlanta. We arrived in Atlanta about noon, and I started looking for a phone to call my bookie. The NFL playoffs pitted the Rams at home against the Vikings at 3:00 P.M. Chuck Knox coached the Rams, and I knew the Vikings preferred cold weather.

A sizeable bet placed here should cover the expenses of the trip. From the first pay phone I saw, I called my bookie, Fruity, and placed the bet. Mission accomplished, I headed to—where else—the airport bar to meet Buffalo.

On arrival, Buffalo was pounding vodka martinis, which are lethal enough under normal circumstances, but both Buff and I had been drinking all night, and neither of us had slept since yesterday. These weren't normal circumstances.

I said, "What are you drinking you fat bastard, martinis? And what the hell are you drinking them out of, a trough?"

His cheeks had the red blush of unripe plums. His eyes were lit with an alcoholic benevolence. He hoisted the enormous mixing glass, smiled and said,

"I promised myself I would only have three drinks before I got back on the plane."

"Why don't you just fill up a bathtub?" I said.

I had told him I knew New Orleans inside out and promised him a good time. But I was already starting to fade, and he was just getting warmed up. Sleep on the plane to New Orleans was out of the question. I had been down this familiar road too many times. I knew the pattern.

For self-preservation, I decided to switch to spritzers. Spritzers are a woman's drink consisting of a glass of white wine topped off with club soda. At least drinking spritzers, I had a shot to stay awake and keep pace with Buffalo.

Buff and I would be inseparable for the next week, but no one would even notice me. Despite having lived in New Orleans two years, I'd be like an oxpecker on a rhinoceros's back.

After more libations in the airport bar, once again we were whacked.

Our flight announced, the Fat Man and me boarded the aircraft that would take us to Louisiana to "begin" drinking.

The flight consisted of a conveyer belt of tiny liquor bottles, most of which emptied at the Fat Man's overstuffed seat. True to my plan, I subsisted on a few white wines carefully diluted with club soda. But even drinking spritzers I was walloped.

God only knew Buffalo's condition.

We landed at 3:30 p.m. and took a cab directly to the French Quarter.

* * *

Off of Bourbon Street, right across from Pat O'Brien's on St. Peter, sat my old haunt, Johnny White's. Johnny was gone, but the feel of the place remained the same. Bartenders, who worked in various saloons in the quarter, stopped in for a pop before and after shifts.

No tourists were in Johnny's, only men who drank with purpose in a town infamous for consumption. As I blew in, the jukebox blasted, "It never rains in Southern California." A second behind me, Buffalo blasted unabashed through the tied-open doors like he owned the place.

"What a sorry bunch of whores. Give everybody a drink, and give me three shots of whatever's in the Absolut bottle."

The customers reacted with mild smirks of the "What have we got here?" variety, but the bartender, Little Joe, looked as if someone had just put his balls in a vise. I wasn't accustomed to the look of fear that masked his face. He retreated to the furthest end of the bar in an obvious attempt to regroup.

I was delighted I knew the bartender, but I was puzzled.

"Little Joe, who do I gotta blow to get a drink around here?" I said jokingly.

Johnny White's rectangular establishment was only a dry heave from Bourbon Street. It had a two-step entrance and a 35' bar on the left side of the room that went from front to rear, a bar with no frills, no food, and no bullshit. Slouched in the stools were men out of a Mathew Brady photograph, hard and grizzled with forlorn faces.

Buffalo threw two 20's on the bar and said,

"Give me $40 for the pool."

I tossed $40 beside his.

Little Joe still cowered at the far end of the bar.

Bewildered, I hollered,

"Hey Joe, how the hell you been doing?"

His answer illuminated.

"Not too fucking bad, Timmy, since you punched me in the fucking teeth last night."

The veil lifted. I understood.

My brother was a lunatic when drinking. He had always been quick with his hands, and he was the lethal combination most bartenders feared most, a guy who liked to fight and could. Take that nightmare and couple it with a 320-pound loudmouth who sounded as if he yearned for trouble, and you understand why Little Joe sought shelter at the far end of the bar. He was looking for a safe place to tell us that he wasn't serving us.

I yelled back, "I'm not Timmy, Little Joe. I'm his brother, Connor. Don't you remember me?"

The look on his face spoke volumes. His eyes and expression took on the countenance of a man who had been constipated for a month and had just had a bowl movement.

"Oh, Connor, I didn't recognize you," he murmured as he sauntered down to take our order.

"What are you two guys having?"

As Little Joe strolled away to get our drinks, with a wry grin, Buffalo said conspiratorially out of the side of his mouth,

"Fuck telling everybody you're Timmy's brother. Just keep your mouth shut, and we'll terrorize this fucking town."

I looked up at the television and saw that the Rams were losing 24-0 in torrential rain. Despite Albert Hammond's song, it did rain in Southern California, and when it did, it poured. The week blew by in a drunken stupor. By day, Buffalo and Timmy got to know each other, and at night I spent some quality time with my brother.

"I finally got a handle on my drinking," Timmy said. "I've been on club soda for a month. I like myself better sober. I'll probably still have a few beers on weekends, but no more four-day loads. Those days are over."

Spending time with a sober Timmy made me realize that I must curtail my madness as well. Despite all my childish foolishness, some deep psychological urge inside cried for stability and a strong moral woman like my mother.

My brother had slowed down. I'd follow suit. Marriage might be just the thing. But the women I ran around with were so wacky that if I had a child with one of them and it didn't work out, a judge would have awarded me the child on grounds of mental stability. The women were that crazy. Besides, I missed Lorraine. I called her in Oregon, and she agreed to return and marry me. I was ecstatic.

Marriage would slow me down and put me on the proper path. No sooner had the sun come up in the East and settled in the West that I, Connor Kelly—compulsive gambler, drunken manic and wanton womanizer—was married.

Now everything would change at last.

CHAPTER TWENTY-SEVEN

Lorraine and I had been married for six months, but I hadn't slowed much. When sober, I did all I could to make her happy, but even one drink obliterated any and all restraints. I was ruining my marriage and my health. Gambling and drinking, not marriage, remained my top priorities.

When I deposited my Johnny Walker Black on the Long Island banquet table's white-linen cloth, the jingle of half-melted ice cubes told me that it was time for a refill. My right hand now free, I tapped the vial of crushed cocaine in my jacket's left inside pocket.

Check.

My other hand lightly slapped my shirt pocket for my Marlboros.

Check.

Not finished with my inventory, I let my fingers slide inside my pinstriped pants' pocket and stroked my three Quaaludes.

Check.

Yeah, I was ready.

Surveying the room again, I couldn't believe how many people I knew. Every live wire, screwball and misfit in Queens was here. Why not?

It was Kevin Quinn's wedding.

Last week I got so twisted with Kevin that when I staggered home, I couldn't even make it up the stairs. I passed out on the landing below my apartment door just like my old man did decades ago.

No wonder Lorraine was livid.

My wife thought I had stayed out all night. Instead, on the bottom of the one flight of carpeted stairs that lead to our front door, I collapsed, curled up into the fetal position and pissed my pants.

But a week had passed, and these shenanigans were nothing she hadn't seen before. In this new dawn, I figured she'd get over it.

Today everybody was dressed in gowns, tuxedos and three-piece suits. At least 10 out of the 30 or so tables seated only bar owners and their staff. Every bar, club, and gin mill that I had been loaded in for the past five years was represented.

Whatta drunk this was going to be!

Kevin owned KQ's saloon on Bell Boulevard. He was short-necked with a permanent grin tattooed on his pie face. A total joy of a man incapable of pushing his bandy legs past a saloon entrance, Quinn could start a party in an empty room.

The catering, cocktails and company were all first class. On top of that, Quinn had booked a great seven-piece dance band with a hot horn section.

My table for 12 sat three other bartenders and their dates. Two of my bouncers and their wives were across from Lorraine and me.

And because of last week's tomfoolery, or my lifestyle in general, at the moment, Lorraine wasn't happy.

The wedding party entered to the usual fanfare, and the festivities began. Kevin spotted me, left the dais, and hurried over for a laugh and a quick belt.

Quinn leaned over and whispered sardonically,

"Stick around. When the wedding's over, I might need a few guys. I'm gonna stiff the band."

We both cracked up.

From a bottle on my table, I poured two quick shots of scotch. We threw them down. I wished him the best, and he hustled back to his place of honor.

The waiters started to serve the salads. As people began to eat, the banquet room quieted.

Suddenly, I heard my name from across the dance floor.

"Connor Kelly, I can't believe it."

Startled, I looked up as a not so old flame charged. She wore black stiletto heels, a painted-on black low-cut blouse and a leather mini-skirt so short that it could have passed for a belt.

Good Christ, I thought,
Where did Barbara buy that outfit, Sluts R Us?
Barbara mesmerized the men at my table.
To nip this in the bud, I leapt up.
"Well, how are you? So good to see you again."
I turned with an open palm toward my wife.
"Introduce yourself to my wife, Lorraine."

She said hello politely, but Barbara's smile faded. She acted like she was on a job interview. A brief awkward conversation followed. The game up, she spent a few minutes swapping small talk then sprinted for her table.

Adding to this disaster, my colleagues gawked at me the way a holdup victim stares at an off-duty cop during a robbery. The whole table wondered what I would do or say next.

They were sure I was busted. They didn't know how clever I could be.

I had this.

I turned to Lorraine with a pained look,
"Isn't it embarrassing when someone knows you, and you can't even remember their name?"

As if part of a rehearsed comedy routine, Lorraine answered,
"If she lifted up that mini-skirt, you'd recognize her easy enough."

Two of my bartenders spat drinks across the white tablecloth.

Busted.

With no way out, I checked my watch.

"Shit, almost 7:30, I gotta find a phone and get my action in."

I scurried from the room and felt Lorraine's stare burning into my back.

* * *

What little credibility I might have had gone, everything I

would say in the future Lorraine would judge a lie. I was like the drunk who told people,

"Everybody else was drinking, not me. I didn't drink. I just had a few beers."

If you say anything to yourself enough times, you'll start to believe it. But no one else will. Obviously, I was the only one delusional enough to believe my own lies.

The party atmosphere poisoned, I spent most of my night checking basketball scores on one of the lobby's three pay phones. Because all four games that I bet had lost, now I was nauseous as well.

Boy did I know how to screw up a party. I had to be the only bar owner in America who needed to borrow $5,000 from his porter to pay his bookie.

* * *

Two weeks later, Lorraine and I went out to dinner and then topped off the evening back at P.O.E.T.S. We were having a few pops in my usual spot at the end of the bar when another gal whom I had had a dalliance with strolled through the front door.

Pam hit my club like it was her living room. Her hair was the same shiny yellow as the satin blouse that she wore with flesh-tight white jeans and purple heels.

While Pam kissed the bartenders hello, a screwdriver magically materialized in her hand. Pam's hazel eyes glanced the length of the pine bar at Lorraine and me. After assessing the situation, her painted face screwed into a shrewd leer. Pam turned one-eighty and headed to flirt with Buffalo.

My wife said somberly,

"Who is that girl?"

I lunged for my cognac, swallowed the remains and casually replied,

"She comes in quite a bit. I think her name is Pam."

Doing her best Agatha Christie impression, Lorraine said,

"Funny, she knows the bartenders, Buffalo, and most of the customers, yet you're the owner. You're here all the time. How come she doesn't know you?"

* * *

Years ago in a bar, an old-timer gave me some advice. A sage of 70, he had seen it all.

"Connor," said he, "I understand you're getting married."

"That's right, Fitz," I said. "Any advice?"

"Well, I know you since you were a kid. I know you're a guy who likes to take a drink. It seems inevitable to me that one night you'll be out past closing time. When this happens, most married men make the mistake of sneaking up the stairs, taking their shoes off at the door, and slipping noiselessly into bed hoping that their wife won't wake up. Wrong approach, she'll wake up every time. Take my advice, barge up the stairs, kick open the door, and at the top of your lungs scream, 'Anyone in this house looking to get laid?' I guarantee she rolls over and pretends to be asleep."

This seemed like sound advice. My problem was that when I arrived home I was usually so drunk I couldn't negotiate the front door. I'd fall asleep in the hallway, in my car, or just pass out at the bar.

For a man with a pregnant wife, this lifestyle was a disaster. One needed not be Nostradamus to see where this marriage was heading. Satan was my chauffeur, and he was driving shit-faced.

I had to stop drinking.

CHAPTER TWENTY-EIGHT

One long, rocky year after Kevin's wedding, I placed my wife and infant son on the plane at Kennedy.

"There are TV dinners in the freezer. We'll only be gone two weeks. I'm sure you'll be okay," Lorraine said.

"Me, you kidding? I'll be fine. I'll be busy with the bar. The main thing is for you two to be safe, and have a good time with your sister in Oregon."

To my mind I had been a model husband. I had gotten banged up a few times, and in an attempt to remain faithful I had even turned down a few no-frills blowjobs. I hung around the airport and watched the plane dab the sky. As soon as it disappeared, my mind took off with it.

My wife was no ordinary woman, no woman ever is. Lorraine was a woman any man would be proud to skip home to. I certainly loved her and had tried to tow the line, but the taste of whiskey and the sounds of fiddles always beckoned.

Two weeks to party, the bar should be slow in the summer anyway.

The theme from the movie "Born Free" blared through my brain. Where to go for a few jars at 10 a.m.? The Airport was a short drive from Kevin's joint in Long Beach, just the place on a Monday morning in July.

* * *

As I walked through the front door of Chauncey's, the long bar seemed to mouth me a welcome. Even at this hour of the morning, six or seven people were cocktailing. The stool I picked was next to the patio that led to the beach.

I ordered a beer from the friendly face behind the bar.

"Tommy, bring me a bottle of Heineken, and throw this in your tip cup in case I get shattered and forget you later."

I tossed a sawbuck at the bartender and then peeled two $20s to begin the long bout ahead. It was one thing to be on a beach with beautiful women in bikinis. It was quite another to be drinking vodka next to a half drunk, half naked fox in a dark bar on a Monday afternoon.

The sand, sun and water lost their appeal fast.

Four Heinekens later, a familiar fog started to descend, and the beach might as well have been in another state. The stool felt more and more comfortable. The guy next to me pointed to the logo on my shirt.

"You go to "P.O.E.T.S." often?"

"Once in a while, why, have you been there?" I asked.

"Yeah, I go there all the time. The owner's a friend of mine."

"Really, what's his name?"

"Connor."

"Nice guy?" I asked.

"Yeah, a bit full of himself but a good guy with a buck. He always buys a drink."

Despite the name Connor plainly beneath the P.O.E.T.S. logo on my shirt, the guy's lips kept flapping. I tuned him out, but he confirmed what I had known since I had gotten in the bar racket.

No one wants to be anonymous. You can abuse customers or laugh at them, but you can never ignore them. People go out to be recognized and feel important.

The beers slid down faster, and the bar filled with partiers who sought refuge from the sun. Any semblance of my sobriety disappeared with the sunset. That night and the next two days were not even memories.

On a three-day bender, I didn't touch the sand or water until Thursday.

This time I had really punished myself. My voice was gone. My throat felt like cotton, and my hands shook so bad that at the diner, I had to lean over and drop my mouth to the cup's porcelain edge to sip coffee.

I spent all day sober on the beach. A clearer head ordered me to get the hell off of Long Island and back to Queens.

The sun and salt water provided a little therapy. For dinner, I savaged a lobster and a bottle of Pinot Grigio. As I cracked open a fat claw, it reminded me that I must dispose of all those TV dinners Lorraine had left me. Dinner behind me, I drove off the island and fortified by the bottle of wine decided to stop and see Kevin.

* * *

I growled, "Hey you fat, miserable son-of-a-bitch. Who you gotta know to get a drink around here?"

Quinn turned, laughed, and shuffled a Heineken at me. I scanned the bar and saw Kevin's usual entourage. I knew four of them, but only an old flame interested me.

"Give everyone a drink, and give Lisa Brennan the title to my car."

After the obligatory chuckle, Lisa sauntered to my end of the bar.

* * *

Two a.m., and thanks to numerous Heinekens, I start thinking rationally. Lorraine and Liam were out of town. Home was out of the question. I turned to a drinking buddy, Shifty, and suggested a four-hour ride to Atlantic City.

"I'm in," Shifty said.

"Me too," said Lisa.

"No Lisa. You're out," answered Shifty. "You're one of my best friend's girlfriends. No way I'm taking you to Atlantic City, especially with Connor fucken Kelly."

Lisa had a sexy twisted lip, like the gun molls in gangster films, and she spilled intelligent sentences out of the side of her mouth with a slight lisp, very attractive. She would definitely have had made this trip more interesting than Shifty.

I tried to salvage the moment.

"Why not? I'm married now. Everything is innocent enough. We're just going for a few laughs."

Surprised that my supposition met opposition from Shifty, I dragged him aside to argue my case.

"This trip will be a lot more fun with Lisa," I pleaded, but Shifty was adamant.

To make it up to me, Shifty said he'd drive.

* * *

We silently cruised the last miles toward the Jersey boardwalk and watched the sun kiss the sky hello. A storm brewed. It colored the sky the blue black of a bad bruise. The waves capped as far as my blurry eyes could see.

We parked and raced to the nearest casino.

At an empty blackjack table, we inserted ourselves into the third base and the shortstop slots.

"Give me $500 worth of chips, and send a cocktail waitress." I said.

I turned to my right where Shifty played shortstop and whispered,

"We've got no drugs. Our best shot to stay awake is the sugar in the booze."

"Good idea. Besides, I can't stand the sight of you sober," said Shifty.

I played a few hands at the ten-dollar minimum until the cocktail waitress arrived. With proper respect to the a.m., juice was in order.

"Bring us a couple of screwdrivers honey. No, wait a minute. We might not see you for a while. Better bring four screwdrivers."

Shifty piped up laughing, "Good idea. Bring me four too."

Good God, this day promised to be another long one.

* * *

I started to count cards, but the booze eliminated any caution or discretion I'd have normally had. Plus, I was still pissed that Shifty squashed Lisa coming.

All the time I had spent with those quiet smiles and sly innuendoes to try and maneuver that beautiful girl into tagging along gone to waste. I was drinking, gambling and, although trying to be faithful, always still thinking about women, and when drinking, I could be an eloquent asshole.

After a few hours, and a few buckets of screwdrivers, sanity took a field trip, but I had one moment of clarity. The dealer had a six up, and even though I was whacked, a voice inside me said, *Get more money on the table.*

"Double down on that one, split those, good on that one," I said.

Playing three hands at $50 a pop should carve up my $500 soon enough.

The dealer turned his hole card, king of clubs: 16. When he took the mandatory hit, he flipped the nine of spades, 25, busted.

I looked down at my chips and did a quick check. I was ahead $500.

Shifty said, "You've doubled your money. Quit."

I said, "No way. I'm hot. I'm on a roll here."

He said, "You're stewed. You're just lucky. Cash in."

"Fuck you. I'm hot. I ain't going anywhere."

Shifty said, "Let's go get a steak and a whore."

I tipped the dealer $10 and left the table.

* * *

In New Jersey, hookers stalked the streets of bad neighborhoods like they do almost everywhere else. Because Shifty was too particular, we weaved the avenue a few times. His drunken brain fantasized that a Playboy centerfold awaited him at the next turn, ready, willing and able to leap into bed for $40. Of course, I was as drunk, or worse, or I wouldn't have been sitting next to him in the car.

The short blast of a siren demanded I peek into our rearview mirror. Shifty pulled to the side of the road. A cop pulled in behind us. The patrol car's lights continued to spin.

"How you doing, officer?" I shouted from the passenger seat. "We're a little lost. I was wondering if you might show us how to get back on the turnpike to N.Y."

"Lost huh? I've been watching you guys for the past 15 minutes. You've pulled over and talked to at least four streetwalkers," he said. "If I see your sorry asses near this strip anymore today, I'm running ya's both in. You've got five minutes to disappear."

"Yes sir, officer. Thank you, officer. We were just leaving, sir, and thank you for the warning, sir," Shifty slurred.

I watched the cop close his ticket book and return to his car. I turned to Shifty.

"This is your fault, ya cocksucka. Who do you expect to find selling her ass out here on the street, Heather Locklear? Just grab a hooker. We're not marrying them. We're renting them. Next one I see, I'm grabbing."

Once the police car passed us, Shifty drove two blocks and hung a right. Three girls, two black and one white loitered beneath a pawnshop sign.

"You gals working?" I asked.

"Yeah, we're working," the white prostitute, said.

"OK." I pointed to her and a black gal. "You and you, hop in."

The other black girl protested.

"Hey, what about me?"

I remembered that I won $500 and said,

"OK. You too. Come on. Jump in."

With the three safely aboard, I raced to the nearest short-time rooming house.

Once inside, Shifty shared a bed with the white working girl, and I found myself with the two black chicks.

I told Shifty, "OK, after you're done, we'll switch."

He said fine, and I concentrated on the business at hand.

No newcomer to working girls, I cut to the chase.

"Look ladies, everybody's got their thing. I don't care what turns you on. I'm sure you've seen it all, and so have I. Let's save us all some time."

As the girls got in position, I continued the briefing.

"You wanna get back out on the street to make a few bucks, and I wanna get off. Here's what you do. I've got to think you're having a good time. Make me think you like it. That turns me on."

The two girls responded in the rack with the right amount of enthusiasm. One used her tongue to massage my chest, while the other focused her hands on more useful endeavors.

Pro that she was, while she yanked my crank, she tried to follow my instructions,

"Give me that big white dick," she chanted. "Give me that big white dick."

With this refrain, I burst out laughing. This little prick of mine has led me a merry chase but was hardly notable for its size. Besides, these were two black streetwalkers in Atlantic City.

"Sweetheart, for $50 I wasn't expecting Merryl Streep, but ya gotta give me something I can hang my hat on," I laughed.

After she finished, I told Shifty that it was time to switch. He refused. I couldn't believe it.

"What? Are you fucken kidding? What, did you fall in love, ya cocksucka? Whatta ya gonna do exchange Christmas Cards?"

* * *

After the girls and a steak, we retraced our steps to the casino. We gambled until 3 a.m. with the inevitable result. We limped out of Jersey with barely enough money for the tolls back to N.Y. The plan was to split the driving, Shifty first and then me. When I couldn't stay awake anymore, I would rouse him.

A few miles out, with both of us half in the bag, Shifty pulled over on the Jersey Turnpike. We both needed to piss. Manhood firmly in hand, I was watering the weeds when I heard the now familiar siren of the Jersey police. Shifty heard it too and reacted quicker.

He zipped up, raced back to our car and jumped into the passenger seat where he stared at me with the devil's grin. I looked at him ambivalently with both disdain and admiration. With prick still in hand, I said,

"Quick thinking, ya cocksucka. Ya got me good." And despite the impending doom, and possible DWI, I roared laughter.

* * *

The sun defied the car's tinted windows. I twisted, writhed and gasped for water. I needed a drink. I grabbed my tortured throat. My head throbbed. I tried to speak. My voice was sandpaper.

Jesus, what happened? What time is it? Where the hell am I?

I straightened up, squinted out the car's back window and saw a familiar skyline. Shifty awoke and wondered how far I had driven but not for long.

"Are you shitting me? That's it? That's as far as you got? We're just barely outside Atlantic City."

I said, "Hey man, you're lucky I pulled over. If I'd tried to drive, we'd be dead. I saved your life."

"Yeah, you saved my life," he said sarcastically. "Get the fuck out of the driver's seat, and let's get the hell out of here. Every time I leave this fucking town, I feel like my mother died."

The six-hour ride back seemed interminable. We scraped together enough money to limp across the Washington Bridge, but Shifty couldn't make Queens without a transfusion at the Jolly Tinker. We stopped, had a hair of the dog, and I borrowed $50 from the register. I sent Shifty over the bridge about 1 p.m. and headed home for some much-needed sleep.

* * *

With Lorraine in Oregon, I arrived home to a mercifully empty house.

I had never been this banged up from alcohol before. Whether psychological or physical, I could feel my liver aching. My hands shook so bad that I couldn't even pour a cup of tea. I plopped my head on the pillow and hoped that when I woke up, all would be better.

I was also consumed with incredible guilt.

What the hell is wrong with me? When I'm drinking I don't care about my family or my health, AIDS or nothing, What if I kill someone when I'm driving drunk? What am I doing with my life? I gotta get fucken help.

As soon as my eyes shut, they opened. I tried again, no good. I was exhausted, but every time I closed my eyes, adrenalin awoke me. I turned on my side determined to sleep, and then they started.

Whispers.

I heard them from somewhere in my bedroom. Like two or three people talking in an alternative universe, a steady stream of distant conversation that startled me enough to raise up on an elbow.

I turned my head 360 degrees, no one in sight. I couldn't believe I was imagining conversations. They were so clear, so vivid.

Wow, I put my head back down, closed my eyes and pulled the covers over my head. That didn't help, more whispers.

Oh Jesus, you really did it this time. You're hallucinating. Not from LSD or Mescaline but from alcohol. This can't be good.

No matter what drug I had stumbled over before, no matter how weird the trip, at least I could count on waking up drunk as a familiar balm, an old friend, as comfortable as the womb. Alcohol never worried me before.

I got to the point that I thought Shifty was screwing with me and breaking my balls. I even looked in my pants' pocket for a hidden tape recorder.

The voices were that vivid.

* * *

Too wired to sleep, I slipped on a pair of pants and walked out on the terrace to have a smoke.

My Irish next-door neighbor, Aemon Mullen, had just finished his commute. As he slammed the door of his Toyota van, I recalled that Aemon was a reformed drunk and sensed an ally.

"Hey Aemon, you were a heavy drinker in your day."

"I nearly drowned in the stuff," he said.

"Tell me, did you ever get the whispers?"

"Whispers?"

"Yeah, you ever close your eyes and there's no one in the room, but you hear voices?" I asked.

"Oh that, sure." He shrugged. "Shuh, the whispers are nothing, boy. I often couldn't get out of bed for fear of stepping on the furry little bastards."

I relaxed and headed back inside. But wait,

If my ears have bought into this delusion, how soon before my eyes join the party? I'm turning into my old man. I gotta stop drinking.

CHAPTER TWENTY-NINE

"Connor Kelly, you sick son-of-a-bitch. I thought I might find you here."

The voice belonged to an old drinking buddy. It had been years since we had shared a jar. What was an AA guy doing in my favorite watering hole?

"Danny, how the hell are ya? What brings you in here?" I smirked. "You still a friend of Bill W's? Are you still in the program?"

He wore a beige three-piece suit. His bright-green eyes appeared a bit antsy, but they matched his tie.

"Yeah, almost four years now. Believe it or not, I drove by the Jolly Tinker hoping to catch you."

"It's even money that my ass will cover a stool here any afternoon. What the hell ya wanna see me for?" I asked.

"You're gonna think I'm nuts, but I gotta do what I gotta do," he said.

I cracked a light joke.

"Jesus, Danny, you sound like a narc or a cop. You haven't gone over to the dark side have you? Lighten up. Take a load off."

I nudged a stool. He dropped on it.

"No, nothing that dramatic, but my conscience would have bothered me if I at least didn't reach out."

"You want a coke or something?" I asked.

"No thanks. I won't be here that long."

I thought,

I better nip this in the bud.

"Listen man. I'm not ready for any 12-step program, and forgive me if I offend you, but nothing's worse than lectures from a reformed drunk."

"No. I'm not here to reform you. I was told to come here."

Danny's mug turned serious.

"Listen, Connor. You have a son, right? Are you going through a divorce?"

I was flabbergasted. What the hell was he talking about? How did he know about my private life? We were more acquaintances than friends, yet his question was a grim reminder.

Fed up with my lifestyle, Lorraine had had enough. She had moved out. No way I wanted my son or the halfway-to-heaven woman who gave him birth to suffer, but I just couldn't stop drinking. I had tried, but powerless, I had always went back.

Suddenly reminded of my frailty, I grinded my teeth, my muscles quivered. I turned sullen and barked.

"Yeah, what's it to you?"

"Don't get offended. We've been friends a long time. Every Tuesday I take my son to see a religious adviser named Trudy. Last week, Trudy told me that someone I know is going through a divorce and needs her help. I said I didn't know whom she was talking about. She prayed, stopped, looked me dead in the eye and said, 'He's an old friend. He gambles a lot and has a son. Any idea now?'"

Danny fidgeted but continued,

"I had no clue and told her so, but Trudy persisted. She was almost obsessed. She said, 'He has loaned you money on more than one occasion and drinks a lot. Think? Any idea now?'"

Danny scanned the crowded bar to avoid my raised eyebrows. I smirked and almost laughed out loud at this bullshit, but he said,

"I've played poker with you, man. Whenever I tapped out, you always loaned me cash, and I know you bet a lot of money on sports. I wasn't sure whether you were going through a divorce or not."

I thought,

What's this asshole's angle?

"What's the punch line, Danny?"

"Trudy told me she wants to see you," Danny said.

I had known Danny a long time. We used to be friends. So as not to offend the guy, I feigned interest. I put my elbow on my knee and leaned forward, as if I'd been waiting to hear his dipshit advice all my life,

"Of course, I'm interested. What have I got to lose? Give me her address," I said.

I grabbed a coaster off the bar, and out of courtesy, I wrote the tripe he fed me.

"Trudy, 204 St. Bainbridge Ave, 7 p.m. Friday. Got it," I said.

After a little more small talk, it was time to give this guy the boot.

"Yeah, I got the address." I said. "No man, I won't lose it. Yeah, thanks very much for stopping by, Danny. Damn nice of you."

He garbled a few more sentences and I said,

"Yeah, well, we'll see. Who knows? Thanks again."

As soon as he left, I crumpled the coaster, let it drop to the floor and ordered a shot of Jameson's to go with my Heineken.

The hours vanished with the coaster.

* * *

Five days later, I climbed into my jalopy, turned the key and, because of a rotten muffler, heard my car's engine roar to life.

On the passenger side floor mat, Danny's crumpled up bar coaster knocked me for a loop. I snatched the wadded cardboard off the rubber mat, smoothed it out, and incredulously read Trudy's address.

I use my car every day. Why hadn't I noticed the coaster before? And why notice it, of all days, on the same day I was supposed to have the appointment?

To top it off, it was 10 minutes to 7, and Trudy's address was only four blocks from where I was parked. Although secular, I believed in odds. This one was a long shot. I had to check it out.

* * *

The address led me to a Presbyterian Church with huge

foreboding brass and oak doors. The buzzer produced a Catholic Nun.

"You must be Connor."

"Yeah sister, but I'm shocked to see you here. Since when does the Catholic church endorse fortune tellers?"

"Trudy is not a fortune teller," the nun said adamantly. "She has a gift."

In front of the altar, two chairs awaited. Wearing white from throat to feet, an obese woman creaked one. Her skin was smooth and unwrinkled like a bleached candle. Her gray hair combed out across broad shoulders.

Trudy smiled and said,

"You must be Connor, sit." She pulled the empty chair closer. "Do you mind if I hold your hands? It helps me see things."

She clasped my mitts, closed her eyes and began to pray. After a few minutes of my skepticism, Trudy suddenly started erupting. She shook violently, almost epileptically and chanted,

"Thank you, Jesus. Thank you, Lord. Yes, Lord. Yes, Jesus."

The smirk left my face. My eyelids chased my eyebrows. I needed to get the hell out of here, but her hands were like vises. My body shook in tempo with her hands.

Her gyrations ceased. Her eyes opened. Trudy hesitated and spoke slowly, softly,

"Someone is praying for you very, very hard. Do you know who it is?"

"Yes, I know," I said timidly . . . "My mother."

"Praise God. Save us, God. Thank you, Jesus."

Her eyes gazed toward heaven momentarily but returned and settled on me.

"You are a womanizer, a gambler and a drunk."

I nodded.

"You were in Laos, when . . ."

These words stole my breath so badly that I didn't even hear the end of her sentence.

How does she know this?

I sucked the air out of my cheeks and nodded again.

She said, "Praise God. Thank you, Lord. Thank you, Jesus."

Trudy paused again. Her chin lifted.

"Think back. Think way back. You heard something."

Confused, I said, "No."

"You heard something that upset you as a child, something, something . . . think, think." She closed her eyes. "Lord, please help him to remember."

My memory stung like a cracked whip. I saw a little boy awake too early for school hearing his Dad's gruff voice.

"You never wanted Connor. You never wanted another child," shouted Big Tom.

My mother shouted back.

"Why would I want another child after the way you acted when Timmy was born?"

In anger, my mother said I wasn't wanted, and I heard her.

I never, ever, thought of this before. Why do I remember this now? What kind of woman is Trudy? What the fuck is going on here?

I blurted, "Yes, I remember something."

"Thank you, Lord. Praise Jesus." Then she prayed aloud, froze and began to shake worse than before, violent convulsions, her whole body, not just her hands. She vibrated like a washing machine on tilt.

I searched for the exit. I wanted her to release my hands.

Abruptly,

"After Asia, you lost your way, Connor. You disavowed your creator and decided to live life without God."

I couldn't dismiss this as coincidence. She knew too much, and in my heart, I knew she was right.

The seer continued,

"Lord, let us pray that Connor stops gambling, drinking and womanizing. Help him straighten out his life. We pray that he sees your holy light."

I chanted with her.

"Amen, Amen."

But I thought,

I gotta get the fuck outta here and get a drink.

Outside the church, I replayed the incident.

Was that on the level? Is there really a God, and if so, why's He trying to reach me, rescue me and for whom, for me, my son, my mom? Why does my mother have to pray so much? Sure, I gamble, drink and do too many drugs, but I don't need prayers. I have all this under control.

I looked at my watch. The NBA jumped off at 7:30. I could bet a few basketball games, shoot out to Queens to see Kevin Quinn, pick up an eight ball of coke and call my current squeeze, Pam.

First things first, I phoned my bookie.

"Fruity? Connor. What ya got in the NBA?"

I bet four games, a nickel apiece, $2,000.

Now I needed that drink.

* * *

At 2 a.m., in P.O.E.T.S. cellar, I crushed a Quaalude and used a razorblade to blend it with lines of coke. The NBA games that I had bet went in the toilet. I was out $2,200 for the evening.

Unfazed, I bet three games Saturday. All went to the shithouse.

I bet six games Sunday. They all went south as well. Thirteen straight losers, I was down over $10 large for the week. What was going on? Ever since that bloody fucken Trudy put a curse on me, not one fucken winner.

Monday night I called Fruity, "What ya got in the NBA?"

"All-Star game tomorrow so no baskets tonight," he said. "But I got hockey."

Disgusted I pulled the glass-vial from my inside pocket and searched my other pockets for the cut-off straw.

"Hockey? Forget about hockey. I mean shit, Fruity, use your head. Basketball's my game. What the fuck do I know about hockey?"

CHAPTER THIRTY

Colored strobe lights struck the disco ball and glistened on the writhing women gone mad on P.O. E.T. S. mobbed dance floor. Gloria Gaynor's hit, "I Will Survive," had become 1979's anthem for single women, and I couldn't have been happier.

My joint was mobbed.

The smug smile darted from my face as I shoveled my scotch onto a coaster, stood and screamed,

"Hey you, Spartacus."

At my howl, his wild eyes jerked toward me. He stood well over six feet and weighed the wrong side of 250. A white fedora covered the loudmouth's bloated, massive head. His index finger stopped pointing at the seated man's face as I ran toward him.

Keeping my back to the intimidated man on the stool, I planted my face inches from "white-hat's" blotchy, red mug.

"Take it outside, asshole. I ain't running a goddamn gym."

Facing two men now, the troublemaker hesitated a moment.

A bouncer appeared, followed seconds later by Buffalo, the heavyweight of all heavyweights. Four men against him now, defiance limped from his face.

When he looked around for support, he saw my three bartenders only feet from the commotion.

Outnumbered by seven, prudence trumped bravado.

I told Buffalo and my other heavyweight,

"This asshole's had enough. Show him the gate."

My bartender, Dewey, snatched the fool's cocktail and tossed what was left of it into the stainless-steel sink. One last gasp of pride calculated the consequences before he picked his change off the bar. My two employees wearing green security shirts "escorted" him to the door.

I warned his relieved adversary,

"You skate this time, but one false move, you join him."

* * *

It was Christmas week, but there was no "peace on earth" in Queens. Patrons in my bar wanted to get loaded and laid. If they didn't get lucky, alcohol fueled frustration and led to beefs.

Fuck it. I wasn't serving holy water.

Funny how the ones who wore the outlandish hats always became a problem as if they were predisposed to attracting attention.

When you have a joint this size, the key is to stop a fight before it starts. Never stand between two combatants. Choose a side. Let your back face the passive guy. Face the aggressor. This puts the odds in your favor.

Trouble averted, I reseated myself at my usual spot at the end of the 60' pine bar. Sitting by the back door allowed me to see the customers, the four bartenders, the three bouncers who roamed the dance floor, and the 300 lb. behemoth taking money at the gate. The front door was where Buffalo usually stopped trouble before it started.

The P.O.E.T.S. acronym provided a catchy logo and a cheap theme. It cost me less than nothing to burden the hand carved shelves with used books. And the framed parched papers with quotes of literary giants that hugged my walls were free.

We built the bar's base with beams yanked out of vacant buildings in the South Bronx. A carpenter pal filled the six-inch thick beams with a herringbone pattern of bricks collected from the same vacant buildings.

We accentuated the base by marrying seven, 20-foot slabs of natural pine and then slathering the bar's crown with 12 coats of polyurethane.

Behind the bar, the shelves were built of hand-carved, ornate pine on which a four-layered intertwining backdrop displayed every variety of liquor on the market. Beneath the stocked shelves, mirrors provided a multiplying effect for our glassware.

Glasses aligned six deep appeared to be twelve deep.

The effect was stunning, a touch of Vermont in Flushing, Queens.

* * *

Bloated from the five or six Heinekens that I had downed already, I switched to cognac neat with a water back. I carefully eyeballed the customers straggling in. I had yet to select the night's "femme de jour."

A blonde walked in with three other girls, and I perked up. She was stunning. A body like mortal sin wrapped in a cheap, tight package, too much make-up and too little skirt, perfect.

She looked up and down the bar, skimmed right past me, and turned to the stage where the band blasted another dance number.

I wasn't on her radar.

I'd change that.

Her pouted lips impatiently implied, I don't buy my own drinks gentlemen. Who's stepping up?

I waved at my bartender,

"Dewey, send the young lady and her friends a squirt."

He smirked and said, "Usual line?"

I nodded.

Minutes after the four girls had their cocktails, I held court with three regulars at the end of the bar. I laughed loud and often. My celebrated caw flooded the room, but I didn't even glance in the stunner's direction.

A stranger to indifference, she marched the length of the bar and used her pink-painted lips to thank me for the drinks. I offered a refill. She sat. We swapped preliminaries.

Within minutes, I realized that Samantha had the insight of an oyster. We were in N.Y., yet she chatted about time spent "up" in Georgia and "down" in Maine. When Samantha said she was Lutheran, my vacuous temptress sealed the deal.

"Oh, a follower of Martin Luther, huh?" I asked.

Samantha's sultry eyes shot me a scornful look. Her mouth snapped,

"Bullshit. There's not one black person in my congregation."

Her beautiful eyes were blue, completely empty and ready to contain anything.

Horny, I smiled and didn't bother to explain. Instead I said, "Dewey, give us a couple more belts of Courvoisier."

I was half stewed already, so Samantha could have told me she carried bubonic plague. I wasn't going anywhere. She was so hot and so deliciously dumb.

After a few more cocktails, Samantha blurted, "At 15, I fulfilled every young girl's fantasy."

"What was that?" I asked.

"I had sex with my best friend's father."

I took a long sweet swig on the cognac. As the alcohol glided down my gullet, I smiled the smile of a 10-year-old boy that had just been told his Dad brought him a pony.

* * *

With both of us well lubricated, and everyone but the two of us long gone, I suggested the obvious,

"I don't go to motels," Samantha said. "Besides, I'm not going to fuck you tonight. I just met you. Do you think I'm stupid?"

"No," I said not very truthfully.

But all I was thinking was,

I wasted almost four hours listening to this idiot's babbling for one reason and one only. I have to close the deal, but if I ever hope to reconcile with Lorraine, I can't have the neighbors see her coming from my apartment.

I rushed the amber snifter back to the coaster and used my now empty hand to caress her thigh.

"Look, I told you I was in a relationship. I can't take you to my place, and you said you lived with your parents."

My hand made small circles under her short skirt, and the closer I got to the "Promised Land," the more adamant I became. I had to fuck this chick, and I had to fuck her right now, tonight.

"You know this feels right. We have to do this. Supposed I lived alone, or in a cabin by a lake, would you come home with me then?"

"Of course," she said. "I want to fuck you too, but motels make me feel like a whore."

I leaned over, took my hand off her thigh and placed it gently behind her neck. I went nose to nose with her and looked into her sultry, inviting eyes.

"So just pretend my cabin is inside my motel room," I laughed. I put pressure on her neck to pull her mouth next to mine. When my tongue darted past her lips and inside her mouth, she responded.

* * *

"You wait here," I told Samantha. "I'll get us a room."

"I still don't feel right about this. Motels make me feel cheap. I wish we were anywhere but here," she said.

"Honey, will you forget about the damn motel? There will be other times. I'll take you to Vegas, to the Caribbean. I'm telling you, it's gonna be great."

When I come back with the room key, she blurted through the open passenger window,

"Did you get the Egyptian Room?"

I thought sarcastically,

Motels make me feel like a whore.

She knows more about this joint than the architect.

Samantha wanted me to think I was her first ice cream cone. She'd explode that myth within the hour. This chick had been around the block.

* * *

Samantha yelled from the motel room's shower,

"Hurry. Get up. I'm late for school. You'll have to drop me off."

Exhausted, I thought,

Wow, what a night. If this chick has scruples, she sure kept them under wraps. She's something else. She's a find. If only she were mute.

Slipping on my pants, I yelled into the bathroom,

"No problem. What college do you go to, St. Johns?"

"College? I don't go to college. I go to Bayside High."

My jaw dropped. She was in high school? I was nearly twice

her age and trying to repair a tenuous relationship with my wife. *I gotta dump her, quick. If Lorraine ever finds out about this, I'm fucked.*

* * *

With all attempts to reconcile with Lorraine failed, the following Christmas I find myself combing the jewelry stores to buy Samantha a gift.

My ex-wife was a fine, beautiful, intelligent woman that any sane man would kill to be with, and somewhere inside me an insistent sense of right and wrong remained. Vows like "for better or worse, and in sickness and in health" meant something.

But love was a bumpy road, and a husband who had unipolar manic depression made it bumpier. Drugs, drinking, gambling and womanizing would wreck any relationship.

Lorraine wanted a husband, not an ensemble of vices.

My excesses had burned the cohabitation bridge, so now I was saddled with this dimwit. Samantha had her good points. She was young, hot and horny, but her dirty-blonde hair adorned a head as thick as a cellar full of smoke. Before our "dates," I needed four Manhattans to fortify myself for the inane conversations that preceded the sensational sex.

My brain was no longer in charge. The little head had pulled a coup. And when it came to Samantha, self-indulgence ruled and refused to compromise. My mania fed on sex, drugs and booze, and at the moment money wasn't a problem.

P.O.E.T.S. packed them in. Cash jammed my three registers, but that wasn't enough. I still gambled heavy and looked for the fast buck.

I was never satisfied. And of course, I was losing.

* * *

At my usual spot by P.O.E.T.S. back door just after midnight, I handed my bookie, Fruity, his weekly envelope. Fruity thanked me and bought a drink for the four people in my party.

I took another beating. Thank God my joint was packed. Dewey filled my snifter, removed the air from my entourage's glasses, and paused only long enough to say,

"That's with Fruity, on Fruity, on the Fruitman."

Dewey was almost finished pouring the round when the barman working the other end yelled,

"Hey boss, you gotta phone call. Guy said it was important."

I ducked under the bar's return, strolled behind the bar, and paused to chat up a few customers on the way to the phone.

I put the receiver to my ear and shouted over the band's bedlam,

"Connor Kelly."

The voice on the other end was the New Orleans Police Department's desk sergeant.

When he finished his second sentence, I felt like someone just tore something loose from behind my eyes. I couldn't see the front door, the stage or even the phone, which now dangled uselessly by its chord.

"No," I screamed at no one. "No, no, no, no. Tell me it's a lie. It's a lie. It's a fucken lie."

The pain in the back of my head felt as if someone drove a nail into my eye. The hung mouths that belonged to the shocked patrons on the other side of the bar barely registered.

All my life I had prepared myself for this call, yet when it finally came, my face had quivered as though I had been electrically shocked. A thousand tiny face wrinkles flattened with rage as I banged my fists on the top of the bar over and over again.

"What happened, Connor? Are you alright?" A customer asked.

"My brother, Timmy, my brother . . ."

But I couldn't finish the sentence.

My shaking hand brushed across my mouth. My eyes streamed water. My heart threatened to burst.

* * *

In the car to the Bronx, I was still bawling.

"How am I gonna tell her, Buff? How can I tell my Mom that Timmy is dead? How do I tell her that her first-born son was beaten to death in a bar?" I moaned.

Buffalo kept his eyes on the road and said nothing. As we drove across the Whitestone Bridge, I looked out at the churning black water and opened the window. The cold air hit me like a mallet.

"I knew Timmy would never comb gray hair. I knew he wasn't going to live long. He really grabbed life by the throat, Buff."

"I know, partner. I loved him too. But you have to think about your mom now. You have to get her through this. We both have kids. We both know that as bad as this is for you, it'll be a thousand times worse for her. Don't wake her up tonight. There's nothing she can do. You're already a mess. One of you will need a full night's sleep to handle the details in the morning."

"But she has to know, Buff."

"Sure she does, but she doesn't have to know at 2 a.m., Saturday night."

I stuck my head back out into the freezing night air and thought,

If I'm not going to my Mom's, where am I going?

After hearing the news, my first instinct had been to get the hell out of P.O.E.T.S. and get close to my mother. But Buff was right. She was sleeping, and I should wait till morning to tell her. I had to share my pain though, and I had to share it with someone I loved, someone who understood the grief I was going through.

Only one person fit the bill, my ex-wife.

"Take me to Lorraine. She's at her mom's."

Between sobs and sentences, I took long, deep breaths from the moving car's window. When my crying exhausted itself, reminisces ran from my mouth.

"You remember how bright he was Buff? When he went offshore, all he did was read and lift weights. Fucken Timmy ate books, man, and boy could he sling it."

Despite my grief, I turn to the huge man behind the wheel and managed a smile.

"When I tended bar in Pat O'Brien's, I'd get off shift and cross the street to Johnny White's for a few pops to help me sleep. Timmy would be sitting there with some chick, and before I could talk and screw him up, he'd wink at me and say, 'Hey, here's my brother, Connor. This is Angela. She teaches Biology at the university. Imagine the coincidence, she teaches Biology, and here I am a Marine Biologist.'"

I reached into my top pocket for a Marlboro Red, lit it, and dragged hard. I thought of those joyful moments and smiled.

"Next night, he'd be a psychologist or a photographer, or whatever it took. But the fucker could pull it off. He read everything, could've been anything. What a fucken waste. If there's a God, he's got some rotten sense of humor."

I emptied my lungs of smoke out the open window. Enraged, I stared at the starless sky and screamed.

"Fuck you, God!"

* * *

The clock in the kitchen read 5:55 a.m. I was still sniffling and uttering the same three words, the poor bastard, the poor bastard.

Before I saw Lorraine, I had used a pay phone to call Tim's roommate who told me that four or five guys who knew my brother had sat and watched it happen.

According to Roy, a drunken Timmy gave a guy some shit, and the asshole sucker-punched him. When my brother hit the floor, the guy heaved up the heavy wooden stool and bashed Timmy's head repeatedly with it. It could have, and should have, been stopped quicker than it was.

I felt like the brightest light in my life had gone out. Timmy was gone. I couldn't believe it, so full of life, knowledge and laughter. No one loved to laugh more than Timmy.

My ex-wife supported me through it all, as I would her. Just because we didn't live together, it didn't mean we didn't still love and respect each other. I was grateful for the memories we created and the child that she had blessed me with.

I was just impossible to live with.

Hours crept glacially. I set 9 a.m. as the deadline to call. How would I tell my poor, saintly mother? To make matters worse, today was her birthday.

Here's a present for you.

Happy Birthday. Your son is dead.

* * *

I called at exactly 9 a.m. . . .

"What's wrong?" Mom asked immediately.

"I have to come up and talk to you, Mom."

"What's wrong?"

"I'll tell you when I get upstairs. I'll be there in five minutes."

"Tell me now, Connor."

"Mom, I'm coming right up."

"Oh my God. It's Timmy. How bad is it?"

I lost it. I couldn't even finish the next sentence.

"Mom, stop asking me. I'm comi . . ."

"He's gone isn't he? My big, strong, handsome son is gone. Oh my God. My Timmy's dead."

When I entered her building's lobby, Mom's screams echoed the hallway.

* * *

The funeral was a blur. Four days of wrenching grief that I wanted to forget forever.

But one moment stood out.

On the ride back from the cemetery, Mom and I sat in the back of the limousine. I controlled my emotions, but Mom's broken heart spilled from her eyes.

After one choking breath, she stopped weeping, and wistfully grabbed my hand. She spoke firmly but quietly, without emotion and with unimaginable prescience.

"It's over, Connor."

"Over?" I asked.

"Understand that you can't bring Timmy back. You have to forget this. You have to move on. Leave this behind you. Let go. Promise me. You must forget him."

I broke down.

The feeling that overcame me was the opposite of any emotion that I should have felt.

I felt the way I felt when my infant son squeezed my finger for the first time.

I felt closer to my mother than ever before. Like I was a child again and she was so much wiser. I was grown, yet her touch, sincerity and foresight reached a hollow part of my heart and made me feel vulnerable.

To this day, I think about how a woman with a seventh-grade education could have such insight.

She knew.

She just knew that I was hell bent on some kind of revenge. I wanted to get even with the guy who killed Timmy, or maybe with the guys who watched it happen, or maybe with someone else or maybe everyone else.

Somebody had to pay.

CHAPTER THIRTY-ONE

I heard once in an A.A. meeting that alcoholism is like diarrhea. If you got it, you got it. You can't tell a guy with diarrhea to shit hard any more than you can tell an alcoholic to take one drink.

My brother's death gave me the excuse I needed to go down for the last time. Within the year, I was determined to drown my liver and join my brother.

After the tragedy of Tim's death, my mother turned exclusively to the only opiate she knew. She dulled her incomprehensible pain with prayer. Her family decimated, she prayed unselfishly night and day, harder than ever before. Not for herself of course, but for me, her only surviving son to finally find the right path.

Instead of the path she prayed for, I broke out the maps, and charted a comfortable course for a destination that I had searched for all my life. I spat in my hands, hoisted the Jolly Roger, and set full sail for maximum havoc.

* * *

To a gambler, money's just how we keep score.

Being broke only hurts because it knocks us out of action. Gambling's about juice, not money. The tension you feel when you hear a siren behind you, the butterflies before a speech, the nervousness before making love to a woman for the first time—that's "juice."

When a bet means life or death, family celebrations, inane conversations and the mundane practicalities of life simply can't compete with the rush.

Gamblers are juice junkies.

Like drug addicts, gamblers live for the moment. We don't worry about 401Ks or security blankets. Once that syringe is loaded, a thumb press whisks a junkie back to the serenity of the womb. That glassine package means everything. Nothing matters but the next high.

Action's everything for us gamblers. Money's just the price of the rush. Gamblers are insular, selfish and obsessed. Normal people can't deal with us, or us with them.

* * *

Lorraine was no different. The divorce finalized, self-flagellation synergized with guilt spurred an outburst. I shrieked defiantly at her lawyer,

"Yeah, and put a clause in there that I'll pay for my son's education too."

I didn't need a lawyer. I represented myself.

The result was predictable.

With a fool for a client, my bravado had managed to secure a settlement that would cost $3,500 a month, $2,500 for alimony and $1,000 for my son.

Time had tarnished some of P.O.E.T.S. glitter, so as a bar owner in '79, I made about $4,000 a month. But I wasn't worried. I was a gambler.

I'd live on my other "assets."

Those "assets" included: $40,000 in owed credit card debt, $62,000 that I owed to bookies, no apartment, and after my deceased brother, Timmy, executed my Austin Healy, a second hand Buick that I bought for $1000.

I remembered Tim's reaction when I asked him what had happened to my beloved sports car. He had driven my car up from New Orleans while stoned on black-beauties. After a 25-hour trip, he showed up in New York frazzled.

He had blow-torched the entire front end of my car.

I screamed, "Timmy, what the hell did you do to my car?"

"What did I do to your car? What did I do to your car? What did your car do to me?" He screamed back.

It was hard to argue with the logic of a screwball on speed.

He prattled, "Every 200 miles I had to change a flat. Something was cutting the tires. I took it to a metal shop and had to burn away the bumpers and the front-end, otherwise I never would had gotten here."

But the car was inconsequential. Timmy was dead, and I was divorced.

Besides I didn't care about material things. I had all this under control. My mania told me that I was well-qualified to handle any crisis. I didn't need help. I had other things going for me.

I was a functional alcoholic-drug-user, a dysfunctional gambler and diagnosed uni-polar manic-depressive. In case you haven't copped on yet to the "disease's" symptoms, the competitive runners who cram my brain wear shorts and sneakers, refuse to wait for the starter's pistol, and never ever reach the finish line.

Never depressed, always optimistic, I see rainbows where others see only black seas of pain. Read Vonnegut's "Slaughterhouse Five." I'm like the Jew in the Dachau boxcar who before he died kept muttering, "You think this is bad? This isn't so bad."

* * *

I swaggered out of the lawyer's office, but once outside, an avalanche of reality buried me. I was screwed.

Desperation spawned an idea. I rushed to a payphone.

"Gobbo, I'm telling you man we can do this. I know 15 or 20 guys that bet, and so do you. Let's take action. Let's get on the right side of this shit for a change. We'll clean up. We'll still get the rush, but instead of paying out, we'll collect."

Even though Gobbo was a cop, he was my best friend in the world. One guy I could always count on, a stand-up guy. If anyone could ever replace my brother, it was Gobbo. My mania gave me one priceless gift—enthusiasm. I could sell the Pope a double bed. Gobbo bought in. We were on our way.

Next I called "Julius," a.k.a. Jimmy Simpson, a former big-time bookmaker on Staten Island. Julius lost everything to his compulsion, but powerless he still gambled. He was the most degenerate gambler I knew. I needed the expertise that flowed from his disease.

* * *

Julius's 300-pound frame paused, turned, then wheezed before sputtering,

"I told you pick a shit neighborhood. I didn't tell you a fourth-floor walkup."

He wore an old gray trench coat, a pair of black, civil service dress shoes and a beat-up Yankee cap.

"Stop whining, you fat bastard. It was the best I could do on short notice," I said. "Of the two available apartments, just pick the one you think is best."

Distracted by the stench of human urine, I rounded the second-floor landing and impatiently plodded upward behind my lumbering mentor. On the landing, indecipherable streams of Spanish invective blasted from an apartment door. I yelled above the shouts.

"Explain it to me again, Julius. It's about the vigorish, right? I mean, I take a $100 bet from Jack and a $100 bet from Jill, lay them off against each other and I make $10 right?"

He stopped midway up the steep stairs, splayed both hands on the banister, gasped for breath and said,

"That's the principle. But it doesn't work exactly like that. Don't worry. If we ever get up these fucken stairs, I'll show you. Just get the players. You can't lose."

* * *

Back at my local, The Tinker, the stool groaned next to me from Julius's weight.

"How many partners do you have?" he asked.

"Two," I said. "Carmine and Steve."

"You need pseudonyms. Never answer a phone in your office with your real name."

"No problem. Carmine's family owned the neighborhood delicatessen. In grammar school for lunch every day, he ate Capicola heroes, so we call him Gobbo."

"That'll work," he said, "What about this guy, Steve?"

"Sometimes we call him, 'Crazy Steve.'"

"No. No. That's too long. When you get busy, you want to write tickets fast. Just call him, Red," he said. "Grab a short moniker for yourself, and then go to a print shop."

"A print shop?" I asked.

"Yeah, you need betting slips. Get boxes of them because you'll need plenty. Nothing fancy, about four inches by four inches, but here's the important part."

I took a sip of my Heineken and leaned forward.

"Get them in carbon triplicate. Write each call you get on a different slip. I can't emphasize this enough. Never write more than one phone call on the same slip. You can write three or four wagers on one slip just as long as they're all on the same call," Julius said.

"Why triplicate?"

"After you take that session's action, separate the slips. Give a copy to each partner. Do the work, the figures, in separate places. This way you have three different checkpoints for the totals. If they match, you'll know the figures are correct."

He reached for his Tom Collins and lit a Newport.

"If you make a mistake, and you'll make plenty, if the error is in the player's favor, he won't say shit. But if you have a discrepancy in the house's favor, he'll bitch immediately. These guys are gonna lose anyway. You don't want them to think they're being clipped."

"So that's it? It seems simple enough," I said.

"Whatta ya think these fucken Guineas are brain surgeons? You don't have to be smart to make money, look at politicians."

My convoluted brain sees alimony and child support as math problems, not moral ones. This day looses the demon that I mistakenly believe will solve all my problems.

CHAPTER THIRTY-TWO

"Nice week, huh?"

I tossed our tally sheet to Red and Gobbo and said,

"Funny whenever we win, as soon as the last game ends Sunday night, I hustle to do the work. The rare times we lose, I can't bear to look at the totals until Monday morning."

We calculated figures weekly and had them ready before the Monday night football game. When the players called to bet that night, we'd read them their totals. Any discrepancies, we'd settle right then and there.

This way, when we collected on Wednesday or Thursday, there was no bullshit. If a player claimed he didn't make a losing bet, we'd play him the tape of his voice.

We followed Julius's instructions to the letter: triplicate, separate slips each call, distribute the slips, do our work individually and then compare.

Divide and conquer and conquer we did.

We wrote each player's totals on a master sheet divided by the days of the week. If one weekly figure didn't jive, we'd check it against the figures jotted down on the dailies.

"We won $66 large," I said.

Gobbo, ever the pragmatist, corrected me.

"We ain't won shit yet. We still have to collect it. Right now, we have $66,000 worth of slips."

Taking the action and doing the calculations was the easy part of this racket. Like drug users and alcoholics, gamblers slide a slippery slope. Bettors usually get in over their heads. The best insurance we had for getting paid was that gamblers would do almost anything to stay in action. If we shut players off, they'd lie, whine or beg to be reinstated.

To compare lines and ensure they got the best price on a game, savvy sports bettors had three or four bookies. That brought up another problem. If a player lost $2,000 to us, how many thousands had he lost to other bookies?

Collecting was always a problem. We'd worked out payment plans and listened to multiple bullshit stories every week. Gobbo and I would listen anyway. Red was less tolerant.

He'd demand his money, and it had better be on time.

"The dog ate your money? What? Fuck you. The dog ate your homework, not your money," he'd say. "I'll be at your restaurant Friday night. That's your busiest night, right? You better have my cash, or nobody's getting served. You understand? I'll kick your fucken ass throughout that whole fucken dining room."

Every now and then, we'd have a customer whom even Red couldn't intimidate. Then we'd need outside muscle. I had the muscle connection, Dominick, but I hated to call him. An inveterate psychotic, once unleashed, like the Kraken, God only knew what Dominick was capable of.

That week collections went well. We split close to $60 large.

* * *

Because we were rolling, Red said,

"Ever been to South America?"

"Yeah, I've been to Caracas, Venezuela," I said.

"Fuck that shit-shop. I'm talking Rio."

"Rio? Why Rio?"

"Whores, coke, beaches, what's not to like? We got $20,000 each. Let's have some fun."

"I like the idea that it's not mardi gras season in Rio. I hate bullshit crowds and standing in line at restaurants. Yeah, fuck it. When you want to go?" I asked.

"If we leave tomorrow morning, we can be back by the weekend."

"You want to go, Gobbo?" I asked.

"Fuck him." Red said. "He never wants to go anywhere."

"Fuck you, Steve," Gobbo said. "You guys ain't married, besides someone has to hold the fort till you slackers get back."

Without Gobbo, this trip could get a bit crazy. I'm nobody's prize, but Red makes me look like an altar boy. Funny, how lunatics attract. I guess if you're in a saloon slamming shots Monday morning at 5 a.m., the guy next to you probably doesn't drive a school bus.

* * *

We landed in Brazil without incident.

From the cab's backseat on the way to the hotel, Steve, never bashful, asked the cabby,

"Where can we get some cocaine and a prostitute?"

The driver was a bit startled.

I tried to smooth the edges.

"Excuse my friend. He's a bit impulsive, but in New York, cab drivers pretty much know where to get everything illicit."

He was a small-boned, chubby man with the indifferent, forgettable face of a grocery bagger, but he was surprisingly cooperative.

"You know you lucky you get Jorge," he said. "Other taxi man might tell police. Prostitute not bad in Brazil but cocaine very bad."

When Red opened with that line, I wanted to kill him but now I thought,

Shit, this guy's English is good. He seems reasonable, so maybe it was a good thing that Red cut to the chase.

From the cabs window, joyless buildings bordered both sides of the road. Filthy tenements with stained sacks of propped-up garbage leaned against their entrances. This was not the paradise that I envisioned when I boarded the plane. But poverty and slums blighted most large cities in South America, and as long as Jorge kept driving, I stayed optimistic.

After about a 20-mile ride, our knowledgeable friend pulled up in front of our hotel. I tipped him liberally and said,

"What can you do for us?"

"What time you want?" he said.

I plunked a Marlboro between my lips and said, "What ya think, Red? Two hours?

"Yeah, that's good."

We made the arrangements and barely reached the hotel lobby before a thunderstorm pounded the pavement.

* * *

The rain finally let up, and as promised, Jorge showed up right on schedule. The cordial driver shuttled us to a brownstone less than 15-minutes away. He handed me an aluminum-foil packet. I unwrapped a solid rock of cocaine the size of a large strawberry.

I flashed it at Red.

He started cackling.

I asked Jose the tariff.

He said, "We talk later. I come back three hours. One price for all."

The moon was up now. The air was heavy with the smell of night-blooming flowers and wet trees. The rain had settled deep into the soil and formed pools around the brownstone's brickwork.

We ascended the short flight of stairs and rang the bell. It seemed to be out of order. I rang again, waited a few minutes and finally punched the large brass knocker on the teak entrance.

I heard muffled footsteps, and then the door creaked open.

Her name was Carlota, and she was business, all business.

The Madam was lean and hard-edged, her manner curiously asexual. Carlotta's clear eyes were rich with purpose, and her hair was the same shiny-black as the satin blouse she wore. The sheen of her top accentuated her tight, black-toreador jeans and purple heels.

"Jorge told me to expect you gentleman," she said without a hint of any particular accent. "Come in and make yourselves comfortable."

The room where she herded us to the right was furnished as if an elderly dowager had decorated it. Way too many porcelain Hummel's crowded numerous tables and cherry-wood shelves.

Antique French-fabric chairs formed two single rows, as if the room were an auction house rather than a whorehouse. Directly across from the two rows was a yellow, antique leisure sofa. Behind the sofa sat the room's salient feature, a 15-foot marble bar. The slightly curved mirror behind it was longer again than the bar itself.

Carlotta offered drinks.

Red and I both had cognac.

She served large snifters with water chasers.

"Have you gentlemen eaten?"

When we said we had, the Madam said,

"Perhaps a little later after you work up an appetite, steak tartare or some stuffed shrimp, something light? Our chef is excellent. Miguel can prepare most anything."

As usual, Red cut to the chase.

"Listen honey, the town is filled with restaurants. We didn't come here to eat. How many girls are working?"

I blasted him a disgusted look, which didn't even slow him up.

"Are all the girls Brazilian, or do we get a variety?"

Carlotta graciously parried Red's rude remarks with a smile.

"Most of our girls are natives, but of the seven available this evening, one is South African and Stephanie is from the United States. If you're in a hurry, I'll have them come down."

When the girls arrived, there was no need for them to pirouette. They paraded in front of us while the enormous concave mirror behind them allowed us to see all angles.

The black girl was big-boned but cute with wide hips and large breasts. The other six girls were toned and athletic. The American, Stephanie, was California blonde.

I ruled out the Yank immediately. I wasn't in South America to sleep with a Californian. I settled on the smallest girl available, Rosa.

Her skin was unblemished and dark in the parlor's shade and her hair as coal-black as an Indian's. Her features and the luster in her eyes were hypnotic.

Rosa led me out past the front door and up the carpeted

flight of stairs to the bedrooms. Once inside her room, she slid a CD into the stereo.

She kissed my neck and eyes while she undressed me. After I was naked, she pushed me onto the bed and began to gyrate to Sade. She stripped slowly, rhythmically.

When down to her g-string and stockings, she turned 180 degrees, bent over, clasped her ankles and swayed her ass provocatively. She peeked behind her occasionally to smile seductively and lick her luscious lips in a hungry way.

She was beautiful, but better than that she was shameless, suggestive and sultry. I was a human volcano, and she hadn't even touched me yet.

* * *

After our bit of mischief, Rosa asked in broken English if I would like to spend more time with her or see one of the other girls. She assured me to ignore her feelings. If I preferred variety, she wouldn't be offended. She said my satisfaction was all that interested her.

I decided to go back downstairs and was pleasantly surprised to find Red chomping on a Porterhouse Steak. I told the madam I'd like one as well. We both sat in blue silk robes and compared notes.

"Mine was amazing," I told Red.

"Mine too," Red said. "This time, I might take the blonde."

"Not me, I'm staying native."

After beef and cigars, we picked two other gals and repeated our performances.

We stayed longer than the three hours allotted us by Jorge, and when we prepared to leave, our clothes were waiting. Covered in dry cleaner's plastic, they hung neatly on a hook by the parlor door.

We both grinned and asked Carlotta how much?

The Madam said, "You'll settle up with your taxi driver."

Now I was apprehensive.

On the drive back to the hotel, Jorge asked, "How did you like the cocaine? Satisfactory?"

Both Red and I signaled thumbs up to applaud his efforts.

"For two cab rides, the cocaine, dinner and the women," Jorge asked emotionlessly, "Does $80 American each sound fair?"

CHAPTER THIRTY-THREE

Our divorce final, Lorraine had moved to Oregon with my son.

On weeknights, besides my thriving bookmaking business, I was tending bar at P.O.E.T.S., and it was killing me. But to be fair to Mike, I had to pour myself into the business.

Because I also managed my joint on weekends, I was there seven nights a week. Although the abundance of women helped ease the long hours, I was working like an illegal, and I missed my son, Liam.

Despite the hours, child support, alimony, my lifestyle and gambling excesses ensured I stayed broke.

One night in August, about 7:30 p.m., too early for any action, three stragglers from the dayshift sipped cocktails at my 60-foot bar.

A heavyset guy came in, sat in the middle of the bar and ordered a martini. I fed him his gin and went about the business of getting ready for the night rush. As I filled the juices and poured ice on the bottled beer, I glanced out the front window and noticed two guys in a double-parked car.

No big deal, except Northern Boulevard was a major Queens' thoroughfare and not a place one normally would double-park. But what really added to my angst was that right now all of New York was paranoid about "Son of Sam."

The crazed 44-magnum killer had shot almost a dozen victims in the last six months.

Less than a week ago, Sam had murdered Stacey Moskowitz. She had been parked outside the discothèque, Elephas, which was only a mile from my nightclub and also on Northern Boulevard.

Why would anyone double-park on Northern?

I checked to make sure I had plenty of change for the anticipated rush and then restocked the beer cooler with two cases of Molson Ale and three cases of Budweiser.

When I finished, the car still hadn't budged.

From the passenger seat, a guy got out and headed for my bar's front door. Because the car remained running with the other guy still behind the wheel, I thought,

Fuck, a hold-up.

The guy floated in, grabbed a stool just inside the door and asked for a draught. I was already memorizing his appearance, so I could describe him later to detectives. He wore a light-tan zipper-jacket with a button down striped shirt. Other than a large, conspicuous birthmark that stained the left side of his face, he looked like a teacher.

As I reluctantly slid him his beer, I glanced out the window and saw his partner heading for my front door too, but their car's engine purred away.

Fuck, now I know it's a hold-up.

I grabbed another coaster and tossed it beside his accomplice's, the guy with the tan jacket and the birthmark.

But when the second guy blew through the door, he ignored his friend and headed to the opposite side of the bar. He sat at a stool 60-feet away.

My heart sank.

I'm fucked.

I quickly surveyed the bar, no likely heroes, thank God. Resigned, I awaited the inevitable.

I didn't wait long.

The birth-marked guy pulled a handgun the size of a howitzer and yelled,

"Don't anyone move. Relax and everything will be fine."

Not relaxed but hardly stupid, I wouldn't play the fool for less than a $1,000 score. I froze and reached for the rafters.

At the opposite end of the bar, his partner stood too, but

instead of a gun, his hand flashed an open wallet. Merciful God, a gold shield leapt from the leather.

"Police," he said, "Everyone stay calm."

Both charged the center of the bar. The two detectives sandwiched my heavyset martini drinker. They frisked him and hauled him into the kitchen.

I seized the Jameson's bottle and poured four fingers. The whiskey found its mark and mustered my moxie, so I charged the back room to confront the detectives.

"Why didn't you flash your badge when I gave you your beer? Jesus, you guys scared me half to death."

The birth-marked detective said emotionlessly,

"We've got a certain procedure. We've followed this guy for three hours and need to ask him a few questions. Get your ass back behind the bar, and let us do our job."

I returned to both the cash register and the bottle of Jameson's muttering,

"Asshole cops think they own the world."

The few lingerers I had in the bar had fled.

Unreal, open two hours and I hadn't rung up shit. To make matters worse, now it was pouring rain. Peering through the plate-glass window, I could barely see the detective's purring car.

Sheets of water pounded the panes of glass. I peeked out at the deluge and thought,

This is going to be some crummy night. I won't make a buck tonight.

I retreated to the solace of the Irish whiskey.

Three drinks later, the two cops finished their questioning. They re-entered the bar area and apologized,

"Just doing our jobs. He fit the description of Son of Sam, but he checks out okay."

They started to walk out the door while the heavyweight suspect returned to his now watered down Martini.

I said, "Wait a minute. You're not leaving this guy alone here with me, are ya?"

The smaller detective, the guy without the birthmark said,

"Yeah, we got nothing on him. We can't hold him. Have a good night."

Have a good night?

Was he kidding? I was half shit-faced. I didn't have dollar one in the register, and it was 9 p.m. I wiped down the glasses and tried to decide how I would handle this guy. Should I bully him or treat him with kid gloves?

One way or another, he had to go.

The minutes crawled.

Fuck this.

Maybe I should just close and go finish my load. Between the slow start, the rain, and the fright pervading Queens over this crazy bastard that's shooting everybody, I won't break any register records tonight anyway.

My silent customer continued to sip his warm, diluted martini. I didn't say shit to him. Maybe he'd get the message and get the fuck out of here.

After an eternity of silence, he glanced out the window, pondered the rain a moment, looked at me though a squinted left eye and uttered one bone-chilling sentence,

"Nice night for a murder."

"What? What did you say? What the fuck did you say?"

I threw what was left of his martini down the sink and screamed,

"Take it somewhere else you motherfucker, you son-of-a-bitch bastard, you rotten prick."

I reached below the bar and grabbed the one-foot section of metal pipe that I had wrapped with electric tape and slammed it hard on the bar.

"Get the fuck out of here, now. We're closed for the night."

He narrowed his eyes and stared at me for what seemed a month. Then he stood, pointed his index finger at me menacingly and mercifully walked out into the rain.

I shifted into high gear.

I locked the doors, killed the lights and counted the cash. I trembled like I had Parkinson's.

Nice night for a murder?

That was the exact same sentence that the other screwball had said to me years ago, when I had hitchhiked in Charleston.

Who was that guy? Were he and the other guy in South Carolina nuts? What was the link here?

Two different states, more than a decade apart, how was this possible? Was this God's work or the devil's? I was becoming a believer.

The cops frisked that crazy son-of-a-bitch, so I knew he wasn't armed. But what if he had a piece stashed? What if he came back to teach me humility with that huge 44-caliber cannon?

I had to get the fuck out of here fast and get a drink. And I knew just the place.

Around the corner from Elephas, where the 44-caliber-killer had struck last, was Bell Boulevard. Because of the abundance of saloons in its five-block radius, every serious drinker in Queens called this strip "Booze Boulevard." I knew five bartenders who worked on Bell, and two of them were like my brothers.

* * *

"Kevin, give everybody a drink. Give me a bottle of Heineken, a double shot of Jameson's on the rocks, and a $200 marker out of the register."

This had started my night on the town. When I stopped at "Black Bart's" to see Buffalo, I grabbed another $200. That should be enough for the night. I was in the business, so every bar that I drank in, I had to "set the table."

"Bouncing" from bar to bar paid everlasting, enormous benefits.

Everybody won. I made some noise. The bartender had a better night, and on his night off, he owed me a stop. Besides new customers, bouncing served as good chum for whatever women might feed in those waters that evening.

I was after girls who bit on cash, and I threw around plenty of bait. Later that night after uncountable cocktails, I found myself two blocks from Bell Boulevard in a parked car embracing a lipstick-smeared enthusiast.

One thing led to another. The inevitable took place. As she

put her head in my lap, I laid back. But despite the anesthetizing effect of the alcohol, I shivered with sudden foreboding. My head periscoped up involuntarily and looked 360 degrees for anyone clutching a paper bag that might have a camouflaged pistol in his hand.

Earlier in the night, I was terrified of Son of Sam. But now with my bellyful of whiskey, my prick was giving the orders. An impatient prisoner, he would have gladly send me skipping across a minefield for a few minutes parole from the confines of my zipper.

So, here, only two-short blocks from Elephas during the "Summer of Sam," I "was taking a shot."

But not from the barrel of a 44-magnum—thank God, not tonight.

CHAPTER THIRTY-FOUR

Here was how our bookmaking operation out-slicked the local gendarmes.

As Super Bowl uneasiness approached, Gobbo decided to rent the apartment directly across the hall. We moved our "furniture" there and left only one phone on the empty apartment's linoleum floor. We call-forwarded that phone across the hall to four-cell phones.

That Super-Sunday, San Francisco played Denver. We played the cops.

The action poured in.

Two hours before game time, a loud pounding like an oil drill drowned out our phones. Bam, bam, bam rang through the hall. Red sprang to our new location's door. He looked through the peephole, turned and held an index finger to his lips. Gobbo and I killed all the cell phones.

Through the door's round glass insert, Red watched and whispered updates. The twin locks across the hall finally burst and six cops exploded into the empty apartment. Then the expletives began. The "shits," "bastards" and "motherfuckers" were collectively louder than the break-in. I gaped at Gobbo the way a wide-eyed cow looks at a meadow.

We had won our Super Bowl two hours before kick-off, and Red and I knew Gobbo was our MVP. To celebrate, we hoisted a trophy bottle of Remy Martin and drained it in short order.

Denver lost the 1990 Super Bowl 55 to 10.

* * *

"Red, are you shitting me? Vegas . . . four days . . . all

expenses paid for the N.C.A.A. Championship? Yeah, I'm definitely in."

Red, my bookmaking partner, made me look conservative. For him, nothing was excessive.

Anytime Red bothered to lift a phone, he'd bet $10,000. He gambled on everything—football, hoops, horses, hockey, baseball, slots—everything.

Red bet with big-time Brooklyn bookie, Dennis.

Because Dennis was a gambler too, he loved Vegas almost as much as Vegas loved him. Dennis took action all year and then "vacationed" by gambling.

Incredible?

Think about it.

Junkies don't take vacations from heroin. Alcoholics don't vacation in the Caribbean, Key West or New Orleans so they can dry out.

When Dennis threw craps, he covered every number with $5,000 and then backed-up his initial bets with another $5,000 by taking the "free odds."

Counting his bets on the pass line, that's $70,000, a roll.

On his way to the men's room, he'd nonchalantly plunk six stacks of five $100 checks on six random numbers at the roulette wheel. That's $3,000 he'd bet on his way to piss.

During a four-day holiday, Dennis would donate dumpsters of dollars to casinos. To reciprocate, hotels treated Dennis magically.

Red's gambling compulsion helped finance Dennis's, so Dennis told Red,

"Come to Vegas with me. Bring anyone you want. Everything is on the house. Just sign my name."

* * *

Red and I were partners and great friends, but no way could I compete with his appetite for drugs, women or gambling.

Red needed a babysitter. He thought that I was right for the job.

He'd unintentionally end up babysitting me instead.

* * *

Tomorrow was the day we were to leave for Vegas. I packed my bag and set the alarm for 6 a.m. I glanced out my three-bedroom ranch house's picture window.

Long wooden decks fingered the water from the sliding glass doors of the high priced suburban homes that surrounded the lake. As I watched the last vestige of sunlight disappear over the trees, I decided that there was no sense in sitting home.

I'll grab something to eat and have a few beers. I'll be home by 10 p.m.

* * *

At 5 a.m., I passed out paralyzed on my couch.

Less than an hour later, the alarm rang. I awoke still stewed, fully dressed and grabbed my bag for Vegas.

The cabdriver dropped me at Stewart Airport and lugged me into the terminal where Red awaited.

"Where the hell you been, man? I was worried about you. I didn't think you were going to make it."

He saw the disheveled clothes, the blood-red eyes and the vacuous smile pasted on my ashen face.

"Oh Christ, it's only 6:30 a.m. and you're shit-faced. How did you get plastered so fast?"

"I'm still drunk from last night," I said dismissively. "I need a screwdriver, or a bloody Mary, or something. I'm fucken dying."

We boarded the plane and sat in the last two seats on the right aisle.

I gasped to the stewardess, "How soon can I get a drink?"

She laughed, "Shortly after we're airborne, we'll start cocktail service."

After we lifted off, true to her word, she started to haul Red and me vodkas and orange juice. We slammed screwdrivers like we were flying to the guillotine. The sugar from the booze resurrected me.

I shifted to full party mode. I laughed loud and hard. Once that started, of course, I couldn't catch my breath. Depending on the amount of whiskey poured, and the time of day, my laugh was either infectious or annoying.

Once a sober woman heard me say that and said, "When does it start becoming infectious?"

Not today apparently. My air intake sounded like a hyena.

After two hours of this, some senior citizens rotated 180 degrees in their seats and nailed me with intense, nasty stares.

Belligerently drunk, I leaned forward and sent them a Bronx cheer,

"Come on, loosen up you old goats. You're on your way to Vegas for Chrissake."

I was so obnoxious even Red was embarrassed.

My grating caw infuriated everyone, not only those at the rear of the plane but travelers up front as well. To avoid the outraged stares, Red strolled the few steps to the aircraft's tail to chat up the two stewardesses who were working the service station.

He bullshitted the stews, and said that he and I were heading to Vegas to bet $200,000 on the championship basketball game. My burly pal concocted a charming fairytale about how his attaché case was stuffed with "mob" money.

In '92, airlines weren't yet politically correct. Both of the knocked-out stewardesses bit on Red's bait.

Red and I pounded more screwdrivers. When one fed-up passenger from the front had finally had enough, a deep foghorn voice startled us.

"Are you the two guys making all the noise back here?"

I peered through a boozy haze. One eye focused at what appeared to be a hairy, dungaree-clad cement truck.

Out of the corner of my mouth, I whispered to Red,

"We're gonna have a beef."

As my vision cleared, I grasped the situation's worrisome reality.

Despite the formidable Red, this guy had us outnumbered. He was the whole sorry package—motorcycle boots, spiked leather wristbands, chains, a 300-pound Hell's Angel dispatched by the devil himself.

Then a surprise,

"You motherfuckers seem like fun. I like that. Hold out

your hand hyena man. Here's my contribution."

He extended his hand and dropped in mine a promising montage of red, blue, and yellow pills.

Relieved to be in one piece, I said, "Thanks man. You're a sport."

Then I chased the handful of tablets down with a generous belt from my screwdriver.

* * *

Where was I? What happened?

I glanced at the ceiling fan and then at the unfamiliar nightstand where four crumpled-up dollar bills had been flung. The bedside digital-clock read 9:30 p.m.

Oh shit the basketball game.

I hacked and clutched my throat. My tongue flopped dryly between my lips.

I needed a drink.

I hit the shower and headed for the lobby. When the elevator doors slid open, I followed the shouts coming from the packed lounge. The circular bar surrounded four TV sets all tuned to the N.C.A.A. Championship Game.

My eyes waded through clouds of tobacco smoke and spotted Red roaring at one TV. The two stewardesses from our flight sat by his sides.

I squeezed next to the blonde.

"What the hell happened?" I asked.

"Oh my God. We thought you'd get us fired," the blonde said, "No one could wake you up. We took you off the plane in a wheelchair."

"Mother of God, a wheel chair? Then why are you two here?"

"Before you passed out, you were loads of fun."

* * *

Halftime rolled around and Mike Krzyzewski's Blue Devils were crushing Michigan, so I finally grabbed Red's attention.

"Fill me in later on how you got me up to the hotel room. Meanwhile, how does this expense account thing work?"

He said, "Just eat or drink anything you want in this hotel, then sign Dennis's name and room number."

"Cool." I gulped the remains of my beer. "Hey girls, you want to have a bite to eat?"

Three hours later, we finished our steaks, wine, champagne, and snifters of Courvoisier V.S.O.P. The check came to $1400.

* * *

After our feast, the girls and I entered the hotel's casino. Three security guards held a drunken, angry Red at the wrong end of their revolvers. I froze at the entrance, spun and said,

"Come on girls. This is no place for us. Let me show you my hotel suite."

* * *

I was swimming on the high tide of others' misfortune, but every wave eventually crashes ashore. The one I rode was long overdue.

CHAPTER THIRTY- FIVE

"Yeah, Tony for Red, here's your repeat. On this call, you've got Dallas minus four, 100 times. Good luck."

I charted the $500 bet and saw we needed the Giants for $30,000. As soon as I cradled the phone, I lifted it again. The voice surprised me. Brian sounded urgent, and the Jolly Tinker's bartender didn't bet.

"Yeah, it's me, Brian. What's up?"

His reply pierced my heart.

"Where? What hospital? How long ago? Oh my God, thanks."

Phone forgotten, I grabbed my jacket and through the rage that roared in me told Gobbo and Red,

"I gotta go to Union Hospital. My mother has been mugged."

* * *

I arrived at the emergency room to find Mom unconscious on a gurney with her teeth shattered, a deep gash on her skull and her clothes speckled with dry blood.

The surgeon said,

"Your mother's in a coma. She's lost a lot of blood. X-rays show that her swollen brain is pushing against her cranium. The safest course of action is to operate now and use steroids later to reduce the swelling."

* * *

In the waiting room, my thoughts were with my mom, but our eyes have no conscience and will always seek something rather than nothing.

I scolded myself when my eyes drifted to the Giant game on TV.

Fuck the game. Your mother is in surgery.
But my eyes kept returning to the T.V. before they stuck.

* * *

Minutes before halftime, the emergency doors flung open, and two attendants in blue scrubs and surgical masks pushed Mom to the recovery room. I followed the gurney.

The recovery room nurse told me that all had gone well and to wait for the doctor's briefing.

I stood over my mother's body and studied her battered head and mouth, and I thought about what a selfless woman she was. The heat rose from my toes, cooked through my chest, and hit my brain with a phosphorous flame of fire and fury.

What kind of an animal would do this to a 75-year-old woman? If you're desperate, steal her purse. But hit her across the head and face with a pipe, and then leave her in a pool of her own blood?

The doctor briefed me, and I settled into a recovery room chair to monitor my mom. Every few minutes, the male nurse would leave the room and disappear through the double-doors at the other end of the hallway to check the televised Giants' game.

My mom hadn't stirred.

Every time the nurse returned, I shamefully asked about any change in score. As the Giants' game winded down, he was leaving more often. Soon, he was gone more often than not.

I thought,

Our office needs this game bad. Mom's unconscious. What harm would a quick trip down the hall do?

But then Mom suddenly moaned. She lifted her head an inch, vomited and began to choke.

With the nurse gone, I dashed over. I lifted her head, tilted her face and used my index finger to scoop out her vomit.

She moaned relief and drifted back to unconsciousness.

Holy shit, if I had went to watch the end of the game, Mom would've choked.

Here, my own mother lay dying, and I'm thinking of checking scores. When I told Tony for Red congratulations about his daughter's birth, I mocked Tony's, "Fuck that, whatta ya got on Dallas" response.

Shit, I'm as bad as Tony. I need help.

When the nurse came back, I read him the riot act, yet I knew that had our situations had been reversed, I would have had been down the hallway as well. The patient in the recovery room, in this case my mother, would have died.

* * *

The second day of her coma, two detectives showed up to question her. One of them had gone to my grammar school. Not exactly a friend, but we had a history. Pat Walsh had been the tallest guy in the class and the best basketball player on St. Philip's team.

I filled Pat in on the what, where and when.

He exchanged a knowing downward glance at his husky partner.

"You don't seem surprised," I said.

"For the last three months, there has been a pattern of attacks in the neighborhood, always Sunday and always senior citizens." Pat said.

"Do you have any leads?"

"Just suspicions, nothing we can prove."

"Has this bastard killed anyone?" I asked.

"No, but last month, a priest was walloped at the top of the metal rectory steps and fell the length of them. We didn't think he'd make it."

My arteries pulsed with pure malice.

I looked past Pat at the numerous IV's hooked up to the multiple wheelchairs down a long hallway of misery, and said,

"I'd love to get my hands on that fucken prick."

"I don't blame you," Pat said. "Just pray your mother comes out of her coma. We'll be back. When she's awake, maybe she can identify the perp."

* * *

Pat returned the next day lugging a large album of mug shots. Disappointed to learn that my mother was still unconscious, he sat and chatted.

"I hate how these drug addicts pray on the helpless and elderly still left in the neighborhood," Pat said. "I remember when you and I grew up. You could leave your door wide open. No one would bother you."

"I wouldn't trade my Bronx childhood experiences for a million bucks." I said.

Pat stood, shook hands with me and shrugged,

"We're not supposed to give you any information about our investigation. But here's the guy we're focused on."

He sat back down, turned the huge volume to the middle and pointed at a picture.

"This kid is a city fireman's son. He lives in Peekskill. He's got a crack habit and goes on weekend benders. We suspect that by Sunday he's broke and needs money for the train ride home."

I chiseled the name Bobby Hanratty into my brain. I thanked Pat for his time, took his card and assured him I'd call him as soon as my mother was conscious.

Meanwhile, I plotted . . .

How many Hanrattys can live in Peekskill? I'll get this parasite.

* * *

By nightfall, I had an address and a plan.

It was pouring rain and a perfect night for what I had in mind. I called Dom and filled him in. He offered his services for free.

"No. I want you with me because I need a wheelman, but this prick is mine. He'll get exactly what he did to my mother in spades. I'll make this asshole think twice before he hits another defenseless old woman."

Within the hour, we were on the road to Peekskill.

The rain splattered Dom's windshield. He squinted through the wipers and said,

"You should let me handle this. I'll tune his ass up right."

"I appreciate it, man, but I gotta do this. I just hope it happens tonight. I figure we'll park outside his house and hope to catch him coming home. I brought sandwiches and a flask of coffee. It could be a long wait. If not tonight, then we get him tomorrow morning. He has to leave his house sometime. One way or another, he's going down."

I reached underneath my long London Fog raincoat, gripped the two-foot length of metal pipe that I had wrapped with electrical tape and thought,

What goes around comes around motherfucker.

* * *

Dom parked within 50 feet of Hanratty's front door. Between sips of coffee, bites of sandwiches and banal conversation, I continually checked the side vent mirror. Butterflies played havoc with my digestion. Hours inched by. The rain stopped.

Headlights appeared at the end of the street. A car slid into the only space available and a medium built man, about 25, got out. He wore jeans, a hooded blue sweatshirt and a canvas jacket with a navy watch cap.

As he headed to his house, I left the car and walked toward him. I had turned up the collar on my Macintosh, and I had a Mets' cap pulled down low on my head. Beneath the raincoat, I had one hand firmly on the pipe. As I passed the creep, my eyes raked his face. I nodded silently.

With Hanratty's identity confirmed, I turned around. My heart pulsed adrenalin. I skipped two short steps and walloped the back of his head with an energy-charged swing of the pipe. His knees buckled. A moment later, the street collided with his jaw.

Pumped full of both animosity and insanity, I rolled the limp body over in the gutter and crashed the pipe murderously down onto his mouth. As his jaw whipped sideways, I heard his upper teeth shatter at the gums. His blood and spittle seeped into a rain puddle.

I clutched my weapon and sprinted the few steps to Dom's double-parked car.

Shaking but smug, I told Dom,

"I got that motherfucker good. Drive over the Tap Pan Zee Bridge; I want to lose this pipe."

All the way home, I replayed my revenge.

I wonder if I killed him?

I convinced myself that even if I did, he deserved it. In this case, vigilante justice trumped the courts and the law.

* * *

After four more days of danger, Mom awoke. The steroids had reduced the brain swelling, and she was allowed to drink liquids. Days later, she could talk.

When Mom was strong enough, Pat returned with his mug shot portfolio and a few questions.

"Describe what happened," Pat said.

"I had just come back from mass. A man about 25 stood outside the vestibule," Mom said. "He was well-groomed and nicely dressed, so when he stepped into the hallway behind me, I took no notice of him."

She reached for a cup of water from the nightstand next to her canted hospital bed. I grabbed it for her and held it to her mouth. She took a few sips.

"He entered the elevator with me, and that's all I remember."

Pat said, "Could you identify him from a photograph?"

Mom said, "Absolutely."

She began paging the tome full of mug shots. Halfway through the book, Hanratty's photograph leapt from a rogue's gallery of recidivists. She casually skipped over him. I stopped her.

"Mom, what about this guy here?" I said and pointed to Hanratty.

She said, "No, that's definitely not him."

"Mom, are you sure?"

"Connor, don't question me. That's not him at all. No way."

I tried to sooth my conscience with a banal aphorism.

He wasn't in that book because he was Mother Theresa. I did someone a favor.

But deep inside, I felt like a character out of Walter Clark's novel, "The Ox Bow Incident."

I had hung an innocent man.

CHAPTER THIRTY-SIX

After Mom's mugging, it was time to move her out of the Bronx. I bought her a small two-bedroom condo in Florida. That year was the best football season we had ever had, so for a change, money wasn't a problem. Bookmaking was the best move I had ever made. I paid alimony and child support with my share of just one day's take.

I partied and traveled the world. There were sailing and diving trips to the Caribbean and the Pacific along with museums, pubs and galleries throughout Europe and Ireland.

Life was better than good, but a wise man once said that it was only a short distance from a halo to a noose. I was due for a fall, and the descent started the day I made a routine phone call to my mom.

"What's that in the background, Mom, 'Here Comes the Sun?' You're listening to the Beatles? Whatta ya getting hip in your old age?"

Her answer caused me to pause.

"Hip? Hip, me ass. If these are the golden years, they can have them." She laughed and then said, "Whatever happened to them anyway, the Beatles?"

"Two of them are dead," I said academically.

"Two dead? Are they? What a shame, just when they were starting to get famous."

I held the receiver in my hand and stared at it.

This didn't sound good. I had better take a trip to Florida.

* * *

After a full week of diagnosis and tests, we found out Mom

had Althzheimer's. I stayed with her a month and realized that her living alone had come to an end, so I found a high-end assisted-living facility in Florida and moved her in. I had businesses to run in N.Y., but getting Mom in a senior citizen home didn't exonerate me of Irish guilt.

On the contrary, it exacerbated it.

* * *

Every time I needed something, Mom was there.

The Florida sun, yellow and hot, climbed my windshield and exploded into a flour white sky. I raised the car windows and switched on the air conditioner. Traffic moved smoother now, the road ahead quiet.

I accelerated, hit the cruise control and swerved into the middle lane. My thoughts raced along with my car.

When it came to Timmy and me, Mom couldn't say no. She'd deny herself, but she would always find a way.

Between my flight and the drive, I'd been on the go six hours. I was up half the night drinking, so Sunday morning greeted another hangover.

Will she know me when I get there? How much has she deteriorated since my last visit?

Before Mom was diagnosed, I knew a little about Alzheimer's, but I didn't know you could die from it. Mom had reached the point now that she didn't even know if my last visit was yesterday or last month. If the disease frightened me, imagine how scared she must be?

When I visited Mom last month, I watched an emaciated old woman rant before a mirror about her own reflection. The poor thing screamed at the mirror for five minutes.

"Stop following me," she said. "I told you to leave me alone."

It scared the shit out of me.

I knew that in the advanced stages of the disease, victims didn't recognize their loved ones.

I expected that.

But for that poor old lady not to recognize herself in the mirror . . .

Please God, if you're really up there, don't let that be my mom's fate.

I remembered the doctor's reply when I asked,

"Doc, I don't get it? How is this disease fatal?"

"The ramifications of Alzheimer's make it fatal, Mr. Kelly. Your mother's appetite will diminish. She'll gradually forget how to chew her food and starve to death."

Starve to death? Good Christ, the doctor recited that sentence like he was talking about getting his car washed.

My mother would starve to death after all her prayers, all her hard work, and all her sacrifices?

Then I got selfish. All drunks are selfish.

If she needs me and I'm wasted how will I live with myself?

Then I had the inevitable alcoholic conversation with myself, followed by self-pity. Where would we alcoholics be without self-pity?

I've turned into a more benign version of my father. A person whom as a child, I vowed I'd never be. That's it. The buck stops here. I've got to quit drinking.

Maybe A.A.?

Nah, I've tried that route. I can't get past that higher power nonsense.

But I really have to get my drinking under control. I've said this before, but this time I mean it. I've tried all the home remedies—maybe I'll just drink weekends, maybe just drink beer, maybe just wine with dinner. All my home cures had predictable outcomes.

God please give me the strength to not let my mother down.

* * *

A few miles later, clouds formed and the sky darkened followed by lightning and thunder. It poured the way only a Florida storm could.

My wipers couldn't shovel the blinding, pounding sheets of water from my windshield fast enough. I pulled into the right hand lane and slowed to a crawl.

No good, I still couldn't see, so when I spotted an exit sign, I aimed for it.

As I anchored at the bottom of the off-ramp, the Ford Focus streamed a wake, and a swollen pool flooded the curb. At the stoplight, I looked for a place to outlast the deluge. Directly in front of me like a great gothic beacon shown St. Jude's Church. I remembered a line from the "Untouchables," where Andy Garcia talked about St. Jude being the Patron Saint of Lost Causes.

If ever there was a lost cause . . . and what the hell, it's Sunday.

As I hurdled up the church steps, the raindrops punished the puddles beneath my feet.

Five people sat waiting between masses. I eased quietly into a back pew, looked down at the scarred, battered wood and saw a St. Jude prayer pamphlet.

The prayer was simple enough. The usual rhetoric followed by an Our Father and a Hail Mary. No stranger to Catholicism, I had seen it all before, but the last sentence struck me as a bit unusual, almost like spiritual instructions.

"Say this prayer seven times every day for a month. Whatever you pray for will be answered."

Being Irish, I was naturally superstitious. I didn't believe in banshees or leprechauns, but I have had my moments. I was already in church, and it was Sunday. What the hell, it was raining outside anyway. The prayer would do me no harm.

Already on my knees, I recited the prayer dutifully seven times and finished with,

"Heavenly Father I pray that I will be there for my Mom when the end comes. I pray I don't let her down. Help me to quit what I can't quit on my own."

I said that prayer without fail for a month.

* * *

Almost a decade now since I stumbled upon that flyer. To this day, I say that prayer faithfully, and except for one near-fatal encounter with human frailty, I pray sober.

* * *

Before I had left the house, I had checked my pockets for chocolate. I remember that, and just about everything else, about that Saturday night because it was special.

We drunks eat plenty of sweets. Alcohol contains massive amounts of sugar. Once we stop drinking, our body screams for what we deprive it of. In A.A. meetings, attendees gorge on cookies or chomp chocolates. Some chase both with cans of cola, anything to avoid tumbling back into an alcohol abyss.

So before I collected in the bars, I always checked my pockets. Without chocolate, I feared relapse.

The long evening ahead would start as usual at the Tinker. I had to pick up two envelopes, leave a few messages, and get the local scuttlebutt.

It was easy to collect money with the network of pubs that I had scattered around New York City. I knew bartenders in three boroughs. On whatever day I designated, customers could drop off their losses anytime between 10 a.m. and 4 a.m.

Both day and night bartenders knew that when I showed up, I'd buy a round and throw $20 in their tip cup and everybody would be happy.

Before I pulled open the Tinker's heavy metal door, I glanced west up the hill that led to the Grand Concourse. With only a glimmer left, the day's red sun dabbed orange-smudges across the tenement roofs.

Once inside, I adjusted my eyes to the saloon's darkness. The face behind the bar stole the air from my lungs and reddened my cheeks.

Colleen was working the stick.

As I approached the mahogany, my mouth went dry the way it used to when I was hungover. Colleen dashed to gracefully flip a coaster in front of me. She had a huge grin and her beautiful emerald eyes glittered.

"Where have you been, stranger? Every time you leave this place, I feel like a light has gone out. You haven't been here in ages. I missed you."

I devoured the compliment, unwrapped a Chunky, popped it into my mouth and said,

"I'd be here more often if I knew your schedule."

Then, because Colleen was more than a score younger than me, I followed the flattery with a deprecating remark.

"I'm young enough to want to believe that bullshit about missing me, beautiful, but I'm too old to really believe it."

"No. I meant it," she said. "Whenever you're around, everyone has a smile on their face."

I was thrilled. She was talking about my mania's favorite subject, me.

"Just give me a club soda with lime, gorgeous."

She swayed to the other end of the bar for a lime. My mania followed.

Maybe I should ask her out? I'm divorced now and sober. She's younger than me, but she's stunning and bright as hell. Why not? All she can say is no.

"What's with the club soda?" she asked.

"I quit drinking a couple of months ago." After a sip, I said, "Never mind about me. How have you been?"

The bar had only a few customers, so Colleen and I had a chance to talk.

In short order, she reminded me that her taut body, striking smile and flashing green eyes were merely a vestibule for a scholar's mind. The more she talked, the more I was captivated. She dismissed all things mundane and didn't concern herself with things that other women usually talked about. She loved books, detested small talk, and used her wit like a spear. She loved to break balls, and she did it mercilessly. I loved it.

A few hours wouldn't screw up my schedule. I decided to go for it, so I asked her to dinner and specified no strings.

"Let's just share a meal and enjoy each other's company."

When she agreed, I felt like I hit Lotto.

* * *

Three hours later, Colleen was drinking white wine with me and enjoying linguini and clam sauce. I was still trying to take her measure. She nonchalantly told me that she played Irish fiddle, had two master's degrees, and a recent scholarship offer for a doctorate from the University of Florida.

I filled her in on my lifestyle honestly and without embellishment.

She seemed as mesmerized by my shortcomings as I was by

her accomplishments. For the life of me, I couldn't figure out why this exquisite, intelligent woman, two decades my junior had consented to have dinner with me to begin with. And the more she learned about me, the more astonished I became.

She said, "You're a recently divorced, struggling alcoholic with a gambling problem, yet you think that everything in your life is fine? Listen to yourself. You're a nut."

We both exploded with laughter.

That night she accompanied me on my collections. At every bar I bought a round, picked up a few envelopes, left $20 and moved on.

"You've got the greatest job I've ever seen," she marveled. "You go from bar to bar picking up envelopes full of money."

In the few hours that we borough-hopped, this gift from God scuttled many of my old misconceptions. In the months that followed, she made it her mission to kick over the prejudices that cluttered my insular mind. For my clarity and self-esteem, she was better than any drug that I had ever taken.

Falling in love with Colleen became easier than anything I had ever done before or since.

CHAPTER THIRTY-SEVEN

When deadbeats "laid down," our muscle changed their minds.

Our office had a 50/50 deal with Dominick. We'd sell him bad debt. How he collected it was his business. He made a buck, and people learned they couldn't rob our office.

Those who knew Dom approached him with caution, not fear but caution. The way you'd walk past a chained-up guard dog or walk around a ladder.

Our office seldom threatened anybody. We were civilians, not wise guys. But Dom had always had a casual approach to violence. Even when I had met him as a child in the first grade, I had sensed he had a screw loose.

Our first "lay downs" were small. We ate the losses or settled things ourselves. But as the office grew so did the problems. One day Red came up with Karl, a new player.

"Karl bets everything, hockey, baskets, football," said Red. "You name it. Karl sends it in."

Established now, we had been in action five years and had over 300 players. We welcomed high rollers. We kept our line sharp and updated frequently. It wasn't easy to catch us napping.

"Cool. Tell Karl we'll take anything up to $25,000 a game," I said.

The first week, Karl beat us for $132,000. We paid him, no problem.

The second week, Karl beat us for $118,000. We paid him, no problem.

The third week, Karl lost $240,000. Came collection day, Karl said, "Go fuck yourself."

Big problem.

If someone lost and cried poverty, it was understandable. If someone got in over his head, nobody wanted to get tough. We just wanted our money.

We didn't want to lose a customer, so we'd work out installments, no juice, just a payment plan.

Gambling was an addiction.

Things happened.

It was part of the business.

But Karl was a thief. He beat us for $250,000 in two weeks. Now Karl had lost $240,000, and he wasn't even bothering to make an excuse.

By telling us to shag off, in effect, Karl was saying that we were not connected. We were nobody. He wasn't paying.

First thing we had to find out was whether or not Karl was a gangster. If he was a made guy, we were screwed. Next we needed to know if he was crazy, and if he was crazy, how crazy?

My partners and I didn't do crazy. That was Dom's domain. If Karl was a head case, or a tough guy, we had to hope he wasn't as crazy as Dominick.

That put the odds back in our favor.

* * *

I had first introduced Dom to my partners two years ago.

As we drove across the main thoroughfare of the Bronx in Gobbo's Honda Prelude, he made small talk.

"Yeah, you see that tree over there in that park? Whatta beating me, Frankie Slick, and Dodo put on some mook over there by that fucken tree. We beat that shine for 30 minutes. What a tough prick," Dom said as coolly as he would talk about the weather.

"This black bastard smiled while we beat him," he grinned.

"I kicked that fucken "moulinyan" until my foot hurt, but he just kept smiling. When we got done beating him, I couldn't sleep. I couldn't think about nothing else but that fucken shine's grin."

Dominick's eyes were lifeless, tiny, dull circles without color. He had the dead gaze of a man whose nerves didn't function when violence reared.

"I knew I had to kill him. So Dodo drove me down here five or six times to look for him." Dom said, "One night, we finally see him alone standing against that tree. So we drive by, and I use my uncle's hunting rifle. I shoot this nigger in the head—boom. Right over there against that tree."

Gobbo riveted me a nervous look. I avoided his apprehensive eyes by looking out the passenger window at the scenery that lined the six-lane road we were cruising.

Instead of thinking about the sociopath in the back seat, my mind drifted to, of all things, the architecture of the Bronx Avenue that we were driving on, anything to avoid my partner's glare.

At one time, the Grand Concourse was the Champs-Elysee of New York. The H-Type apartment buildings, which lined both sides of the roadway, were designed to imitate the Moorish architecture of Spain. The spacious apartments inside these ornate stone and brick slabs once housed luminaries such as Babe Ruth and Milton Berle, but they were a long way from celebrity now.

Mostly minorities, or rent control tenants, inhabited these exceptional examples of art deco architecture now. The neighborhood's drug dealers were the only semblance of notoriety left in these once fashionable apartment buildings.

Once lined with maple trees, the center island split both sides of the boulevard. The trees had long since disappeared, along with the middle class, the neighborhood stores, and the architect's dream. The Grand Concourse no longer remotely resembled the Champs Elysee.

At the moment, I wanted to be in Paris, Dublin or even Newark—anywhere but inside this car. Yet I forced myself to confront the problem at hand. My intuition warned me that things had been too good. We were due for a fall.

My childhood friend in the backseat was borderline psychotic, and I intended to exploit Dom's dangerous mental disorder for my own benefit.

But in the Bronx, we didn't screw our friends.

No good could come of this.

* * *

Afraid of blowback, my partners and I had always used Dom sparingly.

His sheer workmanlike approach to violence boggled the mind. Dominick emanated perpetual foreshock. Although not intimidating in size, you knew any confrontation with this psycho would be a fight to the finish.

As he told us a story about how he had secured employment for his cousin, Dom's dispassionate, distant eyes didn't blink.

"I told my foreman to put my cousin to work.'"

"He told me, 'I don't need anybody right now.'"

"I said, 'My cousin needs a job.'"

"He said, 'Are you deaf? I don't need anybody.'"

"So I went up on the roof, maybe 12 floors. When I saw my foreman down below, I picked up a cinder block and dropped it.'"

"I missed his head by two feet.'"

"When my foreman looked up at the roof, I could see him shaking. I just smiled and wagged my finger at him."

Dom paused. He lit a Newport for emphasis, laughed and said,

"He put my cousin to work."

I said, "Holy shit, man. How did you get that block so close to his head without hitting him?"

He looked as if I had just asked him to split the atom.

"What are you fucken talking about? I wasn't trying to scare him. I was trying to kill him."

His complete indifference to consequence, moral or otherwise, would stun Attila the Hun. He even blew my mind, and I wasn't your everyday citizen.

* * *

Years earlier, Dom had become a foreman. In the old days, the way the mob worked with unions was understood. If you wanted to work, the foreman made you borrow five or 10 thousand dollars at shylock rates. Then you paid the foreman juice every week. If the racket got busted, the foreman didn't get popped for extortion, which was a felony, but instead for shylocking, which was just a slap on the wrist.

Smart.

* * *

Gobbo warned me,

"I don't care how long you've known him. We can't use this guy. He's fucken crazy."

I knew he was right, of course, yet Karl was trying to screw us for $240,000, and none of us were equipped for the job. This problem cried for Dominick's expertise.

First we had to ferret out whether or not Karl was connected. We found out that he wasn't. That was a break.

I had one last chance to get our money the easy way.

I called Karl at home. "This problem won't go away. You're dealing with serious people. What do you think, we're playing games?"

All in the shithouse . . .

I saw no other way out.

I sent Dominick.

In the nightclub business, when you hire a doorman, you hire a gentle giant. You don't want problems. In the bookmaking business, illusion's not enough. Threats must be backed up by cold, callous efficiency.

I should have heeded Gobbo's warning.

The last dance approached. The fiddler would have to be paid.

* * *

I placed that worrisome tune on hold while I sped to pick up the fiddler who I was in love with. Back from a three-week trip to Ireland, Colleen's Aer Lingus flight was landing at Kennedy. I tossed eight quarters into the automated toll-basket and nudged my beat up old jalopy across the Whitestone Bridge.

Even though we had only been dating a few months before Colleen left, I couldn't wait to see her. Her steady wisdom and biting sarcasm were welcome respites from the madness that defined my life. I waited outside customs examining the hordes of anxious, multicultural faces.

Family and friends of the arriving passengers strained and jostled in hopes of spotting their loved ones amid the huddled masses who dragged their luggage through the giant entranceway.

I jigged a bit, when I spotted Colleen. She wore a slightly tilted green tam atop her lovely, long, auburn hair. A short, plaid skirt accentuated an Irish step dancer's legs, and her green silk blouse mirrored her flashing eyes.

In short, she was too bloody much.

Her bag secure in my Buick's trunk and Colleen safely in the passenger seat, I sensed something was wrong. She was a bit too preoccupied, too serious—even grim.

"How was the trip?"

"It was fine, great weather for a change," she said woodenly.

"What's wrong? You've got something on your mind."

She turned and her eyes swelled with tears.

"I have something to tell you, Connor, something that I'm afraid will change things between us," she said.

"Come on, baby. You can tell me anything. What's the matter?"

"While I was in Ireland, I slept with somebody," she said her voice shaking.

Stunned, I said nothing. When I recovered, I asked,

"What happened?"

"I was at a party. Everybody got drunk. When I woke up, this guy was in my bed. I barely remember it." She began to cry. "I'm so sorry," she said.

"You gonna see him again?" I asked.

"Of course not. It only happened because I was drunk."

Drunk was something I understood.

"So, forget about it. You didn't kill anybody."

"That's it?" she asked.

"It was just sex. You were drunk. Forget about it."

"Wow. You're really something. I didn't expect that. I thought you would be hurt, or angry or both."

"Well, I ain't happy," I said. "But what amazes me is that you would you tell me about it. You're never gonna see him again. It was a mistake you made while you were stewed. I'd have never known. Why tell me?"

Now it was her that seemed stunned. She said earnestly, "I had to tell you. If I hadn't, I never could have lived with myself."

I let the impact of that profound statement register, and then the exceptional character of the woman I loved and who currently shared my bed sank in.

"Wow. It's you who are really something," I said. "So does this mean that every time one of us screws up we have to confess?"

I adjusted the radio a moment while I digested her wisdom and decided to lighten the mood.

"So you're telling me I have to dime myself?" I laughed. "Rat myself out?"

"Don't laugh, Connor," she said. "If we don't have honesty, if we're not friends, what do we have?"

She was right, of course, friends first and foremost. That gave our relationship so much latitude in other areas.

Honesty.

What a wild concept.

More than two decades my junior, Colleen is teaching me about relationships. This gal is really something. If only I didn't have this other fucken problem.

But I do. And Colleen or no Colleen, it's not going to disappear.

CHAPTER THIRTY- EIGHT

I was on the phone to my partner. Gobbo was enjoying his first holiday in six years, but not for long. A bookmaker never gets a real holiday.

"Hey man, I hate to ruin your vacation, but we got a situation."

"C'mon, man. I'm in Italy. Take care of it," he said. "Wait, how bad is it?"

"I can't talk over the phone. Come back to the States. It's pretty bad."

"Tell me something . . . anything," Gobbo said.

"Dominick got arrested last night."

"Fuck . . . I'm on my way."

* * *

A week before I had made that call to Gobbo, I had been on the phone to Dom.

"How much will Karl pay?" I asked.

"Half now, and $5,000 a month until he's paid up." Dom said.

Relieved, I said, "Cool. The office will split the first $70,000 with you, and then we'll each take $2,500 a month until he's square. When's the meeting, Dom?"

"I'm meeting him at 8 p.m. Friday in a Westchester park."

I felt like the quarterback for a football bet that I'd given up on had just pulled off a Hail Mary pass.

The risks of sending Dom to handle this were plain.

If Karl couldn't pay, this deadbeat might panic and start screaming for the police.

Dominick's volatility presented another danger. Like the Kraken, once loosed, God only knew how much havoc went with him.

This mission required forceful diplomacy. If Dom harmed Karl, or worse, killed him, we would have been accessories to murder—jackpot—game, set, match.

But Dom had to get the money.

Our office couldn't take this kind of hit, not for these numbers.

Karl should have the fucken bread because in the past two weeks, he had beaten us for $250 large and "only" owed us $240,000.

Counting what we had already paid him and what he owed now, if Karl "came up lame," we'd be out almost $500,000.

When it came to Dom's collection methods, this time I'd wear blinders. If the lights were on, I'd see the roaches.

I knew our office had bugs. I didn't need to study their breeding habits.

* * *

Just like cops, one collection method that "wise guys" used was good thug, bad thug. In front of the deadbeat, one brute would spew hardball and say to the other,

"The boss told me he don't care about the money no more. This scumbag's a thief. Let's just shoot this prick and go home."

The more reasonable monster would say,

"Don't shoot him right away. Maybe it's not too late. Let him talk."

They'd throw the poor schmuck into the trunk of their car and then drive around for an hour or so. Meanwhile, the deadbeat in the trunk would be scared shitless.

They'd stop for coffee.

Once the car stopped, the mark in the trunk thought his fate was decided, death by anticipation.

The car restarted 20 minutes later. The process repeated. When the car stopped again, the deadbeat died again. You know the adage. "The coward dies a 1,000 deaths..."

But even a brave man would crack like a cheap Chinese toy

under that kind of psychological abuse.

When the boys would finally open the car trunk, the victim's soiled pants showed that he was ready to negotiate. The good thug, bad thug act would continue,

"I say we just kill him."

"I don't want to have to kill another guy this month."

Honest concern, accompanied by a few well-timed smacks, usually persuaded the easier cases.

"Hey pal, we don't want to kill you, but the boss has gotta get paid. Why not just give us the money?"

* * *

Friday night the reckoning came. Eight p.m. passed, no word from Dominick. Nine and 10 p.m. passed, still nothing. At 11 p.m., Dominick's clear, clipped voice carried catastrophic news.

"I'm in jail on $300,000 bond. Come get me out."

I was frantic.

What? Why so much? Did Dominick flash a gun? Did he beat the shit out of this fucken guy? Three hundred large, where do I get it? I gotta think fast.

Not from Gobbo.

He's on his vacation in Italy.

Not from Red.

Because he's an insane gambler, Red's broke.

And of course, not me.

Before I met Colleen, I had blown all my cash on booze, broads and drugs.

If Dominick talks, the authorities will get Gobbo and Red on the Rico Act. Both will lose their houses. Poor Gobbo stands to lose the most. Gobbo will lose his job, his police pension and most likely his family.

I don't have shit to lose, unless I lose Colleen. And I don't see that happening. She's a sticker.

I had already lost my wife and house. But the reason I had started this racket to begin with was to pay alimony and child support and to make sure that my son wouldn't suffer the consequences of my insane compulsions.

My manic mind skipped.
No way I can do time.
My blonde hair, fair skin and blue eyes would make me a prison pincushion. I'd have to commit murder to make it through, and then I'd end up doing life for sure.
No way I could rollover on my best friends.
It's Friday night, which presents another problem. The court system in N.Y. shuts down on weekends. I have to get Dom out before he gets pissed. He's a stand-up guy and won't rat, but it's our responsibility to do the right thing. It's on us to get him out. No way I can leave Dom in jail.
I have $100 large from the business in a safety deposit box. I can bang out $70 large in credit cards . . .
Maybe I can reach out to a shylock for the other $130 large?
But the standard street rate is three points. That translates to $30 weekly in vigorish for every $1,000 borrowed. If I can get $130,000 on the street that means the juice is $3,900 a week, and that's with nothing coming off the top.
What am I thinking? I can't worry about juice. I have to get Dominick out.

* * *

The next morning, I grabbed the Westchester papers. The headline read,

"Westchester D.A. Arrests Cop Killer."

What the fuck? Cop killer?

The column read,

"Today the Westchester District Attorney's office announced the shut down of a multi-million dollar gambling ring. The suspect was driving a convicted cop killer's car when arrested."

Multi-million-dollar-gambling ring? Cop killer? Where do they get this shit?

Turns out that Dominick's buddy from the neighborhood, Pete, had gone with him to collect the money, and Pete had borrowed his uncle's car. Because this was a Bronx Italian ghetto, percentages were high that Pete's relative was doing a "bit."

In fact, Pete's uncle was doing a stretch for the worst crime of all—killing a cop.

Complicating this disaster were the political ambitions of the Westchester D.A. She was running for Senator. If she made this look like she'd just captured the Loch Ness Monster . . .

* * *

Since I had returned from Viet Nam, I had been either a bartender or a half-assed gambler. Before I met Colleen, my history was one selfish hedonism.

For some of this, I had enormous regret. For much of it, I had no regret at all. Given the chance, I'd do most of it again without pause, particularly if I didn't hurt anybody but myself.

Self-destruction held little fear for me. I had been on borrowed time since the Mekong River, and I had always been willing to mortgage my future for my present.

It had all been worth it.

I had held mortality at bay with weed, downs, coke and plenty to drink. When the grim reaper rowed me across the great divide, I vowed it wouldn't be from thirst. My boat would carry more than enough to drink.

But screwing my friends and taking them down with me went against everything I believed in.

I was hurting everybody now. I had gotten my best friend, Gobbo, involved, and he was a Sergeant in the New York City Police Department. Red stood to lose his house. I had already screwed up my wife and kid's life, and my childhood friend, Dominick faced a long stretch in jail.

All three of us were close to broke. Besides bond, we had to get Dom a good lawyer and then pray he kept his mouth shut.

I couldn't see any way out of this mess.

* * *

Despite the pressure, Saturday and Sunday, I worked the office. I couldn't shut down. We had to earn.

I was screwed. I couldn't sleep, couldn't eat and couldn't keep my mind on the bets I was writing. Alone and anxious, I paced the floor between phone calls. I pumped iron between games, smoked Marlboros between bench-presses, and turned the crisis over and over in my mind.

Will Dom stand up? Can I get that much money by Monday morning? Do I go to the jail to bail him out or send someone else?

Many issues, no answers, I was glad Gobbo was on his way back. He'd know what to do.

CHAPTER THIRTY-NINE

"Man, am I glad to see you," I said.

Reinforcements had finally arrived.

In my mind's eye, Gobbo was clad in blue and high astride a white horse blowing a bugle. In reality, he wore a blue turtleneck sweater, jeans and a Navy Pea coat.

My partner and I sped from Kennedy Airport, over the Triborough Bridge and up the Major Deegan Expressway toward the Westchester Detention Center.

I drove and filled Gobbo in.

"I don't want you to panic, but the problem's bigger than I said on the phone."

Gobbo grimly said,

"How much bigger?"

"The Westchester paper's headline said, 'Cop killer arrested.'"

"Cop killer? Christ, what the fuck? Where in the hell did they get that idea? Don't tell me Dom actually . . ."

"No. No. No, wait. Hold it. Dom didn't kill a cop," I said.

"Thank Christ."

"No, his friend's uncle did," I said.

Gobbo slipped seamlessly into cop interrogation mode.

"Who? What? When? Whose uncle? What the fuck are you talking about?"

"Wait, easy, calm down. It's not as bad as it sounds," I lied. "Dom took his friend, Pete, with him to collect the money, and Pete borrowed his uncle's car. Pete's uncle is doing time for killing a cop."

With the dazed, empty expression of a man just awakening from a nightmare, Gobbo said,

"Are you shitting me? I feel like crying. Good God, I should have stayed in Italy."

I had gotten my best friend into this, so I felt like crying too. Realizing nothing I said would help, I did what I usually did when I wanted to escape a situation. I opened another door in my cluttered mind. My gaze escaped Gobbo's disgust and lazily wandered out of the Buick's half-open window.

Van Cortland Golf Course bordered the Major Deegan Expressway. I peered through the rows of live oaks that rustled in October's mild breeze and spied a golfer teeing off. I wished I were striking a nine-iron into a clear, cool Bronx sky right then. I wished I were anywhere but here having this conversation.

"Let's get the poor prick out, and go from there," I said.

"You'll have to go in alone, Connor. I'm not bailing out on ya, but it's better if I distance myself from this. If the D.A. even smells that a cop's involved in it, we'll end up on the front pages. She won't let up until she gets us all."

"No, Gobbo, I gotcha. I'll bail him out."

"How did ya raise the bail?" he asked.

"The bondsman wanted collateral for the $300,000, and Red couldn't put up his house, so…"

For a moment I hesitated. I could tell Gobbo anything. He was like my brother, but this one was tough. I cleared my constricted throat to buy time. Finally I turned back to him and gravely spit it out.

"I put up cash. I used the 100 large from the office's bank and reached out on the street for the rest of the money," I said. "Three different shylocks."

"Jesus."

He hung his head and rotated it side to side.

"Do you have an ounce of good news? Any good news at all?"

I grinned inappropriately.

"Well, we won 20 large yesterday."

Disgusted my partner and best friend in the world looked at me as if I were a piece of shit that wouldn't flush.

* * *

I bailed Dom out of the slammer and handed him a tepid container of coffee from a vending machine in the Detention Center's barren, gray reception area. The jailers handed Dom a manila envelope stuffed with his possessions.

From the Buick's backseat, Dom filled Gobbo and me in.

"Me and Pete went to the park to meet this asshole, and he tells us he ain't got the money. I said, 'Why didn't you say that on the phone? Why make us come all the way up here for nothing?' Next thing you know the guy goes crazy."

Dom leaned forward and got wildly animated.

"This cocksucka starts screaming, 'Now you're going to kill me aren't you? Say it. Say, you're going to kill me. Say it.'"

Dom snatched a Newport from his shirt pocket and slid it into his irate face.

"I tell him, 'What the fuck are you talking about. Kill you? No one wants to kill you. We just want to get paid.'"

He lit the smoke, took a drag and said,

"Thank God I didn't bring my piece with me. I almost brought it . . . just in case."

A fog of smoke clouded the back seat. Dom sipped his coffee and continued,

"So this fucken mook, what's his name? This . . . Karl, keeps yelling, 'Say you're going to kill me.' I tell him to shut the fuck up. No one's going to kill you. You need a fucking beating, but no one's going to kill you."

As if to prove that he was a victim here, Dom paused and swallowed what was left of his coffee. As the smoke from the Newport crawled up his wrist, he allowed all he had told us to sink in.

"Madone, it was like I tripped an alarm in hell. The parking lot lit up like Yankee Stadium," he said. "Westchester police and troopers charged out of the woods pointing shotguns and assault rifles at us. A voice blasted over a bullhorn, 'Put your hands in the air. You're under arrest. You have the right to remain silent.'"

Dom said,

"I nearly shit."

* * *

At the trial, months later, we found out that our boy Karl had stumbled on one of life's legal rackets. He busted bookmaking operations . . . a Godsend for a compulsive gambler. He couldn't lose. When he won, he collected. If he lost, he told the bookmaker,

"Go fuck yourself. I'm not paying."

Then off he trotted to the D.A. to testify.

Once Karl strapped on that wire, he became a real fucking citizen.

Suddenly Karl's repeated screaming made sense.

"You're going to kill me. Aren't you?"

If Dom were packing a piece, he and Pete would be facing attempted murder charges right now, and the Senate-seeking D.A. would have had even more fodder to feed the Westchester papers.

This rat, Karl, was a gambler who came up short. Rather than work out a payment plan, he ran to John Law with this sleazy scheme.

Nice racket. The cheese-eater picked up about 100 large a week until he lost. If he took a bath, he baited the bookmaker, and then provoked whatever poor sucker the bookie sent to collect.

Although this "to catch a thief" law enforcement method worked, I doubted that it was standard procedure. Only an extremely ambitious D.A. would have put a scheme like that in play.

Months later, this same D.A.'s Senate hopes were ironically squashed because of her husband's ties to organized crime.

* * *

The tab for Dom and Pete's legal fees came to $120 large, which we split $40 large each. We were also out roughly $500 large from the bamboozling Karl ended up giving us.

This economic disaster and a new city mayoral election combined with the fright we got from the near pinch convinced us to bequeath bookmaking to the gangsters.

When we started our operation five years ago, David Dinkins was mayor. Dinkins was more worried about his tennis game than organized crime. However, New York's new mayor, Rudy Giuliani, made his bones as a crime buster. He vowed to break the back of organized crime. His re-election depended on it.

As a cop on the job, Gobbo couldn't take this heat anymore. He had written his last bet, but Red and I decided to brazen it out and operate till the end of football season.

* * *

In five years of bookmaking, I had never addressed my gambling problem. I used bookmaking to stop losing, not to stop gambling. The more money I won, the more action I needed.

The 10 weeks that followed Dom's bust played out much the same way. Without Gobbo's steadying influence, Red and I were on tilt and completely out of control.

Even though our phones rang off the hook, the calls from other bookies were the ones we were most interested in.

Not because we wanted to layoff action but to bet "hot games" ourselves.

We'd let wise guys rob us of a dime so we had access to their information. On Saturday, a Brooklyn bookie, Brendan, might bet 10 games with us.

He'd win eight or nine.

When he called, we'd write a dime slip for him and then bet $10,000 each on his game. So besides booking $130,000 or so a day, I gambled on games across the board. Only now, I was betting $10,000 a game.

"Hurry Red, Brendan just bet Michigan plus four."

When Brendan called, Red and I immediately stopped everything. It was really frustrating before kickoff. We'd even hang up on customers to place our own bets.

I wasn't taking action. I was mainlining it.

Any sickness not addressed progressed. Red and I excelled at excess. The result was predictable. When the games cooled, our cash burnt. Slippery slopes were one thing, but Red and I were halfway over Niagara Falls.

Broke again, I got out of the business.

So I went from "Guido the gangster" to "back of the line Fred." No longer strutting after my wild ride, and still in debt up to my ass, I melted into the multitudes.

My mania was optimistic about my future though. Despite being laid, relayed and parlayed, I was down but not disgusted. After all, I wasn't dead. I wasn't in jail.

My sickness stared at the sunny road ahead and spawned a scheme. After Dominick's bust, the only resource I had left were my wits. I'd have to put them to good use.

I was done gambling. That was certain. But a man must have some vices, so I shelved that stupid prayer to St. Jude as well.

Because you know what?

A few beers never killed anybody.

CHAPTER FORTY

Throughout Mom's Alzheimer's, I had prayed every day for sobriety.

A year after her death, I was done praying.

I didn't need God.

I needed a drink.

When I left that Westchester bar stewed, it was 2 a.m. and pouring rain.

Despite the nasty weather, I lowered my passenger window and hoped the cold night air would keep me awake. Through my Buick's slapping windshield wipers, I squinted at the flatbed truck paused ahead at a stop sign.

Not obliviously drunk, I slowed up and pulled behind it.

I didn't see the 12-foot pipes that extended beyond the back of the truck.

The steel exploded through my windshield, rocketed past both my ears and out the rear window.

I sat frozen. The silence became palpable and merciless in its depths. The only sound came from my car's radio. The Temptations towed me to tears.

"People get ready. There's a train a coming. You don't need no ticket. You just thank the Lord."

Covered in broken glass, decapitation two inches from both ears, in this windowless wreck, amid sheets of rain, my sodden fingers formed the sign of the cross. But no hypocrite, I refused to pray.

From infancy my drunken gambler's journey flicked before me like a deck of cards.

* * *

Where do I go from here? I thought.

Half a decade of futility had finally convinced me that bookmaking belonged in my rearview mirror. I no longer had the stomach nor the discipline for that racket. I must drive in a new direction, but where?

I had taken my last drink. That was certain.

Another certainty, once I quit drinking and gambling, my life was sure to get better, granted slowly but better. Maybe I should read Jeremiah again. That was what Elijah told me to do way back when God first demanded my attention.

* * *

The next morning, I rummaged through my bookshelves and placed my hand on an old grammar school Bible. I turned to Jeremiah and searched for 29:11-13.

"For I know the plans I have for you," said the Lord. "They are plans for good and not for disaster, to give you a future and a hope. In those days when you pray, I will listen. If you look for me wholeheartedly, you will find me."

Jeremiah's passage gave me hope. Now I needed a future.

Jeremiah surrendered to God. I would too.

So, miracle of miracles, my mother's prayers had finally been answered.

Like Jeremiah, I decided to put my future in God's hands. I followed the Temptations advice and just climbed on board. My hooded eyes tilted skyward. My lips mouthed two words,

"Thank you."

When the horses in my head stopped, my future galloped in. For the first time in my life, I put the past aside. I forgave my father, my Maker and finally took responsibility for the only soul that I could change . . . mine.

* * *

In no small part to Colleen, I always had a reverence for teachers and had always wanted to attend college, but Viet Nam had gotten in the way. Colleen and I were moving to Florida, so she could earn her doctorate. Maybe attending a university would buy me time to figure out what direction I should go in next? At the very least, I'd look productive. Maybe I'd even learn something.

* * *

The University of Florida wouldn't accept me until I attended a community college. I chose Santa Fe, in Gainesville. My first classes were rudimentary mathematics, science and English. Many of the same subjects I had studied in high school.

English 101 was essentially a class to see if I were literate.

Sober and committed to the journey ahead, I wrote, edited and re-edited a term paper about the American invasion of Iraq and submitted it to my teacher. Next day, she told me to see her after class.

"That paper you submitted yesterday was quite good."

I said, "Thanks, professor."

"Do you mind if I do something with it?"

"Do something with it?" Surprised, I said dismissively, "It's only an English 101 paper. What can you possibly do with it?"

* * *

The very next day, I awoke to over 300 e-mails from all over the world. From Dubrovnik to Dublin, readers commented about how poignant and heart wrenching my prose was. Remark after remark praised my style and content.

I don't know these people. What prose?

"Colleen, come here a second. What does this mean?"

"You got published."

"What does that mean?"

"Someone published your work."

"I didn't write anything."

"You wrote something. Trace the comments back to the source." So I did.

It was my English 101 essay. The first time that I had ever put pen to paper without restriction, my piece went viral.

Staggered, yet intoxicated by the attention, I wanted more. Could this be what the black giant, Elijah, had meant? Could this be the gift from God that I had wasted?

"I always knew you could write," said Colleen.

I thought, *she thinks that?*

"What's the fastest way to learn?" I asked.

"Major in journalism, not English. Journalism will give you the tools you need."

And as I gaped open-mouthed at the woman two decades my junior whose infidelity had gifted me with fidelity, I knew then, that right here, right now, at 60-years of age, everything had finally changed.

I realized at that singular moment that St. Jude was right after all.

There are no lost causes.